MW01077352

FRANKLIN HORTON

LEGION OF DESPAIR

BOOK THREE IN THE BORROWED WORLD SERIES

ALSO BY FRANKLIN HORTON

ABOUT THE AUTHOR

Franklin Horton lives and writes in the mountains of Southwestern Virginia. He is the author of several bestselling post-apocalyptic series. You can follow him on his website at franklinhorton.com.

While you're there please sign up for his mailing list for updates, event schedule, book recommendations, and discounts.

ACKNOWLEDGMENTS

Neither books nor writers develop completely of their own accord, even though writers might wish to think so. While each writer brings to the table his own indefinable chemistry that makes him unique, both he and his book are also the distillation of his thoughts and experiences. While I continue to evolve as a writer, I am assisted in that process by the many friends and influences who have shaped me and continue to work their magic on me.

Many of the ideas that I write about were first bounced around in conversations with coworkers. My friends Greg Smith, Bill Wimmer, and Adam Wade have helped live out many apocalypses with me over the years. I want to thank author Steven Konkoly, a master of post-apocalyptic fiction, who continues to answer my questions and keep me focused on the big picture.

I also want to thank the book team who made this happen. My editor, Felicia Sullivan, has been invaluable in providing insight to all levels of this experience. She not only helps develop books, but writers and careers as well. I am indebted to her.

I also need to thank the folks at Deranged Doctor Design, especially Kim, who inspire me with their professionalism every time we work together. There's also the team of readers who helped me correct and clarify: Anita Debord, Dawn Figueiras, Vicky McFadden Bowens, and Carrie Bartkowiak.

Finally, I want to thank the friends and family, both present and departed, who have been part of this life-long adventure. Without the experiences we shared together, there would be nothing to distill and nothing to write.

Franklin Horton
March 8, 2016

PROLOGUE

The past weeks had been difficult ones for the people of the United States. ISIS operatives had seeped through the borders and launched a widespread coordinated attack against the infrastructure of the country. Aided by radicalized Muslims living in plain sight, the attacks were swift and deadly, targeted toward producing long-term devastation.

Trucks bombs were detonated on bridges and in tunnels critical for the transportation of people and goods. Residents of San Francisco, New York City, the Upper Peninsula of Michigan, and the Hampton Roads area of Virginia found themselves cut off from the most used travel and supply routes. In the current economy, it was doubtful those landmark bridges and tunnels could ever be rebuilt.

Several mortar rounds led to the collapse of the Wolf Creek Dam in Kentucky and the unleashing of half a trillion gallons of water from Lake Cumberland onto the folks of Nashville, Tennessee. It was unknown at this point how many people lost their lives to the flooding. The loss of electricity restricted the flow of information, preventing many from learning they were even at risk until it was too late.

Knowing the reliance of modern America on the luxury of electricity, the grid was a primary target of the terrorists. They relished the thought of pushing America back to a prior century. Critical transformers at junctures in the grid were destroyed by explosives and weapons fire. There were no spares available. The transformers were custom-made in Europe and Asia specifically for their location within the grid. They could take up to a year to make, then they had to be transported via ship, rail car, and finally by a specialized trailer to the site of their installation. With dozens destroyed, it was unknown how long replacements would take. Some sections of the country could have to wait years to get their power restored.

With the failing of the electrical system came the unavoidable consequences of power loss. People lost heating and cooling, refrigeration, the ability to heat water and cook on electrical appliances. Those requiring electrical-powered medical devices in order to live were dying. Cities could no longer pump water into storage tanks, nor could they treat it to make it safe for drinking. Certain critical municipal functions could be run off generators, but for how long? There was no guarantee of a steady supply of either diesel or propane.

Besides the electrical grid, the other primary targets of the terrorists' plan were the major refineries that turned crude oil into fuel. Utilizing portable weapons systems, the terrorists precisely dropped mortar rounds onto those facilities. The capacity to create fuel was destroyed, along with the existing inventory of fuel stored in on-site tanks. As this began to sink in, the president issued an Executive Order restricting all sales of fuel to the public. It was now only available to the military, law enforcement, and first responders. The president tasked state governors with this fuel seizure, utilizing their state troopers and National Guard troops.

The result of this fuel restriction was that millions of Americans found themselves trapped on the road. Those fortunate enough to be stranded on the beltways of their home cities faced potentially harrowing journeys home through unfamiliar sections of town. Those unfortunate enough to be traveling when they ran out of fuel were stranded along the interstate highways, at rest areas, and at truck stops.

One group of coworkers from Southwestern Virginia found themselves far from home on the day of the attacks. They were hundreds of miles away in the capital city of Richmond when they awoke to a power outage and only a vague idea of what had transpired overnight. There was a disagreement among the group as to the necessity of leaving town without attending the meeting they'd come for. Some felt that the terror attacks were just a bump in the road that would amount to little more than an inconvenience.

"We survived 9/11," one of them said.

Without fuel and electricity, there were also those among the group who felt that there was the potential for immediate chaos and eventual societal collapse. They had little news to go on. Cell phone connections were becoming sporadic. Even if they could not agree on what the societal effects of such an attack might be, it was eventually agreed upon that they should at least all return home to be with their families in this time of national crisis.

As they started their journey home, they were at an interstate travel plaza when the Executive Order restricting fuel sales was announced. This resulted in a riot which left one of their group dead. When they attempted to escape the chaos of the travel plaza, a man attempted to carjack them and one of the men, Jim Powell, was forced to kill the carjacker with a pistol that he carried concealed, a strict violation of his employer's policy. Unable to obtain fuel, their vehicle soon ran dry and they were forced to proceed on foot, leaving their useless car behind. They spent the night in a darkened, powerless hotel at a highway exit. The night was filled with the sounds of violence that further reinforced to some that societal collapse was a strong possibility.

In an effort to clean up the mess of stranded travelers abandoned along the highway system, FEMA established camps and ran buses in search of the stranded. Some among the group felt this was obviously the solution to their problem. They would go to the FEMA camp and wait for a bus ride home, courtesy of the government.

This contingent was shocked to find that this belief was not shared by all of those in the group. Jim, along with his friends Gary and Randi, opted to not put their fate in the hands of FEMA. Jim and Gary were both prepared and aware individuals who traveled with weapons and carried Get Home Bags just in case an event such as this were to ever befall them. Their plan was to go home along the Appalachian Trail and use its remote footpaths to avoid the more populated – and dangerous – areas between them and home.

Alice and Rebecca did not agree with this plan. They took a bus to the FEMA camp, where they remained until they realized that FEMA really had no plan for getting them home at all. FEMA just wanted them off the exits and out of the hair of the people living along the highways. It became clear to Alice and Rebecca that if they ever wanted to get home, they were going to have to leave the camp and find another way.

This was not a simple request. While leaving was not prohibited, it was not encouraged. No supplies or aid would be given to those who wanted to leave. Readmission was also forbidden. They were only able to leave by stealing some provisions and stowing away on a bus with another camp resident. However, they quickly learned that their new friend, Boyd, was not stable. His behavior was erratic and violent. After an argument, he killed Rebecca and fled in the night, leaving Alice alone on the road. In a cruel twist of fate, as Alice made it back to familiar territory she crossed paths with Boyd again, waking up to find herself tied up in his basement with no idea if she'd ever see her family again.

The journey undertaken by Jim, Gary, and Randi was no picnic. There were multiple violent encounters that left them changed from the people they'd once been. After several weeks on the road, they made it to Tazewell County, Virginia, each of them a harder version of themselves. Gary split off from the group at this point and headed toward his home. Randi and Jim proceeded together and it took them a day longer to reach Jim's home.

Jim's arrival home was not the idealized event that he'd imagined. Instead, he came home to find his family being victimized by Charlie Rakes, a prisoner set free from the local jail when the food ran out. Charlie had taken Jim's mother and son hostage in an attempt to extort food from Jim's family. Within fifteen minutes of arriving home, Jim had killed again, putting a round in Charlie's head and leaving his body for the coyotes that haunted the perimeter of the farm. The next day, Jim was able to fill his diesel truck from the fuel tank on his farm and use it to return Randi to her family.

Throughout their journey home, each anticipated being in the arms of their family. Each had the dream of a reunion that shone like a beacon and kept them walking each long day through blisters, aches, sickness, and hunger. Each imagined a set of smiling faces that would welcome them home. They imagined rest and recovery, sitting outside in a patio chair regaining strength from the depletions and exhaustions of the road. Each had a fantasy.

No one found what they expected.

1

G ary's House
       Richlands, VA

As GARY WALKED the last miles home, his hometown was as quiet as he'd ever seen it. It was the only small town for nearly an hour in any direction. If people wanted food, liquor, or building supplies this was where they came. It was always busy. There was always traffic. As a large coal town, it never closed. In the middle of the night, men in dirty work clothes with reflective safety stripes were driving service trucks, fueling up, stopping for cigarettes, or changing shifts. The sound of trains, the sound of coal trucks, were ever-present.

With the Executive Order that limited the available fuel to authorized emergency vehicles, most folks had already used up the limited supply they kept around their homes for mowing or running generators. Only a few vehicles moved on the streets now. There was a golf cart disappearing into a neighborhood. A shirtless man in shorts and flip flops rode a gas-powered scooter with a cigarette hanging from his lip. It was the kind of scooter that didn't require a license and was favored by drunks who had lost theirs. In some ways the town had shifted backward a century, making it okay again to walk in the center of the streets or ride a horse through town. Yet the congenial atmosphere of those long-gone days, even the hectic efficiency of two weeks ago, had departed. Even the twenty-four hour grocery store was closed, as was every all-night convenience store that Gary passed.

When Gary was a child, his family had moved from their home into one a little larger in another part of town. Years later, he'd had the opportunity to go back to his childhood home. There was a sense of deep familiarity at seeing the home where he'd grown up, yet there was also a slightly alien feel, and the awareness that it was not his home anymore. Things may have looked the same, but they were different too. That was exactly how his town felt now. The same, with a disturbing undercurrent of... *different.*

Gary's route took him through the downtown area where hundred-year-old brick buildings stood three stories tall. The upper floors were typically apartments. With no lights or any air conditioning, folks sat in backyards or brooded in shadowy doorways. Only the children seemed without worry, playing as children always do even in the worst of times. The adults had little to say. Some he passed met his eye or nodded, but none spoke. Even in this southern town where friendliness came naturally and everyone spoke to everyone, the people seemed dispirited. The state of the nation hung over everyone like a dark cloud.

Gary plodded the concrete sidewalk, seeing his town as he'd never seen it. The sound of his steps echoed between the buildings. After two miles, he crossed the railroad tracks and walked by the fire station. A group of volunteer firefighters sat in folding chairs in front of a garage bay. He nodded at them and they watched him pass, their conversation halting while they tried to figure him out. He wondered if they had the ability to respond to fires or if they were just unsure of where else to go. With no phones, unless they saw smoke they would not even have any means of being alerted of a fire in progress.

Beyond the fire station stood the vacant parking lot of a shopping center. A half-dozen kids were weaving on skateboards, feeling free to ignore the NO SKATING signs at this point. No one cared. They ignored his passing, which was the way he preferred it.

He approached the community food pantry and found it burned to the ground. He wondered why it had been burned. To conceal that the food had been stolen or run out? Perhaps it was because thieves were infuriated that there was no food left to steal. Gary recalled how this small town had seen so much change in his lifetime, from the boom of coal to the bust, yet they'd never needed food pantries here until recently. The media kept saying that the economy was recovering, but the lines at the pantry kept getting longer and longer and there was never enough food to give away.

Gary had not grown up with much money, but his family's food pantry had been in the backyard. He and his brothers had to help his parents plant it in the spring and early summer. Then they helped water it when the days were hot and dry. They harvested it together and they helped preserve it for winter. It was what had to be done. It disappointed him that the once-proud people of his community now preferred this handout of stale and outdated food to raising a garden of their own. It was discouraging that such was the world his grandchildren would inherit.

He was less than a mile from his house when he could stand it no longer and the anticipation of his homecoming made him start jogging. His feet were so sore from the journey that it felt as if the small bones within his shoes were broken and grinding together, but he didn't care and he didn't stop. His pack pulled at his already aching shoulders and he felt lightheaded from burning more calories each day than he had consumed. Still he ran.

In ten minutes, he was at the foot of the driveway that his family shared with a few neighbors. He tried to continue running up it, but the half-mile road was too steep and he was too spent. He climbed as quickly as he could. In the years he'd lived here, he couldn't recall ever walking this driveway and he was impressed with the effort it took. Halfway up, he was sucking wind. His legs were cramping and his side ached, but he knew the top of this hill was all that stood between him and his family. He started running again.

He could not stop himself. Emotion welled up in him, threatening to spill over.

In the exhausting blur of his journey home, Gary had dreamt of this moment. There were many times when he, Jim, and Randi had sunken into the dark pool of their thoughts and he knew they were all thinking of the same thing: home. In his mind, he had pictured a reunion worthy of *Little House on the Prairie,* him ambling out of the woods near his home into a field of wildflowers and being spotted instantly by his wife. She would drop the basket of laundry that she was preparing to hang on the line and cry his name. He would step through the high grass toward his family as they spilled from the house.

He pictured his wife, his daughters, his sons-in-law, his grand-daughters, all running toward him in slow motion, their arms outstretched, love radiating from them like a sunny day at the beach. He imagined he would shed his pack into the deep daisy-filled grass and run toward them. They would collide in an enormous hugging mass and his depleted body would absorb it all, the love he'd been missing on those hundreds of miles when all he could think about was the family he'd left behind. He knew it was a little sappy and over the top, but distracting the mind helped the body cope, and that was how he endured the many miles he'd come. It was one of the games he played in his head to make it home.

Gary had three daughters and two of them lived next door to him. He'd cut building lots off his larger parcel of property and gladly allowed them to build homes there when they were married. It was a small price to pay to keep his children and grandchildren within arm's length. A third daughter had not yet married and still lived with them.

As he crested the hill, one daughter's house came into view, then the next one, then finally his own. He stopped and panted, attempting to regain control of his breathing. His heart was pounding in his ears like an oncoming train. It would suck to make it this far and go into cardiac arrest within sight of his home.

He scanned the grounds of the three houses, looking for signs of life. The homes looked abandoned. There were no laughing children. Then he saw his son-in-law out walking around, an AR-15 cradled in his arms. Gary smiled.

"Will!" he called.

Will froze in his tracks, looking around. Gary yelled again and this time Will spotted him. Gary waved, wanting to make sure that the armed young man knew who he was before he started walking toward him. After a moment of shock came recognition. Will waved back and Gary started trotting toward him. He could hear Will shouting toward the house, but couldn't make out the words.

Will must have been announcing his arrival, though, because the front door flew open and his family spilled out. It was like a hole punched in a bag of sugar, an unstoppable pouring forth that spread uncontrollably in all directions. They were all there, all the grandchildren, all the daughters, the young men who'd married his daughters, and finally his wife. While it wasn't the bucolic scene that he'd imagined, complete with golden light, flowers, harp music, and a chorus of angels, it was still a beautiful moment.

He was home. He was finally home.

His youngest daughter reached him first and nearly toppled him over backward with a hug that was closer to a tackle. Gary shrugged out of his pack, dropping it to the ground. His daughter was crying and holding him tightly while his other two daughters plowed into them. They all sagged to the ground at that point, Gary smiling, his daughters crying, then Gary crying too.

At the rear of the pack Gary's wife, Debra, approached with a granddaughter in her arms. Gary's other son-in-law, Dave, was with her, carrying a child in one arm and leading another by the hand. As all the grandchildren got their feet on the ground, they joined the mass, giggling and laughing. It was more than music to Gary's ears, refilling the void within him with warmth and life. It put back nearly everything that he'd left on the trail home. It filled the holes created by the death he'd both seen and the death he'd wrought. He felt himself becoming a human again, becoming all the things these people needed him to be.

Debra dropped to her knees, her face streaked with tears, a sob breaking loose despite all her efforts. Gary pulled himself gently free of his brood and crawled toward his wife. He took her in his arms and she lost all the composure she'd struggled to maintain in his absence. She no longer had to be the only thing that held this family together.

Throughout the reunion, Will, Gary's oldest daughter Sara's husband, stood back from the hugging mass. He held an AR-15 in a ready position and was nervously scanning the tree-line around the property. When Will turned his back to them, continuing his perimeter check, Gary noticed that he carried a pouch on his belt with two spare mags for the rifle. Anyone could sling on a rifle for looks, but the extra mags indicated the expectation of a possible fight that would precipitate the need for reloading. The rifle had been a present from Gary the first Christmas after Will had married into the family. The young man's actions made Gary nervous. Will was not a high-strung kid. He was coldly practical. If he was concerned, there was a reason.

Lana, the oldest of Gary's granddaughters, climbed into his arms and covered his cheeks in her little kisses. She crinkled her nose at him.

"You smell bad, Papaw," she said.

Gary laughed. "I know, sweetie. Trust me, I know. I've not had a bath in a long time."

He let her slide to the ground and she ran back to her mommy. Everyone laughed as she whispered to her mother, "Papaw's stinky, Mommy. He need a bath."

"Let's move it back inside," Will said. "We've been out here long enough. I don't like everyone being exposed like this."

Everyone groaned. It was a beautiful day and with the stress of Gary's absence lifted from them, they were ecstatic and enjoying the moment.

Gary knew that Will must have good reason for his instructions. "Will's right," Gary said. "Let's move toward the house. I'm starving and need something to eat."

Everyone began happily strolling toward the house. Gary hung at the back, while Will continued to scan their perimeter, his weapon held at the ready. Whether it was from stress, sleeplessness, or something else, Gary had no idea, but Will was clearly ready to swing around and open fire at a moment's notice. Something *had* happened in his absence. Will would not be demonstrating that level of paranoia if there weren't a good reason.

"What's been going on, Will?" Gary asked.

Will kept his eyes moving, his focus intense. He was tall and had never served in the military but was experienced with firearms. He'd trained with Gary on a regular basis. His movements were practiced and efficient. He scanned the tree line, the road, and then his eyes landed again on the backs of his family, silently urging them to pick up the pace and get inside. His attention never wavered.

"We've had visitors," he said. "Folks on dirt bikes. They came up the driveway at first, like they were lost. They looked around and then they left. That was a couple of days ago."

Gary could sense there was more to the story.

"That night, the garden got raided," Will continued. "They took as much as they could carry and trampled most of what was left."

"Dadgummit," Gary said. It was about as close to swearing as he normally got. "That's aggravating. Not just the theft, but the waste."

"I know. There's still a few things left but not much," Will said. "The tomatoes in the planters didn't get taken. It was too much of a coincidence, though, that those guys showed up and then the garden gets wiped out."

"I'm guessing you didn't have a guard posted?"

Will shook his head. "Up until that point we didn't think we needed one," he said. "We were just a few days into this whole thing and people were pretty much treating it like the aftermath of a snow or ice storm. Everyone was walking around socializing and the mood was halfway friendly, like a town sharing a crazy experience. Then the mood turned sour after the grocery stores closed and people realized this might be serious. There's been a lot of shooting. It doesn't sound like hunting, it sounds like gun fighting."

Gary nodded. He'd seen the same thing happening during his

travels.

"I thought I heard someone trying to break into the storage buildings last night. I shined a spotlight around but didn't see anyone. First thing this morning we moved some of the important supplies out of the storage buildings," Will said. "All that stuff is in the garage now. It's a mess but it's safe."

Though exhausted, Gary tried to process what he was hearing. "So are you thinking this is all from the people on the dirt bikes or just different, random groups of people?"

"It's hard to say," Will said. "There's a lot of people just wandering around for lack of anything else to do. Folks have been coming up here on the hill nearly every day. I think some of them are just casing the houses. They're looking to see what we have that they need."

"You really think so?" Gary said. He looked out over his property and that of his neighbors. They lived on a flat hilltop of about twenty acres. Gary had about six of those acres and had cut off one each for his married daughters. The remaining property belonged to the neighboring families. The road that came onto the property formed a circle, rejoining itself before going back out the way it came in. It would have been easy for those folks on dirt bikes to drive in and make the circle and then ride back out.

"I've never seen so many people walking around up here," Will said. "I think some of them are just taking a shortcut out of the housing project back there. As for the others, I don't know who they are or why they're here, but they all have the same look, like they're shopping for things they can use."

Will kept scanning the woods. The kids were all inside now. Gary's wife and daughters were filing through the door. With them no longer in the open, Will visibly relaxed. "The way that the guys on dirt bikes were stopping in the road and watching us, it seems like they were challenging us. It got to the point yesterday that I geared up and went outside with my AR. There were folks standing at the end of the driveway just looking at the house. I asked them if I could help them with anything. They never answered, just turned away and left."

"You think those dirt bike riders took the food from the garden?"

Gary asked.

"I think so," Will said. "You can hear those machines running up and down the main road all night. I don't know where they're getting the gas to do that. I haven't been able to buy any."

"They're not buying their gas, Will."

"Of course they're not," Will replied. "I should have realized that. I'm just getting stupid with exhaustion."

"Don't worry about it now," Gary said. "Let's get inside and we can deal with this later."

THE EVENING with his family was beyond words. Gary's wife and daughters prepared what looked like a feast after the deprivations of the road. Gary ate until he could eat no more, but it was not the food that fed him, it was the presence of his family.

Although Gary did not have Jim's level of paranoia, he'd read all the same books Jim had read. The effect on him had been nearly the same as it had been on Jim. He long ago began making preparations in the way of storing food, water, weapons, and emergency power. Much of it was stored in the nooks and crannies of his home. Other items were stored in his various outbuildings. Still other items were stored in undisclosed locations because the items were expensive and he wanted to conceal the purchase. It wasn't that he had any reason to feel guilty for making the purchases; they had the money. It was more of an issue that he was innately frugal and felt guilty about spending money. For that reason, some of his purchases were either disguised or hidden in plain sight.

Part of those preparations he made were in the way of long-term food storage. They had clearly not reached the point where it was necessary to dig into those supplies, though. They were still eating the fresh refrigerated foods and items from their everyday pantry. This was because, like Jim, Gary had installed a transfer switch on his house that allowed him to hook a generator up to run essential circuits, like the refrigerator and freezers.

While Jim stored his in an outbuilding and only brought it out when needed, Gary had gone the extra step of installing a permanent generator housing out back so that the generator could be left in place all the time. All Gary needed to do was go out back and start the generator, then flip a few breakers on the transfer switch to restore power to the circuits he wanted to energize. Gary had no long-term experience with this, but his theory was that alternating between running the generator for four hours and then letting it sit idle for four hours would keep the frozen food frozen and the refrigerated food cool enough that it wouldn't go bad, as long as people stayed out of those appliances as much as possible.

Gary had explained his theory of generator operation to Will many times and was certain that Will had been responsible for doing this in his absence. Because of the items on the dinner menu, it had obviously been working. Gary reminded himself that he'd need to check the fuel supply later and see how it was holding out. He'd had intentions of purchasing a tri-fuel generator that would run off various fuel sources, but he'd never done it. He owned a gasoline generator, which had been substantially cheaper, and he stored cans of stabilized gas in his outbuilding to run it. He kept about twenty-five gallons at all times, rotating it through his mower or vehicles as it got old and replacing it with fresh.

LATER, as they were cleaning up from the meal, Gary asked Will if they'd been maintaining a watch at night.

"Like I said, until recently, there's not been any indication that we needed to. There just hasn't been any trouble."

"We'll need to look at that," Gary said. "It might be time to start one. We just need to be careful. With everyone scattered out over three houses, I don't want anyone wandering around outside where they could be shot by mistake."

Will nodded as he considered this.

"How's Dave dealing with all this?" Gary asked.

"He's doing pretty well," Will said. "I don't know if he's completely onboard yet, though."

"Meaning?"

"I'm not sure if he's grasping the seriousness of it all. He's still worried that he's going to be fired for not showing up to work, even though there's no fuel for getting there. You and I have talked about disasters ever since Sara and I started dating. We've always thought alike. Dave never had any idea how fragile things were until he and Charlotte got married and he started listening to our conversations. He's trying but I think he might still be in shock or something. He just seems to think he's going to wake up one day and everything will be back to normal."

"There's a lot of people that think like that. Had a couple on our trip. I'll talk to him," Gary said. "Check in and see how he's doing."

"That's probably a good idea," Will said. He looked at Gary seriously. "You know that I would kill to save anyone in this family. I would not hesitate to pull the trigger to save any one of them. I am not sure Dave is there yet."

Gary yawned and rubbed his eyes. "I'll have to deal with him tomorrow. I'm exhausted right now. I think I could sleep for a week."

"Do you want to start a watch tonight?" Will asked.

"I'm not sure it would do any good tonight," Gary said. "With us scattered out in three houses, we'd need someone awake in each house to cover all this ground. We'll figure something out tomorrow. For tonight, everyone just needs to make sure their house is locked up tight and that weapons are as accessible as they can safely be kept. And no one should come out after we're all home for the night. Like I said, I don't want any friendly fire incidents."

NOT LONG AFTER DINNER, Sara and Charlotte left with their families. The children needed to be bathed with baby wipes and those tasks were best done while there was still some remaining daylight. After that, stories would be read and the children would be tucked in for the night. While Jim's home in Russell County had a backup water source in the way of a spring, and had a well that could provide water under generator power, Gary really had no water source other than what they stored. Their property had public water which had saved the expense of drilling a well when he built the house. It had seemed like a good thing at the time. Then, as Gary started making emergency preparations a few years back, it began to seem like a liability that would be difficult to overcome.

For three years now, Gary had kept every two-liter soda bottle that had come his way. He carefully washed them, then refilled them with water and stored them in his basement. He had hundreds of them sitting on shelves with the fill dates written on them. His plan was to refill them when they got to be around five years old. There was no real science behind that number, it just sounded like a good idea to him.

He had also purchased a blue plastic drum in which he could store larger amounts of water. A hand-operated pump allowed him to pump water out when it was needed. He had the materials on hand to collect water from the guttering on his home too, but he'd never put the system in place. That would have to go on his list of things that needed to be done pretty quickly.

As he thought about the long-awaited fantasy of settling into his own bed that night, the thing that he wanted *almost* as much was to take a long, hot bath. If he had an unlimited supply of spring or even creek water he could have heated it over a fire and gradually filled a tub, just as people had done in the old days. Without any immediate idea of how he was going to replace the water that he used from his supply, Gary did not feel like he could do anything so frivolous. Feeling guilty and wasteful, he took a single two-liter bottle, poured it in a pot, and heated it on the burner of his gas grill.

He went to the nearest bathroom and lit a battery-powered lantern. By that light, he peeled off his crusty clothes and washed the miles from his body. It took a while. He continued scrubbing long after any dirt was gone, as though trying to scrub away the things that couldn't be seen, the experiences he no longer wanted to have in his head. The bath did not help with that, though. Only time could wear such things away.

When he was done, he looked at the pile of clothes in the floor. He knew that he could never again wear them without remembering the smell of death on them and the images of where that smell came from. He emptied the pockets and removed the belt from the pants, carefully held the reeking pile of clothing away from his body and carried it out the back door to the fire pit in the backyard. There was a bottle of charcoal starter fluid sitting on a nearby pile of firewood. He squirted some on the clothes, then struck a grill lighter to it. As the flames rose, Gary imagined the whole nightmare of the past weeks rising into the sky with the black smoke. He wanted those memories to leave him but knew they never would.

While the physical trials of his trip home had been enormous, his group also found themselves experiencing additional stress from the lack of information. Rumors and conspiracy theories were rampant in everyone they spoke to. Even those with official connections to public information knew very little. Gary had thought constantly of getting home and digging out his Baofeng HAM radio and speaking to other HAM operators. In a disaster, they were always the most reliable source of information. No spin, no cover-your-ass denials, only pure person-to-person shared information.

Gary retrieved his Baofeng from the gun safe. He didn't know why he kept it there, but he did. It was a $20 radio and he had six of them, but still that's where he kept them. He turned the radio on and let the extended range antenna stick out the window and located a commonly used frequency in his area.

"CQ, CQ, calling CQ. This is WNFZ960. Whiskey-November-foxtrot-zulu-nine-six-zero."

No one responded. He changed frequencies.

"CQ, CQ, calling CQ. This is WNFZ960. Whiskey-November-foxtrot-zulu-nine-six-zero."

There was an immediate hit. "WNFZ960, WNFZ960, reading you loud and clear. Where you coming out of?"

It was strange that the person responding did not offer his call sign, so not wanting to be too specific, Gary responded, "Tazewell County, Virginia."

"Well, Tazewell, you got Piney Flats, Tennessee, here."

"How are things in Piney Flats?"

"We've had a lot of traffic. Folks west of us got a little scared that things were getting hot in Oak Ridge. You know, hot as in *nuclear* hot. People were trying to get away from anything nuclear in case the terrorists blew it up."

"Did they?" Gary asked. "Did the terrorists hit anything in Oak Ridge?"

"No," the man said. "I've spoken to someone that lives there in Oak Ridge and he says it was all just paranoia."

"What about other nuclear sites?"

"There were some nuclear sites hit, but the folks I've talked to said there were no releases. Some of the plants got knocked offline and can't send power out onto the grid, but there were no leaks or discharges that I've heard of."

"That's good to know," Gary said.

"They did flood the shit out of Tennessee, though," the man said. "Nashville is now Lake Nashville since they blew that dam."

"I've been out of touch for a couple of days," Gary said. "I'm just trying to catch up on what I missed. What's your call sign, Piney Flats, in case I need an update in the future?"

"Just call me Jack," the man said.

"Okay, Jack. I'm Gary."

"Well, Gary, I wouldn't be using your call sign anymore if I were you. Perhaps I'm just a paranoid old man, but considering the state of things, it's probably best not to be broadcasting to the powers that be that you have a working HAM setup."

"Surely no one cares," Gary said. "There have to be a lot of sets out there, right?"

"Maybe no one cares," Jack said. "Maybe they do. Maybe some sectors of the government thrive on chaos and they don't want the sharing of news to dispel some of that chaos."

That made sense to Gary. "I'll keep that in mind," he said. "Hopefully we'll talk again."

"Okeydokey," Jack replied. "Take care of yourself and hang onto your scalp."

Gary set the radio down on his desk. Tomorrow, he would inventory supplies. He would dig out his family band radios and make sure each house had one, talk to the neighbors about securing the road into their property, and try to figure out how they could set up a watch so that they wouldn't be so vulnerable at night. For now, for tonight, he was doing nothing more than crawling into bed with his wife. Tomorrow was a new day.

As fantastic as his reunion with his family was, his reunion with his bed was also a special moment. His pillow remembered the shape of his head and his bed welcomed him like a long lost friend. As much as he'd complained about his sleeping conditions since Richmond, he hadn't realized until just this moment how deeply and truly he loved his bed.

Before tucking himself in, he made sure his Glock lay ready on the nightstand with a flashlight beside it. He had retrieved his Smith & Wesson M&P-15 from the gun safe and it was propped against the nightstand too. He put the Baofeng earpiece in place and listened to the radio as he lay there in bed, hearing bits and pieces of regional news, filling in some of the gaps in his knowledge of the disaster. It was nothing that provided any comfort. Instead, it scared him a little. There was so much to do, so much to prepare, but his reunion with his bed – and the wife he'd finally come home to -- became all-consuming and he drifted off to sleep in her arms.

GARY SLEPT like the dead until the whine of engines woke him. He was heavily disoriented, trying to remember where he was and who he was with. As someone who had grown up with a dirt bike, he recognized the sound of a two-stroke engine through the fog of his mind. He knew these were the riders Will had talked about. He jerked awake and sat up in the bed. In the dark, he listened carefully, trying to figure out what was going on. It was difficult to place exactly where the riders were because there were several of them and they were separated. The sound told him nothing, muffled by trees and bouncing off houses. The men could be anywhere.

He rose from the bed and stumbled to the window. He was still out of it, so used to waking up in the woods in the presence of his coworkers. Being inside a house felt different. He was sheltered, but realized he was still vulnerable. This was not what he'd expected from home, not what he'd hoped for. He stood to the side of the window so that he would not be visible if light splashed across it. He leaned from cover and looked out.

His bedroom window faced out toward his two daughters' houses. He could see the erratic movement of light in the trees and across the houses. It looked like the riders were just doing laps around the houses, circling back and forth through the yards.

"Why are they doing this?" It was Karen, his youngest daughter, and she'd just entered the room.

"Stay over there with your mother," Gary said. "Don't get in the window. They could have guns."

Karen sat heavily on the bed beside her mother. Debra was sitting up silently, her back against the headboard. Gary could tell that she was afraid but trying her best to be brave.

Gary then remembered what Will had asked him earlier, about how these riders still had gas to do this. He knew they were stealing it, they had to be. While all this activity was taking place on this side of his house, all of his fuel was on the *other* side of his house, where his cars were parked and where his outbuildings were.

He turned away from the window. "Is your window open, Karen?"

"Of course. It's impossible to sleep around here with them closed. There's no air at all."

Gary picked up his AR. It had a light on it, but the flashlight on the nightstand was more powerful so he grabbed that too. "You all stay here."

"Don't go outside," Debra warned.

"I'm not," he said. "I'm going to a window."

Gary stepped quickly down the hall, the hardwood floor creaking beneath his bare feet. When he got to Karen's room, he approached the window cautiously, then glanced quickly out from the shadows. At first he saw nothing, but as his eyes adjusted to the low light he noticed a pair of legs extending from beneath Karen's VW Jetta.

He didn't like to curse, but tonight he only applied that to saying them out loud. In his head, he let them roll. If the man was under the car, his intention was obvious. He was puncturing the tank so that he could steal the fuel inside it. Gary did not want to let that happen.

"Crap." Gary felt his frustration boiling over, both at being awakened in the middle of the night and for having his return home immediately be disrupted by people who couldn't stay on their side of the fence. Still, Gary did not want to kill a man for this. Jim might have, but Gary wouldn't, not over gas. He was not that kind of man and he was trying hard not to be.

He drew his rifle up to a firing position and activated his red dot sight. Resting the barrel on the windowsill, he fired a round near the extended feet. He waited for the feet to jerk up beneath the car, but they didn't.

Gary fired another round.

The feet still didn't move. Although Gary could hear the bullets ricocheting off the asphalt, he assumed there would be some lead splatter spraying the man's legs. It would hurt like hell. The man did not move, though. He should have been running like a scalded dog by now.

"I'm coming down there!" Gary yelled. "If you're still under the car, I'm shooting you. This is your only warning."

Gary drew back further into the room and watched. He was giving the man an opportunity to run but the idiot didn't take it. He went back to his bedroom and saw immediately that the dirt bikes were pulling off and heading back down the driveway. It was possible they had some kind of communication and the man under the car had warned them he'd been busted.

"I'm going downstairs!" Gary yelled to his wife and daughter. "Lock the bedroom door and do not come out."

"Don't go, Gary!" Debra yelled. "You just got home. Don't take any chances."

Gary was already gone, though, scuttling down the steps barefoot. He ran to the kitchen, onto the tile floor, and came to a stop at the door. He looked through a crack in the blinds and tried to see what was out there. Aside from the man beneath the car, he could see no one else.

It crossed his mind that this could be a trap, an effort to draw him outside. Still, he whipped open the door, raised his rifle, and depressed the switch that activated his weapon-mounted light. From the cover of the doorway, he played the light around his immediate surroundings to make sure no one was lying in wait for him. From what he could see, there was no one. Beneath the Jetta, the legs still protruded. Gary doused his light, crouched, and approached the car.

Gary kicked one of the scuffed boots, then immediately backed up, expecting to be shot through an ankle. Not seeing the man's hands made him very nervous. "Out of there!" he ordered. "Get out now or I shoot."

The man did not move.

Gary kicked him again.

No reaction.

Was the man passed out drunk? He'd heard of things like that happening, criminals who passed out mid-crime. They go to rob a house and fall asleep like Goldilocks in one of the bedrooms. Usually those people were on drugs or drunk. Gary needed a hand free. He held the rifle single-handed, the pistol grip in his hand, the stock pinched between his bicep and his body. The safety was off. This was not an accurate firing position but surely he could hit someone within arm's length this way.

He crouched and grabbed an ankle, planning on pulling the man from beneath the car. He wasn't sure what he was going to do then. Interrogate? Threaten? Shoot? He pulled as hard as he could with one hand, backing his body up and using his legs to pull. The man was holding on, though, and wouldn't let go. He could not pull him out with a single hand.

"Let go, you bastard," Gary hissed.

Frustrated, he moved from the front of the vehicle to the passenger side where he would be even with the man's head. He dropped onto his side in the driveway so that he could peer beneath the car. He leveled his rifle at the man's head and activated his light.

Gary sucked in a breath and stared in horror. It looked like a zombie from a movie, peeling skin, exposed skull, ragged and damaged features. The man's entire upper body, face, and head were abraded to the point that he would have been difficult to recognize had Gary known him. Through the blood seeping from the man's crusted face, Gary could see a rope leading from his distended, broken neck and knotted around a section of exhaust pipe. He imagined the man must have been dragged to death behind one of the motorcycles.

No wonder he couldn't pull him from beneath the car. These sick maniacs had tied the man here. But *why*? Then he realized the simple and obvious answer.

To keep him occupied.

Suddenly his paranoia spiked and blew through the top of his head. Gary rolled away from the vehicle and rose to his knees, scanning his surroundings with the light. Aware that his light made him a fully illuminated target, he quickly got to his feet and backed into the house. He had the vague fear that someone may have slipped into the house while his back was turned, but he didn't think so. He ran upstairs and stopped before he got to his bedroom.

"Are you all okay?" he called through the door.

"Yes," Debra responded, her voice strained. "Are *you* okay?"

"I am," he said. "You can come out."

Debra threw open the door and hugged Gary tightly. "What happened?"

"You don't want to know," he said. "We're going to have to change some things around here tomorrow. I think I just got played."

2

Boyd's House
Bluefield, VA

ALICE KNEW she should be afraid, but really, she was too tired and too depressed to muster the energy to be more scared. She felt defeated. She just wanted it to be over with at this point. This day, this journey, maybe even this life. She wanted to be home with her family and she couldn't take much more of this nightmare. She was drained. If Boyd was going to kill her, she just wanted to get it over with. She couldn't take another day like yesterday.

"What do you want, Boyd?" she asked.

He stared down at her, an obscure, menacing presence that absorbed all of the light in the room. He reached into his pocket and removed something, tossing it toward her. She tried to recoil, but she could not. Between the zip ties binding her and her stiffened muscles, she could barely twitch. The object clattered off the floor and bounced into her thigh.

Body lotion?

"It rubs the lotion on its skin," Boyd said, his voice a stiff falsetto.

"What?" she asked in confusion.

"It rubs the lotion on its skin!"

You got to be kidding me, Alice thought. *Silence of the Lambs? Really?* She looked up at him blankly.

Boyd smiled. "Just messing with you," he said. "I loved *Silence of the Lambs.* Always wanted to use that line on someone."

He was clearly screwed up royally in the head. Who else would do something like that? Who would find this the time to make a joke? Then she realized that she had already answered that question. Someone crazy.

"Why am I tied up here, Boyd?" she asked, her throat parched and her voice cracking.

"I didn't want you going anywhere before we had a chance to talk," he said. He dropped to the ground and sat cross-legged across from her. "I prefer a *captive* audience." He smiled at his own wit.

"Were you following me?"Boyd studied her, watching her face. She couldn't understand why he was looking at her so intently. Although she had not been sure it was possible, his gaze made her even more uncomfortable than she already was. It gave her a glimpse into the blackness of his interior. Into his madness.

"Or did you just luck up and find me sleeping in that car?"

"I came across you sleeping there inside the car, sound as a baby. I was looking in cars, as you know I'm prone to do, trying to find supplies, and I found you in there. You were starting to stir, so I just slipped under the car and waited for you to step out."

"Why?"

"I'm assuming that what you mean is why did I *collect* you, and the reason is because we need to talk. I guess I could have sat down with you in the car and talked but I didn't think about that. I was kind of thinking on the run and hiding under the car was the first thing that crossed my mind. I apologize for the abruptness of it."

"I don't even really know you," she said. "What could we possibly have to talk about?"

He stared at her again, as if trying to read her mind and see what she was thinking. Then it hit her. He was trying to figure out if she knew he had killed Rebecca.

He didn't know where she went that night. He didn't know if she ever saw Rebecca's body or not. As far as he knew, she could have been long gone by that morning and never seen what took place there.

At the memory of the blood, the brutality, it was on the tip of her tongue to start screaming at him, curse him, and call him a monster. What would happen if she did? She knew what would happen. He would kill her. Her life would be over. Her family would never even know what had happened to her.

She would have to play innocent. "Where's Rebecca?" she asked. She did her best to sound genuine. "Is she upstairs having a good laugh at my expense?"

He continued to stare at her, as though trying to sniff out a lie.

"I thought you two were travelling together," she added.

He fiddled with his shoe lace, twirling the bow around a meaty finger. She noticed the crescent of dirt beneath the nail. "No, she's not here. We *were* travelling together, but we're not now," he said. "You know how she is. She got in one her moods. She became hard to get along with. I couldn't deal with her anymore. We parted ways."

Alice nodded. "Oh," she finally said. She tried to sound resolute, as if she both fully believed his statement and was satisfied with it.

"You haven't come across her?" he asked, raising an eyebrow.

Alice shook her head, which was not exactly easy lying with her head resting against a concrete floor. Her forehead rocked against the cool floor with the effort. "I wasn't exactly looking for her, though. I decided to just get myself home. She could find her own way. Never really liked the bitch anyway."

She hoped this comment might somehow endear her to him and put them on the same side. It was a risk, though. If he felt bad about killing Rebecca, he may lash out at Alice for this slight against her.

Boyd nodded. "I'm sure she's well on her way home," he said. "She'll probably be there any day now, if she's not already."

"I'm sure," Alice agreed. She closed her eyes. Her body felt so heavy. She didn't have the energy for these games. "What do you want from me, Boyd? I have a family I need to get home to. A husband. A son."

She'd always read that you should humanize yourself if taken hostage. Make it harder for the kidnapper to see you as an object. Take every opportunity to express that you were a person, not an object.

"None of that matters anymore," Boyd said. "Your son and husband are part of your old life. You're going to have a new life. With me."

Alice cracked her eyes and stared at him. "I have a life. I have people that care about me. People that I care about."

Boyd smiled at her, then shook his head, a look of pity in his eyes. "Not right now, you don't, Alice. Now you have nothing. But you do have an option. You can have the life I give you or you can have nothing at all."

"What do you mean by *nothing*?" she croaked.

"Nothing," he repeated. "As in *no life*. As in I kill you in this basement and you never see another day on this miserable Earth."

She clamped her eyes shut and lay there. She would not give him any tears.

"You think about it," he said, rising from the floor.

"Take these zip ties off," she begged. "They're cutting off my circulation."

He stomped loudly up the wooden steps. "Consider it an incentive to think very carefully."

"I'm hungry!" she cried.

"More incentive!" he called back to her.

ALICE LOST consciousness after he left. She was too miserable to sleep, but the weakness from her deprivations pulled her into blackness. It was like the fevered sleep of the flu, where you lost all orientation to time and place.

When she awoke, she opened her eyes and saw nothing. She moved her head, looked in all directions. More blackness. She listened and heard nothing. For a few moments she thought she had passed away and was dead once and for all, then gradually the throb of her raw wrists and ankles crept upon her and she knew that she was still alive.

She felt the need to urinate, which was surprising to her since she had not had anything to drink all day. She started to just let go and pee on herself, then she decided this might be an opportunity to appeal to Boyd's sympathy and see if she could gain any ground with him. Showing that she needed him would give him the feeling of control over her and he seemed to want that.

She cleared her throat and called his name. "Boyd."

What came out was little more than a hoarse whisper. She worked her mouth, trying to distribute what little moisture remained there.

"Boyd," she called. It was slightly louder this time but she still suspected it could not be heard beyond the basement.

"BOYD!" she yelled, louder this time, stronger.

"WHAT?" he bellowed.

She jerked in terror and nearly lost control of her bladder.

"WHAT?" he repeated, screaming in her face.

Where had he come from?

A powerful flashlight came on just inches from her face. She contorted, tried to crush her eyes closed, the pain from the beam making her head explode. He must have been sitting there in front of her this whole time, in the dark, just...staring.

"Turn it off!" she pleaded. "Please turn it off."

"You yelled for me," he said, his voice reverberating off the stone walls of the old basement.

"You're hurting me," she said, twisting her body, trying to get her face out of the beam of the powerful light.

"You don't know what hurt is," he said. "Yet."

He turned the light off and the pain in her head disappeared as quickly as it had come. She was breathing erratically, her heart pounding. "Thank you," she gasped. "Thank you."

He said nothing for a moment and she lost track of him in the darkness. She felt him, though. Knew that he was there now, knew that he was within reach.

"What do you want?" he asked. His voice was different now. It was a voice she'd never heard from him before. Before he'd almost been playful, though still clearly crazy. He'd displayed a sense of humor.

This person here in the darkness with her now sounded demonic. She felt that he was right on the razor's edge between continuing this game with her and slaughtering her as he had Rebecca. This was the man she'd seen choking Rebecca in the luggage compartment of that bus, and no doubt the man that killed her as well. It was the shadowy, evil man that lived inside the other. She had to pull the other back somehow. She had to make the monster retreat back into the cave and leave the other man, the man that she might have just the slightest chance of outwitting.

"I need to go to the bathroom," she whispered. She tried to make her voice as non-threatening as possible, adding a note of embarrassment, of desperation. She wanted to make sure he knew he was in the position of power in this interaction. It was the only way he would possibly go for it.

"Then go," he said. She could tell from his voice that there was some of the old Boyd in there. This was the voice of the sarcastic smartass, not the killer. Still, there was an underlying rage and hostility that scared her.

"I don't want to go on myself," she said. "I smell bad enough and I don't have any other clothes. Can't I just use the toilet?"

"They don't work anymore," he said. "There's no running water."

"Then where are you going?"

"The yard," he said, as if it were the dumbest question he'd been asked all day.

"Can't I use the yard too?"

He was silent. She could hear him breathing. She could feel him thinking, the rusty, encumbered wheels grinding.

His flashlight clicked on and she shut her eyes tightly. She heard Boyd stand and move about the room. Items were moved, a plastic bag rustled. Suddenly hands grabbed her and rolled her over onto her face. She heard the rattling of a chain, then felt something around her neck. She heard the plastic ratcheting sound of another zip tie and felt one bite into her neck. She gasped in panic, thinking he was going to tighten one around her neck and kill her. Though he stopped short of that, she could not push the thought of dying that way from her head.

She heard a metallic click, then a pulling at her wrists as that zip tie was cut. Soon, her feet were free too. She sagged onto the floor, limbs outstretched, feeling the blood restored to her aching extremities.

"I thought you had to pee," he said. "Get up."

She stood awkwardly, staggering. She was dizzy and her feet were still numb. She felt a tugging at her neck. It wasn't hard, but it was enough to stop her in her tracks. Then Boyd tugged harder and he was at her back, whispering over her shoulder, his mouth inches from her ear.

"I have you on a leash," he said. "I ran the zip tie through a link of this chain so you cannot get loose. Don't even try. You can do what you need to do in the backyard, but I'm not letting go of this leash. If you try anything at all, I will tighten it and watch you die."

She thought this over for a moment. "I'm not sure I can pee with you standing right there," she said.

"This is the last time I'm asking," he said. "Do you want to go or not?"

"I'll go," she said quickly, not wanting to take a chance on him changing his mind.

He used his light to get them to the stairs and then turned it off. Boyd went ahead of her, walking with a sure step up the dark stairs. Halfway up, her leash tightened and he yanked. She had no choice but to start feeling her way up the stairs using her hands. On all fours, trying to negotiate the unfamiliar stairs, she indeed felt like a dog on a leash. She resolved that she would make him pay for this if she ever had the opportunity.

At the top of the steps, Boyd swung open the creaky old door, stepping into the house. When she joined him, she could see nothing. She involuntarily put her hands on Boyd's arm, using him as a guide through the unfamiliar terrain of the house. In a moment, he pushed against the metal latch of a storm door and they stepped onto a porch.

"Where?" Alice asked.

"Not on the damn porch!" Boyd said. "Down the steps. Into the yard."

Not wanting to raise further ire, Alice felt around until she found a porch rail, then felt further until she found a rail descending. She followed it to the end of the leash, unbuttoned her pants, and peed in the grass. She felt her neck, noting that Boyd had threaded the zip tie right through a link in the chain, just as he'd said. There was nothing she could feel that would allow her to escape the leash without a knife.

She must have lingered too long because a sudden yank on the leash nearly pulled her over.

"I ain't got all night," he said.

When they re-entered the house, Alice's heart filled with dread at climbing back down into the dark basement. She feared that she'd never make it out of there again.

"Do you want to talk some more, Boyd?"

He laughed. "I'm not ready to talk to you now. I will be later."

He led her back down the steps, using the light and keeping her on a tight leash.

"Can you not tie me so tightly this time?" she asked. "Please?"

In the end, he left the leash on her neck, tying the other end to one of the support posts. He also put a fresh zip tie on her hands, but left her feet free this time.

"We'll talk tomorrow," he said.

"Can I have some water?" she asked. "I'm thirsty. Hungry too."

"Maybe I'll feed you tomorrow," he said. "Maybe I won't."

3

T he Valley
Russell County, VA

IN A VALLEY alongside the Clinch Mountain range there lived a man named Buddy Baisden. Buddy had a larger ranch-style brick house that he'd built in the 1980s. The light in Buddy Baisden's life went out two days before everyone else in Russell County lost theirs. That was the day his daughter Rachel died of an OxyContin overdose.

Buddy had already lost his wife three years earlier to some kind of female cancer that he didn't know much about. All he knew was that it took from him the woman who made his house into a home for him and Rachel. His daughter had been a senior in high school and he began losing her the day his wife died. She spent less and less time at home, giving him vague answers about where she was and what she was doing. He gave her curfews that she ended up breaking. His punishments had a limited effect and only served to push them further apart. He gave up punishing her eventually, hoping he might preserve his relationship with the only other person in this world that he gave two damns about.

Rachel had still looked healthy, but she came home often without that glow in her eye that he lived to see. She staggered around the house and bumped into things. Several times she had lain in the bed and urinated upon herself, so high on pills that she could not even get up to use the bathroom. He had tried talking to her, which only made her mad. After those talks she would stay away from home for days to punish him, so he quit saying anything.

She'd been with her latest boyfriend for several months. He was of a cut that Buddy didn't care for. He drove a banged up late-model Camaro in an unattractive teal color. He was forty but seemed to think he was twenty, running around with girls Rachel's age and partying when he should have been working. Buddy wondered if he was a drug dealer, but he didn't know enough about such things to know what the signs were.

Then one night, Rachel died outside of the Emergency Room doors at the local hospital, where she'd been dumped like garbage. She was not immediately noticed, laying there in the dark, but a nurse on a smoke break eventually found her. They tried everything they could, including administering opiate blockers, and were unable to bring her back from the dead. The police never figured out where she'd been or who she'd been with. No one was talking.

Buddy wasn't talking. He knew who she left home with and he knew where to find him. There was some justice better administered by a father than by the court system. It was a matter of love and of honor.

Her funeral was on the very day that the lights went out. With the condition of the country and the concern about more terror attacks, no one but Buddy showed up. They buried her on a sunny day in the cemetery in town. Buddy gave her his plot, right beside his wife. He figured he'd just have to buy another for himself. He'd never counted on needing more than two.

On the way home from the funeral, Buddy stopped at the local

Chevron to fill up his truck. When he pulled in, he found the pumps roped off with yellow crime scene tape. A deputy was sitting in his car, watching Buddy. A sign on the bank of pumps said: Pumps Closed.

Buddy got out of his truck and approached the deputy. "I hear the generator running," he said. "Why ain't they selling gas?"

"Haven't you been watching the news?" the deputy asked, squinting up at him.

Buddy hadn't had his television on since the police came and told him about Rachel. "No, don't reckon I have."

The deputy frowned at this, unable to imagine anyone who could not know what was going on in the world right now. "Terrorists are blowing shit up all over the country. They say it's ISIS or Al Qaeda. They blew up the big refineries and it's going to take a while to get them back online. The president has stopped all fuel sales except for police, military, and other first responders. It's for emergencies only."

Buddy nodded. He didn't have the words left in him that day to argue or ask questions. He was too numb. He walked back to his truck, started it and drove off toward home.

BUDDY'S FAMILY was not originally from Russell County, but from nearby Wise County. His father had been a coal miner for most of his life. In 1958, Buddy's father saw his own brother crushed when a slab of un-cribbed slate dropped from the mine roof. The two men had been discussing going deer hunting the next day. As they walked in the stooped posture required by low coal toward the shuttle car that would take them out of the mine, there was a thud that shook the ground and a puff of displaced air that pushed gently against Buddy's father's back. He turned and found that his brother was no longer behind him. Only a hand and forearm extended from beneath the car-sized chunk of slate. He dropped and took the hand in his, but despite its warmth there was no life left in the limp flesh. Buddy's father left the mine that day and never went underground again.

Shortly after that, Buddy's father bought an abandoned house on an empty stretch of dirt road far from town. He spent several months gutting and remodeling the house until he had fashioned it into some semblance of what was locally known as a "beer joint." When the interior of the building was done and all that remained was repainting the old house, a mining friend stole ten gallons of yellow safety paint from his job. Buddy's father painted the house and all the exterior trim with that color. The paint had the added benefit of high reflectivity, a feature that enhanced the safety aspects of the product, and the result was that headlights would illuminate the building brightly when they landed on the lone structure in the remote countryside. Buddy's father aptly named his new establishment The Yellow House.

Over the next several years, Buddy's mother and father ran The Yellow House with modest success. They developed a reputation for good quality meals at a fair price. Cold beer could also be had at a reasonable price. While hard liquor required a license that Buddy's father did not have, he kept such spirits under the counter and would sell them by the shot to men that he knew. For those that appreciated the novelty of untaxed clear liquor, the highest quality local moonshine was also available by the shot or by the jar.

Despite taking liberty with the letter of the law, Buddy's father did not flaunt his under-the-counter offerings. He even developed a regular clientele of deputies and state troopers who stopped in for a free meal and a coffee mug of their preferred beverage, which was as apt to be moonshine as coffee.

The Yellow House thrived until a fall day in 1963. Buddy's mother opened up for the lunch shift while Buddy's father ran into town to make a bank deposit. His wife had opened the lunch shift on her own many times over the past couple of years and had never had any problems. The lunchtime opening of a drinking establishment, though, can represent Happy Hour for a man who has been working the night shift and has not yet made it home to bed.

Buddy's mother, as she did nearly every day, served beers to such men, who would drink them with their meal and go home to sleep until their next shift. On this day, she only had a few customers and most ate their lunches and then left promptly. One man did not. He continued to drink and made comments to Buddy's mother of an insulting and inappropriate nature. She cut him off, having served him a half-dozen beers already. This made him angry and he refused to pay, issuing vile promises to Buddy's mother before left. These were emphasized with a firm hand encircling her wrist, a gesture that made her all too aware of the man's strength and, at the same time, of her own vulnerability.

She had stopped her crying and shaking by the time Buddy's father returned. She could not hide that she was upset and wilted under the pressure of her husband's stern gaze. She told him the entire story. Buddy's father knew the man she spoke of, and in fact had passed him walking home a few miles down the road. Buddy's father walked out of The Yellow House and sped off, gravel spraying from beneath the tires of his black Buick Electra.

It took him no time to find the walking man, who'd turned off the main road by this time and was following a narrow dirt road along the Levisa River. Buddy's father slid to a stop and got out of the car. The man must surely have sensed who Buddy's father was and why he was there, but he reportedly said nothing. Buddy's father withdrew a .25 caliber Colt automatic from his pocket. He shot the drunk man in the face until he fell and kept shooting him until the gun was empty. When he left the scene, Buddy's father made a tight turn, backing over the body twice before his car was pointed in the right direction.

Buddy often wondered why his dad did not attempt to hide the body, but he made no such effort. The body was found and reported before the day was out. While the face of the dead man was not easily recognizable, the reek of alcohol was, and that led the police right to the door of the most likely place that the alcohol had been obtained -- The Yellow House.

When asked if he'd seen this particular man today, Buddy's father replied that he had.

"When did you last see him?" the trooper asked.

"When I killed the son-of-a-bitch," Buddy's father said.

His father was sentenced to twenty years and sent to the Virginia State Penitentiary in Richmond. Buddy was less than a year old at the time and had vague childhood memories of visiting his father there. Buddy's mother kept The Yellow House running in her husband's absence, hiring various folks over the years to fill positions.

One night, shortly after Buddy's father had been convicted and sent away, the trooper that had arrested him came into The Yellow House and sat right at the bar in front of Buddy's mother. She held no ill-will against the man; he'd just been doing his job.

The man placed a brown paper bag onto the bar top and slid it across.

"What's that?" Buddy's mother asked.

The man nodded toward it. Buddy's mother hooked a finger in the opening and tipped the bag toward her, leaning over to peer in. Inside, she saw the Colt .25 automatic.

"With the trial over with, we won't be needing that anymore," the trooper said in a gesture that would seem quite alien in this day and time. "But if you're going to keep this place open, *you* might need it."

When Buddy's father was released after ten years for good behavior, The Yellow House was still open and waiting on him. He worked that bar until he died of a heart attack in 1977.

Buddy still had the gun his father had used to kill that man. In his family, the act had never been portrayed as murder. There were just certain actions that a person took in life that brought about a particular set of consequences. The rules of this were as set in stone as sums in arithmetic. A math problem only has one answer, as do some problems in this world. When that drunk laid his hands on Buddy's mother, he set in place an unavoidable consequence, given the times, the region, and the man whose wife he'd touched. It was the natural world at work. There was only one answer.

The same had been done when that man drove off in his teal Camaro with Rachel and had not brought her home safely. There were unavoidable consequences. Buddy had no other course of action available to him. If the world was collapsing around him anyway, that would just make it easier for Buddy to do what he needed to do.

4

Gary's House
Richlands, VA

WHEN THE MORNING sky began to show the first signs of graying, Gary felt a little better. He'd stayed on high alert for the remainder of the night, trying to maintain a watch on his home and hoping that his sons-in-law were doing the same at their homes. He'd been stupid to not send them home with radios. He'd thought that formalizing their security measures could wait another day, and found it wasn't the case. If he wasn't careful, his stupidity was going to get someone killed.

His family didn't even know about the worst part of the night yet. They were not aware of the mangled body still in his driveway. The big question that hung over Gary's head was to understand why these people did what they did. He was sure it was a decoy maneuver of some kind and he'd fallen for it hook, line, and sinker. More stupidity on his part. Now that morning was coming and he could see without a light, he had to find out what the riders had done while he was distracted. Surely they didn't just tie a body under his vehicle for laughs. If that was the case, they were a higher caliber of scumbag than he'd been expecting.

Armed with his AR and his pistol, Gary checked the garage first. Karen's Jetta was parked at the side of the house and the door that led to the garage wasn't visible from there. While he'd been occupied with that body last night, someone could have pried open the deadbolt and had access to their fuel and other emergency preparations. When he checked, he found no indication of this, though; no signs of forced entry.

He went to his outbuildings next. Although Will had said he'd emptied them of all the important supplies, the riders would most likely not have known this. They may still have thought they might find gas cans or other useable items in there. The buildings had not been tampered with. He opened each with the keys he carried in his pocket and looked around. Though things were a little disorganized where Will had hurriedly transferred the more important contents into the garage, they didn't look like they'd been burglarized.

As he exited the last building, the sun finally broke over the hilltop. The rays of golden light hit his yard and reflected off the dew, illuminating a pair of deep tracks that led across his yard from the road. That got his attention. They were not the heavily lugged tracks of an ATV tire, nor were they narrow dirt bike tires. He followed them to where they crossed his sidewalk. The tread pattern was more visible where the vehicle had tracked mud across the concrete and he thought he recognized it.

Golf cart.

Realizing that the directions of the tracks meant they could only lead one place, he ran furiously around the corner of the house. At the most remote side of the house, where it would have presented less of an eyesore to visitors, Gary had stored their Generac generator in a small housing specifically built for it. The housing lay upended from where it had been rolled.

The generator was gone.

Enraged, Gary kicked the empty housing several times. He finally let out a long sigh and closed his eyes. This was a blow. He knew that fuel would run out eventually but he felt like the generator had been a critical component of his emergency planning, giving them more options.

The fact that it had been stolen told him several things. It could mean that his home had been watched enough for someone to know that he had a generator and where it was stored. It could also mean that his plan to bug-in at home was fatally flawed by virtue of their location not being safe enough. For certain, it meant that he was becoming more of a victim each day, with the theft of his garden and now his generator. He didn't like that feeling one bit.

REGARDLESS OF HOW dire the circumstances, a little daylight always made everything more manageable. Coffee would help even more. Gary went back to the kitchen to regroup, process, and plan. He started a pot of water boiling on the side burner of his gas grill. He had other means of heating the water, but the gas grill was the quickest until he got things better set up.

Like much of his gear, his various cook stoves had been stored away in the garage and his outbuildings. With Will moving things into the garage in his absence, he wasn't even sure where to start looking for his most critical items. When he'd gone to bed last night, it had been a priority to get some of his preparations set up today and start transitioning over to using them, and now the theft of the generator left him unsure. Was it even safe to set out equipment like solar panels or would they just be stolen? It looked like security would end up being a bigger priority than sustainability.

With the coffee water heating, he took a moment to enjoy the morning view of his yard. He'd missed this sight while he'd been gone. He enjoyed it for all of about ten seconds before he caught sight of the feet sticking out from beneath his daughter's car and realized that this had to be dealt with before everyone got up. He didn't want his children or grandchildren to see it. He couldn't help but want to insulate them from the ugliness of the world.

He knew the body would be heavy, literally *dead weight,* and while he would have preferred Will's help in moving it, he didn't want to take the time to go find him. In the meantime, he could at least hide the body somewhere and Will could help him dispose of it later. He decided that pulling the body on a sled might be easier than just dragging it. He stored his children's old sleds under one of his outbuildings. He went to it and retrieved one of the plastic ones, hoping he could roll the body onto it and then pull it through the wet grass.

First, he cut the rope loose that held the body under the car. He'd stuck a Kershaw Cryo in his pocket that morning and he fished it out. Though he wasn't excited about getting under the car with the body, he didn't see any other options. In the tight quarters, the body reeked. With the corpse so closely resembling a movie zombie, Gary also had to deal with the irrational fear that the corpse would latch onto him as he worked and try to sink its teeth into him. He was relieved when he finally got the rope sliced and could put some distance between him and the body. He rolled out from beneath the car and pocketed the knife.

In short order, he dragged the body out by the ankles and rolled it onto the sled. It was nasty, disgusting work that he couldn't imagine ever getting used to. He'd handled several dead bodies over the last couple of weeks and he hoped this wasn't developing into a pattern. Despite the unpleasantness of it, he took a good look at the guy's face in the light and it wasn't familiar to him. He didn't know the man, which made the whole process just a little easier. It spoke volumes about the state of the world that a dead guy wasn't a big deal unless he was someone you knew.

He leaned down to pick up the rope and start pulling the sled across the yard, startled to notice Debra and Karen standing in the doorway watching him with morbid fascination. They were clearly aghast at the circumstances, seeing Gary roll a dead body onto a sled. Having been sheltered until now from the horrors that were being visited upon the rest of the world, the look on Debra's and Karen's faces said a lot. In seeing the casualness with which Gary dealt with this corpse, they must have begun to realize how truly awful Gary's trip home must have been.

Gary felt that in allowing them to see this, he had somehow let them down. It disappointed him. Still, they *had* to see this kind of thing eventually. They *had* to know what was out there waiting for them. And for that matter, what was not just waiting for them, but now knocking at their door. He could not protect them if they didn't realize how dangerous the world was.

They all just stared at each other for a moment, so many thoughts and looks racing between them.

"Do you need some help?" Debra finally asked, breaking the silence.

Gary nodded.

After they got the body behind the building and covered it with a sheet of black plastic, Gary walked around the house checking for other signs of damage that may have occurred either last night or in his absence. He was pleased that he found none. He did find one of his neighbors outside, likely doing the same thing. Gary raised a hand and waved at the man. When he waved back, Gary walked down his drive and followed the common driveway toward the man's house. The neighbor met him along the way and they shook hands.

"I see you made it home," the man said. He was tall and effeminate, with a dismissive tone in his soft voice that always implied a dissatisfaction with whatever was being discussed. It had irritated Gary at first until he realized that it was the man's way and not something directed at him personally.

His name was Scott Rose and he was a self-proclaimed minister of some sort. He and Gary were polar opposites on many topics but they were in agreement where it was important. Both liked their privacy and wanted to keep their neighborhood peaceful. There were six houses total, with three belonging to Gary's family and three belonging to Scott's. That made it easy to make decisions affecting the neighborhood. Most of them could just be worked out between

Gary and Scott. No Home Owners' Association, no bylaws, just two guys standing in the yard over a glass of sweet tea making any decisions that had to be made.

"I did make it home," Gary replied. "It wasn't easy. I can't say that I'm happy to come back home to a bunch of idiots out here riding in my yard and stealing my stuff either."

Scott nodded. "Yeah, they hit me the night before. I didn't catch them. Did you shoot one of them last night? I heard a shot."

"I shot at one of them," Gary said. "Scared him off." Gary didn't want to go into the whole story with Scott about the dead body and the stolen generator.

"Should have blown his nuts off," Scott mumbled.

"Trust me, I've seen enough killing recently to hold me for a while," Gary said.

Scott looked at him with a question in his eyes but it never reached his lips and Gary didn't elaborate. Despite their years as neighbors, they weren't close enough to talk about personal matters. Theirs was strictly a meat-and-potatoes relationship.

"I was wondering about closing the gate on our road," Gary said. "If you got a key and I got a key that about covers everybody, doesn't it?"

Scott nodded. "I reckon so. That may slow them down. Probably won't stop them. You can drive around it."

"Do you know who they are?" Gary asked. "I haven't been able to get a look at any of them."

Scott shook his head. "All kinds of possibilities. There's the public housing project over the hill, then there's also hundreds of houses up and down the main road. They could be coming from anywhere, really. There's no shortage of Godless troublemakers."

Gary mulled it over, staring at his house in the distance. "Things like this have a way of getting out of control," he said. "I've seen it a lot recently. With no police to call, little conflicts grow into big conflicts and people get killed."

Scott reached into the pocket of his brown polyester pants and withdrew a snub-nosed revolver. "I got no problem enforcing the law myself when I have to. Some people need killing."

Gary stared at the gun, then raised his eyes to Scott. It was easy to talk about killing when you'd never had to do it. "You ever shot a man, Scott?"

The man met his eyes, shaking his head. "No. Never had no call to. You?"

Images of violent episodes from his journey rushed to fill Gary's head. He saw the shocked expression of the people he'd shot on the Blue Ridge Parkway. He saw the way that life faded to death, like a flashlight losing power. He remembered the smell of the decomposing bodies they'd found on Mount Rogers, the family killed for their food and supplies. He remembered the smell of a man shot in the gut, the contents of his intestines mixing with blood and pouring from his body in a black torrent that the man's clutching hands could not slow.

Had Gary shot men? Yes. He'd killed them and he would forever be changed by it. It was not something he cared to talk to Scott about, though. If Scott ever had to make those decisions, he could see for himself that it was not something you went around bragging about.

"I'll shut that gate," Gary said, turning and walking off. "You take care of yourself."

BY THE TIME Gary made it back to his house, his entire clan was assembled in the kitchen and working on breakfast. They were discussing the events of night, using enough coded language that the grandchildren wouldn't be able to tell what they were discussing. They were serving eggs, sausage, biscuits, butter, and jelly. Gary could not immediately tell what was made from fresh, canned, powdered, or freeze-dried ingredients. That was a good sign. Unfortunately, though, with the generator gone, there would be no more refrigeration. He hadn't yet shared that tidbit with his family. It was only when a cup of coffee was placed in front of him that Gary realized he'd walked off and left the water heating on the grill burner earlier. He opened his mouth to say something about it, but his wife cut him off.

"That's okay," she said. "I kept an eye on it."

He smiled. The beauty of being home and back among family was that they did things like that for you. They kept an eye out for you so that you didn't have to be so hyper-vigilant all the time. That said, it was now time for him lay out the ideas he'd tossed around in his head this morning as he'd maintained a watch.

Once breakfast was prepared, Gary had everyone sit in the kitchen so that they could discuss their situation together. They'd never had a family meeting before.

"I want you all to know that being back here with you is beyond words. This is all I thought about while I walked across the state. I missed you all more than I can ever tell you." He took a breath. His emotions were flaring up and he felt his eyes watering.

"I'm more than a little concerned about what our neighborhood is turning into. I think we might need to literally circle the wagons," he said. "There's no way we can defend three homes with the few people we have. I think we all need to move into this house until things are safer."

Sara frowned. Her reaction didn't surprise Gary. Sara's house was new and she'd just finished getting things the way she wanted them. Of course she didn't want to move out of it. "Why your house, Dad? I just got moved."

"Simple. Our house is brick," Gary said. "The other houses are vinyl siding over wood. Brick offers some degree of ballistic protection. Vinyl does not."

This was a solid argument. Gary expected debate as to why they needed *ballistic protection* but there was none. They were all reasonable enough to see that this might truly become the case. Just because no one had fired on the house yet didn't mean that it wouldn't happen at some point. The fact that they were already having to carry guns around on a regular basis meant that conditions were escalated, to say the least.

"The wolf couldn't blow down the brick house when the pigs hid there," Lana offered, looking up from the toy she was playing with.

"Exactly right, Lana," Gary said, stroking her head. "I think you all should spend the morning gathering what resources you have and shuttling them over here so we can consolidate things. Bring sleeping gear, batteries, flashlights, weapons and ammo, food, all of your emergency stuff," Gary continued. Then, with a glance down at Lana he had a thought. "We can take turns watching the kids so everyone can get packed up without having the kids try to help. That would be more efficient."

"How long will we have to stay like this?" Charlotte asked. "I like my house."

"I know you like your house, baby," Gary said. "We have to think differently now. You have to leave behind your everyday mindset and adopt a survival mindset. This is not about comfort, it's about staying safe. There's no way I can tell you how long we'll have to alter our lives. Just remember that stuff doesn't matter. What matters is in this room right now."

"But we *will* get to go back to our regular lives, right?" Charlotte asked. "Things will get back to normal, won't they?"

Gary was silent for a moment. They were not up to speed on the situation in the world. They did not realize the full implications. They had not seen what he'd seen. He had to be gentle about this. That was the problem Jim always had in communicating the serious-ness of the situation to people who weren't getting it. He had no subtlety. He had been the perfect example of how not to have this conversation.

"I would love to pat you on the head and tell you it's going to be all right. As your father, I would like nothing more than to be able to offer you that reassurance. We have to be realistic, though. It could be years before everything is completely normal again," Gary said. "We don't know the extent of everything that's gone on yet. There is phys-ical damage that has to be fixed. There are communication channels that have to be repaired before we can coordinate a recovery effort on a national level. There are a lot of things that have to happen. If it's sooner than a year, I'd be surprised."

There was a collective moan from the group.

"A year? *Really*?" Charlotte asked. "What about my job? What about school for the kids?"

Gary shrugged. "I don't know what to tell you. My role right now, as I see it, is to keep all of you alive and not to maintain some illusion for you. You are all adults and will have to accept the reality of this situation the same as I do. I cannot tell you the...horror of what I saw out there. I do not want that horror to become part of our lives. At the same time, you all will have to accept that there will be inconveniences. There may be struggling. There may even be suffering. I will do my best to minimize that and try to make sure that we thrive. I have prepared for that, but there are no guarantees."

Gary's wife cleared her throat and the room became silent. Everyone turned to her. "I have complete faith in you, Gary," she said. "I did when I married you and I still do now. Do we have what we need to thrive and stay safe here in this house? If we all move in here together, can we weather this disturbance and stay safe? I know you made preparations, but are they enough?"

Gary was silent. This was going to be difficult. They would probably not like this answer. "I'm not sure if we can or not," he said honestly. "By the time I became concerned about societal collapse and began making preparations, we were already invested in this location. We had already built this house and established ourselves here. I thought about us moving to a more sustainable location but I just wasn't sure I could go through that whole process again. Building a home is so emotionally exhausting. I have discovered there are shortcomings to this property that we might not be able to overcome if this is truly a long-term disaster."

Debra sighed as if preparing herself for a blow. "Such as?"

"Water for one," Gary said. "There is no water source up here. Town water was available when we built so we didn't have to put in a well. That was a plus at the time because it saved us money on building the house, but it's not so much of a plus now. There's not even a creek nearby. The closest spring water is on Kent's Ridge Road and it's about a mile from here. We could certainly drive up there and collect water if we had to, but do we want to use up all the fuel we have left just on getting water? How much water could we collect on a bike? Could we push a wagon or wheelbarrow two miles round trip each day to retrieve water? Would it even be safe to do so? Could any of us even pull a wagon of water up that steep hill coming up the driveway? I'm not sure I could."

"That spring is also on private property," Will said. "If water becomes a problem, who knows if there will even be free access to that spring anymore? They could close it off and start charging for water. I'm not sure if it was mine if I would just allow anyone and everyone to come on my property and take water."

Sara glared at Will, obviously not appreciating her husband adding his gloomy insights to the conversation.

"Good point," Gary said. "I'm just not sure that you all have any clue how much water we all use on a regular basis. My mother told me that when I was a baby their well dried up during a drought and they had to haul water from a spring two miles away. Even using a vehicle, they had to get water twice a day just to keep a baby clean and cloth diapers washed. If we run out of disposable diapers, how much water do you think it will take to keep three children bathed and in clean diapers? We're talking lots of water, plus what we'll all need for cooking, drinking, and bathing ourselves."

"Diapers would have been something good to purchase in advance," Charlotte said. "Both disposable and cloth. Too late now. You should have mentioned that earlier."

"I didn't mention it because I took care of it. I have plenty," Gary said, smiling. "I probably have several hundred disposable diapers stored in one of the outbuildings and a few dozen cloth ones. Just in case."

Charlotte didn't appear relieved by that. She was probably picturing herself scrubbing cloth diapers in a washtub and was not thrilled by the image. "I'm guessing you have a washboard stored out there somewhere?"

"Better," Gary said. "I have a prepper washing machine."

"What's that?" Charlotte asked, not sure she wanted to know.

"A five gallon bucket with a hole drilled in the lid," he said. "You put water, soap, and dirty clothes in it. You stick a plunger handle through the hole in the bucket lid, then put the lid on the bucket. You agitate it like you're churning butter. It's not perfect but it's easier than a washboard."

"A clean plunger, I hope," Sara said.

"It's a new one," Gary said. "Never used. Don't worry."

"Is that it?" Debra asked impatiently. "Is water the big problem?"

"Water is probably the biggest, but not the only problem," Gary admitted. "Security would be running a close second."

"But we're up here on this hill all by ourselves?" Sara said. "Isn't that secure enough?"

"Was it secure last night?" Gary asked. "It didn't seem like it to me. We only heard those folks because they were on noisy machines. What about all the folks who might just walk in here on foot? How many folks have already been in here creeping around at night and you've just not heard them?"

"I don't think that's likely," Charlotte said.

"I do," Gary said. "Someone stole the generator last night while we were all distracted. I didn't hear them take it."

The group look surprised.

"How did they find it?" Debra said. "It was hidden around the side of the house."

"They probably heard it running at some point," Gary said. "Then they just watched until they found it."

"Now you're saying that people have been watching us?" Sara asked.

"Probably," Gary replied. "There could be people watching us right now."

"What people?" Sara asked. "That's just creepy."

"There's an entire public housing project close by," Gary said. "Hundreds of apartments of people who are probably already out of food and water. People who need what we have."

"That's nearly two miles away," Sara pointed out. "They have closer neighbors than us. Wouldn't they just steal from them first?"

"By road it's two miles, yes," Gary agreed, then gestured toward the back of their property. "If you walk over that hill there, you come out in the middle of the complex. It's probably not even three hundred yards away."

"I never realized that," Charlotte said. "I guess I never thought about it."

"It was a lot smaller when we built this house," Gary said. "They've added four new buildings since then. We have to take all of that into account when trying to assess the long-term viability of this location. Just as those people came in last night, there could be more people walking in. We need to be on guard against visitors from all sides."

"This is making me sad," Charlotte said.

Gary couldn't help but smile, seeing her pout just like she did when she was a little girl. "I'm sorry, sweetie. The good news is that in an hour you'll be way too busy to dwell on it. Let's just be glad that we're all alive, we're all safe, and we're together. There are many families that aren't."

TRUE TO HIS WORD, Gary soon had his family distracted enough by the task at hand that they could no longer dwell on the unpleasant possibilities that they might be facing. They started at Sara and Will's house, which was the farthest from Gary's. Gary hooked a utility trailer to his lawn tractor, his most fuel efficient vehicle, and they used that to shuttle loads back and forth. It wasn't like they were going a long distance and couldn't ever return home, so they prioritized the loads with the items they would need the soonest and most often. As with any parents of small children, that meant starting with baby stuff: diapers, formula, baby medicines, clothes, toys, a playpen, and highchair.

"Surely that will be enough to hold a baby for a day," Gary said. "I don't think your mother and I ever had this much stuff when we raised you girls."

"Sorry, Dad," Sara said. "They just make more stuff now."

"Then they shame you into buying it," Gary said.

"Hey, we didn't buy all this," Sara said. "I remember *you* buying a lot of this."

Gary grinned. "First grandchild. I couldn't help it."

"It's okay," Sara said, hugging him. "It will all get used and worn out before we girls are done having babies."

"I hope we're never done with babies," Gary admitted.

Sara patted him on the back. "Dad, get moving," she said. "I'll have another load on the front porch by the time you guys get back."

While Will and Gary shuttled the first load to Gary's house, Sara started working in the kitchen. She and Will did not have a generator like her parents so they'd not been able to keep the refrigerator and freezer going long enough to save their food. They'd eaten what they could and taken some things to her mom's house. They'd still been forced to clean out the refrigerator several days ago when everything started reeking. There were probably things that needed to be thrown away anyway, like the leftover mustard from a cookout that no one was ever going to eat, the horseradish from a failed coleslaw experiment, and the bottle of wine they'd received as a housewarming present that had tasted like crap when they tried drinking it. Now the refrigerator door was propped open to prevent mildew and the inside was clean and bare.

Sara made a quick pass through the kitchen and boxed up the contents of her pantry. She considered for a moment that she might need to leave some food for the point in time that she and Will returned to living in their own house, but if they were going to pool their resources she needed to be all in. She would take everything worth taking out of this kitchen and they could deal with restocking it when that time came. As much as she hated to admit it, there was also the possibility that they might not be able to return home anytime soon. She would not think about that now, though. She was more practical and realistic than Charlotte.

As she passed the sink, Sara glanced outside through the single kitchen window. The window looked out across their sparse backyard to the boundary of weeds on the hill behind them. Their lawn looked pitiful. She and Will had sown grass and planted trees, but it had been a busy summer and the children needed their attention constantly. Yards took time to fill out and mature. Perhaps by next summer the yard would be more presentable.

She turned back to her work, then froze. Something outside had caught her eye and was only now registering with her brain. She backed up. There had been something else there, something out of place.

She scanned the yard close to the house but it was so bare that anything unusual would have been readily apparent. She looked higher onto the hillside, where the knee-high weeds merged with the woods that bordered their property. Her breath caught in her throat when she saw three men standing there.

These were not normal men. Besides all of them wearing black clothing from head-to-toe, they were also wearing masks. They were pullover cloth masks that covered the wearer's face from the eyes down. The masks were printed with a skull pattern that made them appear to be leering at her from the hillside. In another time and place the getup might have been laughable. Now, with full knowledge of what type of people would be wearing such an outfit and why they would be wearing it, it filled her with terror.

They made no attempt to hide themselves as they watched the house. She was nearly certain that they could not see her because of the glare off the window. She backed away slightly, just in case, putting her body off to the side of the window. She watched to see if they would walk away but they continued watching.

She ran to the front door in a panic. She looked out and couldn't see her dad or Will. They were probably unloading the trailer into the garage for now and the garage wasn't visible from her front door. She could yell for them but it was several hundred yards. They probably wouldn't be able to hear her. She started to run out the front door and toward her parent's house but with the yard bare of any concealing vegetation she would be out in the open. What if they came after her? If they took her, no one would have a clue where to even start looking.

She found that the idea of running away did not set well with her. She did not want to be afraid in her own house. She wanted to stand her ground. She had been raised to do that. She was not a victim and she would not *let* herself become a victim. This was *her* house. She needed to calm down and take control of this situation. She had not seen any visible weapons. If she could calm herself, she could take care of this.

She closed the front door and locked the deadbolt, then made a quick pass around the lower floor of the house and confirmed that all of the doors and windows accessible from the ground were locked. She ran back to the kitchen and glanced out the window again. The men were still there. One held a long knife in his hand now and was using it to point. It looked like he was pointing toward the French doors that led from her dining room to the patio. Surely they couldn't think the house was abandoned. If they'd been watching it for any time at all, they would have seen her father and husband leaving with the trailer full of stuff. Maybe they knew it was still occupied and didn't care.

She ran up the stairs, taking them two at a time. Though they planned to take all of the guns with them to her dad's house, they'd not started moving them yet. They had a gun safe in the bedroom that her dad had bought them as a housewarming gift. She punched the code into the digital lock and threw the lever. The weapon that both her dad and Will had encouraged her to use if she ever had to defend her home was the 12 gauge shotgun. It was a Mossberg 590 tactical model and they kept it in the front of the safe with the tube magazine loaded and the chamber empty. All she had to do to ready the weapon was to rack the pump and chamber a round. If the sound of the pump action cycling was not sufficient enough to deter these trespassers, then perhaps a chest full of 00-buckshot would do the job.

Shutting the gun safe, she ran to the window of Lana's room and peered out the curtains without disturbing them. The men had come closer and were at the edge of her straw-covered lawn. They had crouched down and continued to study the house. She wondered if they were trying to figure out if anyone was home or not. They were clearly on her property now. They were trespassing and were not well-intentioned or they wouldn't be lurking in the weeds behind the house. They wouldn't be wearing masks. She had to make it clear that this was the wrong house to mess with.

She returned to the front door, unlocked it, and slipped out. She looked back toward her parents' house one more time and still saw no one. Though two weeks ago she could have called over there, or even called 911 for help, now there were fewer options. As she'd considered before, she could run, but that would not send a message of strength. That would not be a deterrent. Panic resurfaced and she had a brief thought that she should run to her sister's house for help, then she remembered Charlotte and her husband were not there because they were at her dad's house looking after all the kids, waiting on their turn to empty their own house. She would have to deal with this alone.

Dropping off the side of the front porch, she walked along the red mulch and foot-high shrubs toward the side of the house furthest from that of her sister's or parents'. She chose this side because she assumed the men would be splitting their attention between studying her house and keeping watch toward the other houses. There was nothing on this end for them to be concerned with. No other houses, no other neighbors. They would not be expecting anything from this side. She was counting on that.

She listened at the corner and heard nothing. Even so, she raised the shotgun to her shoulder, placed her finger on the safety and stepped around the corner. She'd been taught to do this in such a manner that you didn't lead with the barrel, allowing an intruder to grab the barrel and take your weapon from you. She stepped away from the house, putting some distance between her body and the corner, but there was no one there. She released the breath she'd been holding and approached the back corner of the house.

She knew this time would be different. She knew there was definitely someone around this corner. Three someones, in fact. She paused, keeping her body close to the wall. If they had handguns on them and opened fire, she would have to duck back quickly and hope that the house could absorb the bullets.

She shouldered the weapon and leaned around the corner, glaring down the barrel at the men. The ghost ring sight lay on the chest of the middle man. At this distance, without the protection of her locked house around her, the masked men terrified her. She had never been so close to killing a man purely out of fear.

They had not yet noticed her. She sucked down her fear and let her anger rise. How dare these men try to rob her home? What if her children had been there?

"Don't fucking move!" she shouted, her voice as loud and authoritative as she could make it.

The men flinched, startled. She could see their eyes moving, their brains spinning for traction. With the masks on, only their eyes and close-cropped heads showed. She saw now that the masks were like those that SWAT teams wore on raids to conceal their identities.

"What are you doing behind my house?"

One of the men was whispering under his breath. She couldn't make out what he was saying but she knew he was talking to the other men. She hoped they weren't planning something crazy. She didn't want to have to kill them, but she would. She snapped the safety off, wanting to be immediately ready to fire if she had to. This did not go unnoticed, the slight metallic click carrying loudly enough across the silence of the yard.

As she drew a breath to tell them to leave while they still could, they all heard the sound of a lawnmower start up. While she didn't take her eyes from the men, the sound distracted her for the briefest moment, delaying her reaction. The men took this opportunity to dive into the tall grass and scurry away. They were only visible for seconds before they disappeared into the thicker brush at the edge of the yard. She had no doubt that she could have put easily put buckshot pellets into painful locations as they crawled away but she couldn't make herself do it. Instead, she raised the barrel just over their heads and fired into the trees. She pumped the action and fired again, then a third time. She hoped that the sound of pellets crashing over their heads and dropping leaves on them would make the men think twice about returning.

What she hadn't considered was the immediate effect that the shotgun blasts would have on everyone else in their neighborhood. As she retreated back to the front yard, she found that her father and Will had abandoned the mower and were running across the yards as fast as they could, pistols in hand. Beyond them, she could see her brother-in-law Dave sprinting toward them with an AR-15 in his arms. While she could barely make out their faces, she could see their eyes wide with fear.

The Mossberg had a sling and she threw it across her back, raising both arms to wave toward the approaching men that she was okay.

Will was the first to reach her. "Are you okay?" he practically shouted. "What happened?"

"I'm okay," Sara said.

Gary took in Sara's appearance, seeing no blood and no obvious injury. "What's wrong?" he gasped. "Why were you shooting?"

Sara felt a change in her body chemistry when she opened her mouth to speak. A second ago she'd been completely calm, cool, and collected. Now, she felt like she was going to pass out and burst into tears all at the same time.

"Do you need to sit down?" Gary asked, his father's intuition going off. "It's the nerves baby. You'll be okay."

Will led Sara to the front steps and she sat down. As she did, she noticed that her legs were shaking uncontrollably.

"Tell us what happened, Sara," Gary said.

"I saw three men out the kitchen window," Sara said, fighting to keep her voice from quavering. "They were in black and wearing these creepy skull masks."

"Did they hurt you?" Gary asked.

Sara shook her head. "After you all left, they came out of the woods and were watching the house. They came down into the yard and were looking like they were going to break in. I got the shotgun and surprised them."

"Did they have guns, baby?" Will asked, rubbing Sara's back reassuringly.

"Not that I saw. They were just crouched there in the backyard watching the house. When I got around back, they came a little closer. I had the shotgun on them but they took off running when you all started the mower."

"Did you hit any of them?" Gary asked.

"No, I...I tried not to. I shot over their heads. I just wanted to scare them. Make them think twice about coming back."

"Good girl," Gary said. "I'm going to take a look and make sure I don't see any blood."

"I'll go with you," Will said.

Gary shook his head. "No, you stay with Sara. She needs you right now. Dave can go with me."

Dave trotted up about that time, panting and heaving, the AR dangling from the single-point sling over his shoulder.

"Dave, come with me," Gary said.

Too winded to speak, Dave bobbed his red face in a nod.

"Take this, Dad," Sara said, extending the shotgun toward him. "There should still be four or five rounds in there."

Gary leaned over to kiss his daughter on the head. Then he turned to Dave. "Let's go."

Gary led the way back to the corner of the house where Sara had confronted the intruders. Seeing nothing out of the ordinary, he advanced through the scattered straw and sparse grass to the weeded perimeter of the yard. Keeping the shotgun in a ready position, he scanned the brush carefully but didn't see anyone. What he did see, though, was what looked like a well-worn trail leading away from their property. Where the trail ended at the edge of Will and Sara's yard, there was an area of flattened weeds where several people had obviously sat. There were beer cans and crushed cigarette butts. Some of the cigarette butts were stained from having sat there through rain. Gary knew it meant that people had been watching them for a while. It was an unsettling feeling.

"Stay here, Dave," Gary said. "I think I know where this trail comes out but I need to make sure."

"Are you sure?" Dave asked. "What if they're waiting on you?"

"I'll be fine," Gary assured him. "You just stay here in case something happens."

While Dave was thinking that over, Gary trotted off down the trail. His intention was not to catch up with the men who'd been lurking here but to verify where the trail came out. He walked the rough trail, finding himself concerned that there was even a trail at all. Trails required frequent travel to stay beaten down. He knew that there had once been a shortcut from the public housing development to a nearby convenience store that had cut through their property. When their neighbor Scott first bought this hillside to build his home, he'd had a few encounters with trespassers who'd been intent on continuing the practice of cutting across the hillside.

Eventually, though, folks realized that dealing with Scott was more trouble than it was worth and found another way to get there. With that, the trail should have grown back over and merged with the forest but that was clearly not the case. Some folks were apparently still using it. It made Gary think back carefully to things that had turned up missing over the years: a shovel, a water hose, some toys. While he'd always assumed that he or the kids just misplaced them, had people been stealing from him all along?

In less than five minutes, his question as to the trail's destination had been answered. The trail brought him out in the woods behind the public housing development. He remained in the woods and scanned the grounds but saw no one out moving around. He saw no men that might have been their visitors, nor anyone who might have witnessed them returning. He withdrew back into the woods and walked back.

When he and Dave rejoined the others in front of Sara's house, they found that their neighbor Scott was also there, his revolver tucked into the waistband of his pants. Gary nodded at him.

"Find anything?" Scott asked.

"A well-worn trail between here and those apartments," Gary said. "There's also some trails beat down in other directions. It's practically a highway back there."

"I wonder who's been using it?" Scott asked.

"Besides today's visitors, I'm not sure," Gary said. "I've never noticed people back there before. It does concern me, though."

"It makes my decision a little easier," Scott said.

"What decision?" Gary asked.

Scott looked around at the group. "We're leaving," he announced.

Gary thought this over. "I hate to hear that," he said. "I was kind of hoping that we might be able to work together to put a little better security in place around here."

Scott shrugged. "I'm sorry, Gary, but I just don't know if there's much we can do about that. This place is too close to town. There's probably ten thousand people who could get here in less than a fifteen minute walk. How do you protect against that?"

Scott was telling Gary what he already knew. "I've been wondering the same thing," Gary admitted. "So where are you going?"

"Our church has a camp in the woods," Scott said. "We do revivals and retreats there. There are cabins and bunkhouses, showers, a dining hall – everything we need. It's even got spring water and outhouses. It's on about two hundred and fifty acres over in Bland County. Some of us are going to go over and open the camp up. More folks will probably come out after we get it going. We're going to pool our fuel together and try to make a few trips in the church bus so that we can haul more people. Some of us are thinking that pooling our resources will be the best way for us to survive this. Otherwise the elderly and the shut-ins won't make it much longer."

Gary knew he was right about that.

"When are you going?" Will asked.

"Today," Scott replied. "No use delaying it. Everyone is packing up right now. I went through every gas-operated machine and vehicle I own and scraped together enough fuel to fill my truck up. We're going to load all our stuff into that old horse trailer and fit all the people in the bed of the truck. It'll be a load but hopefully we can get there with no problems."

"And no trouble," Gary warned. "I hope you've got more than that revolver to protect yourself."

"We do," Scott said. "My sons are armed. They'll be watching while I do the driving. The men of the church know to bring their weapons as well. Our camp will not be relying on prayer alone for protection. There's also a time and place in God's world for Smith and Wesson."

Gary extended his hand. "Good luck, Scott. We'll try to keep an eye on your place but I'm not sure we're even going to be able to keep an eye on our own places."

Scott smiled at him. "Don't worry about it, Gary. Without the people I care about inside it, it's just another house. Remember that."

Gary nodded. He would have to make sure his family remembered that. Scott shook Will's and Dave's hands, then hugged Sara. He made Gary promise to give his goodbyes to the rest of the family, hitched his pants up, spat, and walked off.

Things were quiet for a moment, then Gary turned to his family. "So these guys had masks on, Sara?"

She nodded. "They were those kind of masks like soldiers wear. Like tubes that you pull over your head, but they were black with a skull print on the front."

"Have you all seen those folks before?"

"No," Sara said.

"No," Dave replied. "Not me."

Will was hesitant.

"Will?" Gary prodded.

"Yes," Will admitted. "It's the guys with the dirt bikes. They were in creepy black clothes with those masks when they rode up here before. I didn't say anything because I didn't want to scare anyone. It's why I've been so jumpy, though. People don't hide their faces unless they're up to no good."

"Right," Gary said. "I guess we need to get back to work. I don't want anyone working outside of the house again without radios. We probably have a dozen cheap walkie-talkies with plenty of batteries and we're not using them. I thought about it last night and meant to get them out first thing, then we got busy. That's just the kind of dumb decision we can't afford to make anymore. If Sara had one, she could have called us. We got lucky this time. We can't count on luck to save us every time. Let's get those radios before we do anything else."

5

B oyd's House
Bluefield, VA

ALICE SENSED it was mid-morning but only the faintest light filtered into the basement. Outside, the hills were steep and the houses crammed closely together, blocking out all but the overhead light of midday. The tiny basement windows were so grimy she doubted they had ever been cleaned. The insides were smeared with a greasy film that diffused the light. The outsides of the ground level windows were crusted with grass clippings and splashed mud.

The house above her had been silent all morning. She had nothing to occupy her physically so all she could do was obsess on her plight. She thought of her son and husband, how they must miss her, how they must wonder what had happened to her. She didn't know if she'd ever see them again. It was impossible to know. Nothing could be certain in this violent and unpredictable world. She also thought of Boyd. Why had he taken her? What did he want from her?

Would she end up like Rebecca, brutally stabbed and bled out until her skin was white as paper?

At some point in the morning, the floor creaked above her and she heard the solid clunk of a sliding deadbolt being thrown. The door at the top of the basement stairs opened and a pair of feet made their way into her limited line of sight. As she expected, it was Boyd, and he was carrying a bucket of water and a wadded up towel.

He set them on the floor near her, then reached behind his back and withdrew a knife, looking at her expressionlessly. She moved her eyes from his and looked at the knife. Her dad had owned many knives and had told her that you could tell a lot about a man by the knife he carried. Was it a tool? Was it a weapon? Was it a cheap, flashy knife that would not hold up to use? Was it a serious, no-nonsense tool?

This one looked like an older hunting knife, the handle made of antler. She knew from her father that many of those older hunting knives were made of a softer grade steel than modern knives. Though they would not hold an edge as long, they could be honed to cut like a razor. It was impossible to look at such a knife in the hands of someone so obviously crazy and not feel your guts curdle with fear. It was a knife designed for skinning and flesh removal.

Was that what he had in mind for her?

"Stick out your hands," Boyd croaked, his voice raspy from disuse.

Alice hesitated, then did as he said. Boyd slipped the blade between her hands, tugged upward, and easily cut the ties that held her hands. They fell apart. She rubbed her wrists, trying to massage life back into them. There were marks where the zip ties had cut into them which would take a long time to go away.

"You fucking stink," he said. "As my grandfather would have said, you'd knock a buzzard off a shit-wagon. Clean yourself up."

Alice looked down at herself. She was filthy. Her clothes were disgusting, stiff and caked with body oils, sweat, and urine.

"Do you have something else I could wear?" she asked.

Boyd stomped up the stairs, and returned in a moment with his arms wadded full of clothes. He'd not had time to search for anything. He had obviously just picked up a pile that was already up there for some reason. He dumped them on her, then turned and went back up the steps without a word. At the top, he slammed the door ridiculously hard, as if trying to make a point that was lost on her, then latched the deadbolt back.

She could hear him talking as he walked off, although she assumed that he was alone. She'd not heard anyone else in the house. It was likely that he was talking to himself. That was not particularly concerning, a lot of folks talked to themselves, but it sounded like he was arguing with himself.

Alice rolled the stack of clothes off of her and reached carefully for the bucket of water. In the dim light, she could see tiny things floating in it, as if the bucket had not been washed before being filled. It was clear, though. She leaned over it and smelled. There was no odor to it. Thirst overtook her and she tilted the bucket to her lips, gulping at the water. It ran down her face. There was a slight pain in her shrunken stomach as it received the water. When she could drink no more, she turned back to clothes Boyd had left her.

They smelled clean, but vaguely stale, as if they'd been stored for a long time. It was like the smell of an old steamer trunk. In the dim light, she sorted the stack. They reminded her of the clothes she'd seen in pictures from the 1960s – knits, polyester, silky floral blouses. They were the clothes of women with beehive hairdos and long cigarettes. Toward the bottom of the pile she found a shapeless cotton dress that had probably never been in style, even when it was new. Of all the clothes, it was the only thing that would fit her comfortably.

Although maneuvering was awkward with the heavy chain still zip-tied to her neck, she undressed as efficiently as possible. Fortunately, she was wearing a button-up shirt, otherwise she'd have had to tear it loose since she couldn't pull anything over her head. When she was naked in the killer's dark basement, she felt as vulnerable as she'd ever felt. Despite that feeling of vulnerability, she found no room for terror in her heart. At this point, she had little control. Her only choice was to go with what happened until she could find a crack and hope that she could exploit it.

When Alice had cleaned herself as best she could, she set the bucket and towel to the side and dressed herself. She was glad that she didn't have a mirror. With her unwashed and uncombed hair, wearing this old and ill-fitting dress, she was certain her own appearance would have brought her to tears.

She sat down at the base of the support pole, her chain held in her hands to keep the weight from pulling at her neck, and waited for Boyd. Unaware of how long she waited, the shadows slowly changed direction and eventually evening came.

SHE MUST HAVE NODDED off because a sound startled her awake. She sat up and listened. She heard the sound of the steel bolt unlocking, the door creaked loudly, and then the stairs groaned.

"Are we all ready?" Boyd called down. He almost sounded like a game show host, throwing a playful lilt into his voice

Alice wrinkled her brow. *Ready? For what?* "Yes," she said brightly, not wanting to anger him.

He seemed pleased with this answer, skipping down the stairs and smiling broadly at her.

"We're having dinner," he said. "I fixed it myself."

Alice was normally picky about whose food she would eat, but these were not normal times. She was at the point that she'd fight a crow over a rabbit carcass. Whatever he laid in front of her, short of human flesh, she'd eat.

"Great," she said. "I'm starving."

Boyd pulled the knife from the back of his belt and pointed the blade at her. "I am going to cut you loose. I have a gun in my pocket. If you try to escape, if you fight, or even if you just piss me the fuck off, I will kill you. Do you understand?"

Alice nodded, not trusting her voice, certain it would betray her terror.

Boyd edged the hunting blade closer to her. Alice watched it, afraid that even the slightest twitch would result in the blade slicing into her flesh. Boyd met her eyes and stared into them, enjoying the effect that the blade had on her. Fear fed the monster inside him.

He found the gap between her neck and the black zip tie and slid the knife into it. Turning the knife slowly until the blade was against the plastic, Boyd sliced and the tie fell away. Alice felt the tension drain from her body. She could have fallen over if she wasn't so afraid of provoking his wrath.

His knife hand swept into a gesture directing her toward the stairs. Alice rose unsteadily to her feet, slightly dizzy from the lack of food. She couldn't remember the last time she'd eaten. Taking the handrail, she climbed toward the upstairs, finding it brighter than the last time she'd passed through here.

"To the right at the top of the stairs," Boyd said from behind her.

She followed his directions and found herself in a cluttered kitchen that clearly was the domain of an elderly lady. It was decorated in a manner that only an old lady could do, with little tea towels, framed embroidery, and decorative plates on the wall. Everything was old enough to be considered vintage, even though it was clearly still being used, from the chunky aluminum canister set, to the crackled ceramic cookie jar, to the 1950s electric range.

"Excuse the décor," Boyd said. "My mother's touch."

Alice nodded as she looked around. "Mother? We haven't met," Alice said. "Is she still around?" Translation: *Don't be telling me that someone has been in this house with you the whole time that your psycho ass has had me tied up in the basement because that would really piss me off.*

"No," Boyd said. "She passed...suddenly."

"Hmmm," Alice said. She didn't even want to know how that happened. She would not have been surprised to find that Boyd had his mother in a back room making a suit from her dried flesh. He definitely had that vibe going on.

"So, sit down," Boyd said, gesturing toward a Formica table. It was also vintage 1950s, and Alice decided that Boyd's mother had probably purchased it new.

She seated herself. In front of her were a variety of open cans, the lids jagged and still attached, folded back and exposing the room temperature contents of the cans. There were black beans, corn, tuna, and beets. There was also a jar of store brand peanut butter, the jar open and a spoon stuck in it.

"It's not much but it's what I've got," he said. "Go ahead."

She didn't have to be told twice, understanding that the tides could turn at any moment. Boyd could suddenly and irrationally become angry with her and send her back to the basement. She needed to cram in as many calories as she could. She took a can and held it over her plate. She picked up a fork and started to scoop some tuna out.

Boyd cleared his throat. "Aren't you forgetting something?"

She looked up at him, still standing beside her. She wasn't sure what he meant. "The prayer?"

"No, silly," he said. "The *man*. You haven't fed your man first."

She bit her tongue, not wanting to make some sarcastic comment that would result in the food being taken from her. "How silly of me," she laughed. "I'm not thinking clearly. I get that way when I'm hungry."

My man? Acid rose into her throat. The thought was almost more than her stomach could handle.

"Damn right you're not thinking clearly," he said, joining her in her laugh. "Cause this is a fucking test and you were pretty damn close to failing it. I won't be giving you any more of the answers. That was a freebie right there."

Boyd took his seat and handed her his plate. She dutifully filled it from each can. "That's more like it."

She smiled at him. "I sure don't want to fail any test, Boyd. But what happens if I do fail?" She had been unable to keep that thought from coming out of her mouth. She had not wanted to ask, but now it was out there. She looked at him, waiting for an answer.

Boyd scraped together a forkful of corn and tuna. "Let's not dwell on the negative," he finally said. "Let's just assume that you're going to pass. The alternative is unpleasant and makes me sad."

She scraped beans from the can and began eating some of them. They were cold and had not been rinsed of the liquid that they came in. She'd never eaten them that way, but her body needed whatever protein she could get. She ate them eagerly.

"Focusing on the positive instead, what happens if I pass?" Alice asked.

A strange expression settled on Boyd's face. He looked down at his lap. He could not meet her eye. He pointed to a coffee cup on the table, overturned on a saucer.

She looked at it. "What is it?"

Boyd still didn't meet her eye. "Look under it." He had a smile on his down-turned face. It was a bashful expression, though Alice could not be sure if it was genuine or not. She didn't know what to think or what to do.

"Go ahead," he urged.

She lifted up the coffee cup. Underneath was a wedding ring. The gold band was dull yellow and worn thin. Someone had worn it for many years. The stone was small, barely a chip. "Can I?" she asked, gesturing at the ring.

He nodded.

She picked the ring up and examined it. There was dirt on it and something else. She scraped it with her fingernail.

"It was my mother's," he said.

She realized that it was blood she was scraping off. Dried, brown blood.

"Oh, it may need to be cleaned," he said, observing the look on her face as she rubbed her fingers together. "I had a little trouble getting it off."

The hunger had slowed her thinking to the point that she had not been able to put the pieces together. Those pieces slammed together suddenly, though, and she realized what this meant. This was his mother's ring and somehow he had taken this ring off and it had involved both blood and dirt. Had he cut it off her dead finger? Was she buried outside? Alice didn't want to know.

Then the last piece hit her as Boyd looked up from his lap and his eyes met hers. It was broadcast from his expression, a mixture of shyness, adoration, and confusion. He wanted her to be his wife. That was the test. Was she *wife material*? Her immediate thought was to throw the ring at him, to get the vile thing out of her hands as quickly as she could, but she could not know what reaction that might provoke. Her life depended on handling this matter delicately.

She leaned forward and set the ring gently down on the saucer. "That's a beautiful ring, Boyd," she said, her voice rigid as she fought to control it. She was not certain if she was convincing or not.

Boyd shrugged. "You'll probably find this surprising, but I've never been married," he said. "I never needed to be. For most of my life it was just me and my mom. My dad died when I was a kid and I don't really even remember him. My mom took care of me for most of my life."

Alice tried to eat calmly, taking large bites, trying to shove in the calories. "You must miss her," she said.

"Sometimes," Boyd admitted. "She'd probably still be here if she'd continued to do her job and love me instead of turning against me."

Alice felt a chill. She'd unwittingly steered the conversation into dangerous territory. Now she had to find a way to navigate back out. *Reflective listening*, she recalled. That's what the counselors did at work when they wanted to acknowledge a person's feelings without necessarily agreeing with them. "She turned against you? That must have been very hard for you," she said, staring down at her food.

Boyd set down his fork and looked across the table at her. She could not meet his eye, instead focusing on the fork she was bringing to her mouth. "It was her job to take care of me. I was her son, her little boy, and she sent me away. We sat right here at this table and I looked at her just like I'm looking at you now. She went from loving me unconditionally to fearing me. What am I supposed to do with that? How can a person cope with the idea that their mother is scared to death of them?"

Alice was silent for a moment, carefully contemplating her answer. "I have no idea, Boyd. I don't know what to say." She reached for the peanut butter, hoping to get at least one spoonful of the calorie-dense food in her mouth.

Boyd suddenly grabbed her wrist and she raised her eyes to his. "You aren't afraid of me, are you, Alice?"

Alice could not pull her eyes from his. She could not say anything. She felt totally exposed. Could he see it? Could he see the terror?

"My mother sent me away, Alice," Boyd said. "She told the court that I was crazy and they sent me away. I had been sent off before, when I was younger, but this time was different. My mother had bought a gun, the same one I have in my pocket now, and she told me that she would use it to kill me if she had to. Can you imagine? Your own mother threatening to kill you?"

Alice didn't ask what he had done to provoke that reaction from his mother. She didn't want to know.

"Then she hid the knives," Boyd continued. "Both to keep them away from me and to make sure she always had access to a weapon. I kept finding them taped behind doors, hidden in the laundry, under the couch cushions. She told me it was so I couldn't use one to kill her and so she had one nearby if she had to defend herself against me. That's a bunch of bullshit. I think *she* was the crazy one. If I was crazy, I inherited it from her.

"So they locked me up," Boyd spat. "They sent me to Central State Hospital. I stayed there until the lights went out. When they had trouble getting food for the patients, they started letting some of us go. I was only considered at moderate risk to harm myself or others so I was released. I was on my way home from there when I met up with you ladies."

Boyd let go of her wrist and Alice tucked her hands into her lap. She clutched them together tightly, wishing that she could wash his icy touch from her skin. It occurred to her that perhaps his mother had taped a knife under this very table, concerned that she might have to fight Boyd off. She casually brushed her hand along the underside of the table but found nothing taped there. What she did find, though, was a thick wire lever. She had seen these kind of tables before. The lever was for releasing the two sections of the table so that they could be pulled apart and a leaf added to the center.

"When I got home, my mother and I had to... work out our differences," Boyd said.

Though he continued to talk, Alice paid no attention to his words but instead focused on the wire lever in a manner that would not allow him to notice what she was doing. While it was not as handy as a knife taped there and waiting for her, she wondered if she might be able to break it loose and use it as a weapon. She pushed it experimentally with a finger, trying not to let the effort show. The lever yielded to her touch, bending slightly.

That was encouraging. It meant the old steel was soft enough that she might be able to break it loose if she worked it back and forth a few times. While Boyd spoke, she continued to look at him, doing her best to look interested and conceal her movements. Beneath the table she bent the steel lever one way, then the other. Back and forth. When she felt the movements were requiring less effort, she knew that she had weakened it sufficiently and it was ready to come loose. She could only hope that what came loose was in some way helpful to her. It was all she had.

Alice could sense that when Boyd's monologue was over, this dinner was over too. If he had sensed the fear in her, as she suspected, her whole trip home might be over. He would feel betrayed by her, as he had by his own mother. She needed to turn the conversation back to the future he imagined the two of them having together. She wondered, though, if that was the right step to take. If she calmed him down, she'd no doubt go back in that basement for another day and continue to live only at his whim. She could not let herself go back down there in the darkness. Gun or not, this had to end today. She would not spend another day at the mercy of someone so completely unhinged.

She continued to work the lever, the movements requiring less effort. The end had a loop on it that acted as a handle. She threaded her fingers through it, hoping that she would not drop it when it broke loose. That would be devastating. When she finally felt the thick wire sag into her lap, she knew she'd been successful. She could feel that it was about ten inches long. With her fingers threaded through the loop handle, she knew that she could stab with it if she had to. While it was not an ideal offensive weapon, it was something. She hoped it would be enough.

She thought about the weapons he had on him. There was the gun in his pocket, which he could not get to easily while seated at the table. There was also the sheath knife behind his back, which he could get to pretty readily. That could be her biggest problem, besides his strength. She had not fought anyone physically since she was a child, although she was raised with brothers and that toughened a girl. She had never killed, though.

Could she even do that?

There was not a single doubt in her mind.

Boyd violently shoved his chair back, slammed his fist on the table, and stood. "You're not even fucking listening to me!" he shouted at her.

"I am, Boyd," she replied, smiling and pouring as much honey in her voice as she could.

"You are not!" he screamed. "You think I haven't seen that look before? That 'humor the crazy man' look!" He towered over, his face reddening, slobber spraying from his mouth as whatever demons lived in there rose to take control of him.

He was at her side in an instant. "Stand up," he commanded.

"Boyd, you're scaring me," Alice said, trying to buy herself time to think. She didn't know what else to do. Her mind was racing. His vital areas were too high with him standing and her seated. His throat, his heart, they were all out of her reach. Before she could get the wire that high, he would grab her arm and hold it while he drew his own knife. He would kill her then and that would be the end of her journey.

"You're going back to the basement," he said. "You need more time to think."

"But what about the ring?" she asked desperately. "What about our engagement?"

His expression turned cold. He looked at the ring in the saucer, then back at her. "You want the fucking ring?" he asked. "You want it!"

He grabbed the ring from the saucer, turning over cans and knocking things from the table. Cold corn spilled into Alice's lap. She recoiled from his rage. Boyd lashed out and grabbed Alice by the jaw, pressing his thumb into her cheek until her mouth opened. He shoved the ring into her mouth then closed it, pressing so hard to close her mouth that he pressed her head against the wall, mashing her lips hard against her teeth. She tasted blood.

"Swallow it," he hissed. "You want the fucking ring, take it."

Her hand clutched the wire she'd found. His hand over her mouth and nose made it difficult to breathe. She thought the pressure of his hand would crush her skull. The pain was intense, nearly blinding. She knew something was going to break. In the midst of this, trying to come up with a plan of attack, she somehow recalled her Uncle Howard, who bled to death at the sawmill where he worked. A large sliver of wood had shot out from the three-foot circular blade, penetrated his leg, and severed his femoral artery. She knew what she had to do then.

As Boyd mashed her face into the wall, screaming at her to swallow the ring, she grasped the wire and stabbed it between his thigh and groin, hoping beyond all hope that the broken end was sharp enough to penetrate clothing. Apparently it was. When Boyd froze with the shock of pain, she plunged the wire around, repeatedly jabbing and tearing, hoping that she had found the artery and somehow managed to cut into it. She was rewarded with a warm gush as his blood sprayed onto her body.

Boyd screamed and exploded upward from her, his face a mask of rage and surprise. Alice instinctively sensed that her only hope for survival was to latch onto him in a bear hug that he could not escape. She spat the ring from her bloody mouth, then wrapped her arms around his chest, locking her hands tightly behind his back, twisting her body to get her legs around him. Boyd still rose, trying to get his hands on his knife, but the manner in which she gripped him limited his range of motion.

Boyd lifted her from the chair. He staggered, his balance thrown off by the addition of her body weight. He crashed into walls, clearing them of pictures and knick-knacks. Realizing that he could not get to his knife, he began raining blows down on Alice's head. He was attempting to drop his powerful elbows onto the top of her head, though with her body pressed against him he was not getting the effect he wanted. Still, with each blow, Alice saw stars and knew that he would eventually knock her loose. She would die when that happened.

Boyd staggered again and made a move for his gun but it was crushed between their bodies. He could not get his hand into his pocket. Alice felt him weakening, then he slipped in the growing puddle of his own blood and fell hard to the ground. Together they writhed on the blood-soaked linoleum, Boyd attempting with less and less effort to pry her from his body. As they rolled, she felt her grip giving way. The blood made her hands slippery and she couldn't hold on much longer. Although weak, she was afraid he could still kill her. He pushed on her and she slid down his body. As she did, her hands fell upon the sheath of his hunting knife.

Without hesitation, she yanked the knife from its sheath and, with a yell, plunged it into his back, puncturing his kidney. Boyd moaned but there was little strength behind it. She plunged the knife again and again, the long blade nicking one lung and his liver. Boyd rolled onto his back, pinning the knife to the floor and not allowing her to pull it free.

"I'm going to kill you," Boyd said groggily, reaching to slide his hand into his pocket for the gun.

Alice scanned the debris that their fight had knocked from the wall. To her left, she saw a cast iron skillet, a weapon of lore among housewives for centuries. While Boyd tried to untangle his hand from his pocket, she brought the heavy skillet down on his head over and over until he stopped moving. She slumped to the floor, exhausted and bloody. She noticed his chest still moving. She could not leave him alive. She pulled Boyd's hand from his pocket and found the gun he'd been trying to reach. She clutched the revolver in her shaking, blood-stained hands, aimed for his face, and pulled the trigger.

6

The Valley
Russell County, VA

BUDDY SAT at his kitchen table. There had been a time in his life when sitting at this table was the highlight of his day. It was the place where he, his wife, and his daughter reconnected at the end of a day of work and school. It was where he ate breakfast with his little girl before school. Those were some of the best memories of his life. Across from him, at the place where she always sat, his wife smiled at him from a framed photograph. When Rachel quit coming home and having dinner with him, he'd placed the photo there for someone to talk to.

Buddy had not slept that night. He couldn't. To try to sleep with all that had happened seemed almost a blasphemy. Instead, he worked. Buddy had been a smoker for most of his life. His wife had also smoked up until she got sick that last time. When she quit, Buddy quit. He didn't wean himself off. He just laid them down and never picked them up again. Since they both always bought them by the carton to get the best price, there were several dozen packs of cigarettes still laying around their house. Buddy had gathered them all last night.

Over the course of an hour, he sat with a razor blade, slitting each cigarette open and extracting the tobacco. When he'd done them all, he had what appeared to be about a quart jar full of tobacco. He'd dumped that into an old soup pot with enough water to cover it up and boiled it, adding more water when he felt like he needed more. After about two hours, he used a slotted spoon to scoop out all the tobacco into the trash. He threw the spoon away when he'd gotten it all. He boiled the mixture until all that remained was a dark, sticky syrup, then he set it aside to cool.

He went back to the kitchen table and dumped out some of the hundreds of pain pills that had been prescribed for his wife. There were a variety of tablets, all of strengths sufficient to bring rest to the pain-wracked and cancer-stricken. Buddy spread the pills into a single layer on a cookie sheet.

When his wife passed, Buddy hid the pills in a rusty old toolbox out in his storage building. His daughter had not started using drugs at that time, but he didn't want them in the house. He was concerned that Rachel might use them to commit suicide because of her sadness at the loss her mother. That she would ever enjoy taking a pill designed to ease the suffering of a cancer patient had never occurred to him.

Over the last few months he'd seen indications that she had been looking for them. He would come home from somewhere and find things out of place, a drawer not shut completely, or the closet door left cracked open. He suspected that it was the pills she was looking for. Whenever he checked the toolbox, they were still there. When he realized she had started looking for them, he considered flushing them down the toilet just to keep them out of her hands, but he didn't. He suspected that he hung onto them only because he wanted to maintain an easy way out for himself just in case his own suffering became too much.

He went to his garage and got the respirator mask he wore when he sanded paint and donned it, along with stout rubber gloves. He removed the soup pot from the stove and placed it beside the cookie sheet of pain pills. With a toothpick, he placed a single drop of the nicotine syrup on the back of each pill. That would be all it took. Buddy remembered folks he knew as a child getting the "tobacco sickness" from picking wet tobacco. What they were really suffering from was nicotine poisoning. In its concentrated form, which Buddy had spent the night producing, a single drop would produce central nervous system depression and eventually respiratory failure.

"Live by the pill, die by the pill," he whispered.

Buddy set the pills aside to dry. In front of him lay a cleaned and oiled Colt 1911. Although the weapon had never been issued to him in Vietnam, he'd learned to maintain and shoot the weapon while in the Marine Corps. He'd bought one for himself when he returned to the world and got a steady job. Despite the fact he was not really a gun person, he owned several. To him, they were tools. He had no desire to collect or covet them. He just wanted them available if he needed them. In the America he knew, having a gun in the house was like having a car in the driveway, a flashlight in the junk drawer, and a Bible in the living room.

The yellow box of Western Super-X rounds was so old that that the paper felt like the worn leather of an old wallet. The 1911 had two seven-round magazines, which he understood to be a bit smaller than the capacity of more modern handguns. The only holster he'd ever owned for the weapon was a leather Bianchi shoulder-rig that allowed him to carry the weapon under one arm and a spare mag under the other. Buddy slid the holster on and spent a few minutes straightening everything out. Once he had the holster squared away, he shrugged on a flannel shirt over his t-shirt to see if everything was concealed properly. It was.

He picked up the handgun from the table, popped a magazine into the weapon, and chambered a round. Then he ejected the magazine and replaced the round that he just used from the magazine, topping it off. He put the magazine back in the weapon again. He took his flannel shirt back off and slid the weapon in the holster.

After snapping his spare magazine in the leather case on the other side of the rig, he dumped out ten spare rounds from the box and dropped them into his pants pocket.

Buddy wasn't sure what he was going to do today. He didn't care if he died, but he didn't want to die until he had carried out his one objective. That was to kill the man who killed Rachel. He briefly wondered if he should take more weapons. The Marines had also trained Buddy to fight with a knife, and the only fixed-blade knife he ever owned was the one they'd trained him on – a Ka-bar fighting knife. He retrieved the knife from the top drawer of his dresser, removed the knife from the sheath, and examined the edge in the light. It would do.

He got a roll of electrical tape and taped the sheath upside-down against the pistol holster. It would not interfere with drawing the pistol but it would be readily available and concealed should he need it.

He went to the bedroom and stood in front of the dresser, looking at himself in the mirror.

"Son, you almost look like a fucking Marine," he said aloud. "Almost." Someone had said that to him a long time ago in another life.

That gave him an idea, and in fifteen minutes he looked a damn sight closer to being a Marine again. Buddy had been blessed with a metabolism that had kept him roughly around the same size for most of his life. Once he'd dug them out of his old footlocker, Buddy had been able to slip right back into the Marine fatigues he'd worn in Vietnam. The pants were olive drab, worn with an olive drab t-shirt when he'd been there. He'd assumed the pants would be dry rotted but they weren't. He even had his jungle boots, although they were stiff from being mashed up in the foot locker with other stuff. If he was going to war today, he might as well dress the part.

Simply lacing those boots back onto his feet brought back a flood of memories. He'd been a single, young man in that war, unaware of where life would take him if he ever made it home. Had he known the pain that he would face with the loss of his wife and daughter, he wondered if he might have been better off dying there in the jungle mud. If he could have looked forward in time and seen the blackness that awaited him, he might have taken more chances and volunteered for the suicide missions, as some men had done. If he had done that, though, he would have never had the happy moments. Maybe there would be a day when the good times weren't so bound to the sad times, though he couldn't imagine how he'd get there.

Buddy looked at himself in the mirror, dressed again like the Marine he'd been nearly fifty years ago. He was startled, both that he was so old and that the war had been so long ago. Until he married, the war had defined him. It was his only story, his only experience. When they were with him, the presence of his wife and daughter had pushed the war further back into the past. He looked at his face and saw that he was an old man now. When he looked harder and met his own eye, he saw in those eyes that he was not *just* an old man today, he was also the angel of death.

THE CREATURE that had dumped his daughter like trash lived in a section of the county known as Macktown. He lived in an old white farmhouse that had once belonged to his grandparents, according to what Rachel had told him during a rare, talkative moment. The house was in ill-repair, with peeling paint and plastic-covered windows. The yard was waist-high with weeds that were never cut, despite three mowers sitting there idle. A muddy trail led from the driveway to the front door.

About a quarter-mile before he reached the house, there was a wide spot at an intersection. Buddy parked there on the gravel shoulder, not wanting to pull in the driveway and announce himself. He left the truck sitting there with the keys in the ignition. At this point, he didn't care if someone stole the truck or the gas. He functioned with single-minded determination. There was only the moment and nothing else. The moment was about one thing. It was about death.

He walked the shoulder of the lined blacktop in his fatigues. The stiff boots rubbed his feet in all the wrong places. Though there had been a day when he'd done thirty-mile patrols through mud in those boots, those days were long gone. He'd been a tough bastard, made tougher by life in the jungle. The pain in his feet was lost in the greater sea of pain within him.

As he came upon the house, he could not immediately tell that it was occupied. In its overgrown condition, the stately old house loomed wild and unkempt on the roadside. The teal Camaro was there, as were several other beat-up vehicles. There were also a few mopeds and bicycles, the preferred transportation of those that had lost their driving privileges. He stood still by the road, listening. Some windows were open and he could hear loud talk that came unobstructed across the silence of the day. With no power, what else could people do? A month ago they'd have been blaring AC/DC from a stolen CD player. Now they just had to enjoy each other's conversation.

He hoped that one of those people inside was the one he came for. His plan was a simple one. He walked from the road through the grassy parking area and to the muddy path that led to the door. Seeing no one in the yard or in the windows, he continued toward the front door, carefully placing each foot as he climbed the painted green steps so that he wouldn't make too much noise and alert them.

Breaching the door was simple, since it wasn't even locked. He turned the knob and he was in. Buddy had assumed that this might be the case in a house where people were constantly coming in and out, only staying long enough to get high or buy their drug of choice. He eased the door closed behind him and floated down the hall like smoke. Approaching the large, high-ceilinged room that had probably once served as a parlor, Buddy knew that this was where everyone was. All of the voices rolled from there and down the hall toward him. He pulled his pistol and stepped though the sliding pocket doors.

All conversation immediately came to a stop. The presence of a man with a gun could have that effect on people.

The man Buddy had come to see was sitting in a threadbare wingback chair across the room. He was smoking a joint and looked at Buddy with red, angry eyes. "Who the fuck are you? G.I. Joe?"

There was some laughter. Buddy considered replying with a gunshot, but he had a plan to follow and he was going to stick to it. He kept his pistol on the man, meeting his eye, waiting to see if recognition dawned on him. Buddy assumed there was no room inside himself for more anger, but he was wrong. The man's lack of recognition made him swell with a cold fury.

"You don't recognize me?"

The man leaned forward and set the joint in an ashtray. His forearms were roped with muscle. It looked like his preferred poison was steroids. He raised his eyes, slowly blew out smoke, and stared at Buddy again. A look crossed his face and he relaxed back into his chair like a king holding court from his decrepit throne.

"You that chick's dad?" he asked.

The .45 boomed and the arm of the chair erupted into a cloud of bloody spray and wool padding. The man cursed loudly, hugging his damaged hand to his chest, blood pouring steadily from where the hollow-point round had severed two of his fingers.

"Wrong fucking answer," Buddy said.

"*Rachel's* dad," the man corrected, grimacing and forcing himself to say the words clearly. He leaned forward and pulled a wadded bandana from the coffee table, gently wrapping his damaged hand. "What the fuck do you want with me?"

"I don't have anything to do with this," said a scrawny man, scooting forward on the couch. He wore a tank-top and was missing his teeth. "This ain't my fight. I'm getting the hell out of here."

"Stay where you are," Buddy ordered. "Ain't nobody leaving, yet. You move, you die too."

"What do you want?" the bleeding man repeated, his voice louder.

Buddy sighed, fighting to control his emotion. He'd never voiced what he wanted. He didn't dare. "What I want is my little girl back," he said. "And you can't make that happen."

The man in the chair groaned, the shock of the trauma starting to wear off and the ache of his injury starting to move in. "I didn't make her take that shit. She did it of her own free will."

Buddy shook his head. "Does it matter? The end result was still the same. The part I cannot forgive is how you dumped her out at the ER like you were disposing of a deer carcass at a roadside dump. You've left me only one option."

"What's that?" the man asked through clenched teeth.

"To kill you," Buddy stated.

The man somehow managed to snicker. "You really think that all these people are going to sit here and let you kill me? Without me, they got no dope and they can't live without it. They can't live without *me*. You're outnumbered. There's more people here than you got bullets."

Buddy looked around. There were nearly a dozen people sitting around the dim room. Men, women, some respectable looking, and some pure trash. He figured most had some kind of weapon on them. The man was right. If he went to reload, they'd kill him. Thankfully, he had a plan.

"They'll not likely do anything," Buddy said.

"You sure about that?" a man asked.

He looked like a biker, wearing a leather vest, leather gloves with no fingers, and filthy jeans. He had a short length of chain slung around his neck. The ends of the chain hung at chest-level, a pair of fighting knives hanging from each. Of all the men in the room, he was the only one to fear. He knew how to fight. He *liked* to fight. Buddy could tell all those things, so he killed him without another thought.

Not interested in wasting any more time on a pissing contest, Buddy used his free hand to reach into his shirt pocket. He withdrew two amber pill bottles, something that instantly had the attention of everyone in the room.

"My wife died of cancer," he said. "I've been meaning to get rid of her medications but I just never did. There's a hundred OxyContin in each of these bottles. She died before she ever opened these."

Buddy looked around the room. The only eyes not glued to the medicine bottles were those belonging to the man across the room. He was still looking at Buddy, curious about what was going to happen. He probably suspected that Buddy was going to offer the pills as payment for one of his associates turning on him and killing him.

That was not Buddy's plan. He turned to the open window and threw both bottles outside. The reaction was instantaneous. People threw themselves toward the window, diving across each other, scrambling and scratching to get to the pills. They had no more control over their actions than Buddy had over his. No one came toward Buddy, though, preferring the window to the door since using it meant passing within reach of the armed man. Outside, Buddy could hear fighting and yelling. There were gunshots and screams. He didn't even look in their direction.

He met the eye of the man sitting across the room from him. He could not wipe the image from his head of his daughter getting into that man's car and leaving with him that last time. The man sensed that death was imminent and began looking to each side, seeking an exit. Before he could find one, Buddy crossed the room and struck him across the face with the .45, knocking him out cold.

THE MAN WAS AWAKENED by a searing pain. He screamed and writhed. He was on his stomach and felt a pressure on the back of his legs that prevented him from moving. He twisted his neck around and looked over his shoulder in time to see Buddy draw a long knife across the back of his ankles. He screamed again and bucked hard enough that Buddy stepped off him and let him flop around the floor.

"What the fuck did you do to me?" he asked, sobbing.

"Cut your Achilles tendons," Buddy said. "Can't have you going anywhere."

The man tried to raise himself with his arms and crawl away but his arms would not cooperate.

"Your arms won't work," Buddy said. "I cut the biceps. Somehow you slept through that."

"You're a sick bastard!" the man cried. He continued to move about, unable to find any position that eased the pain in his limbs. He tried to get up again, his hands and feet curling uselessly under the weight of his body. He sobbed in horror.

"Didn't cut very deep," Buddy said. "Can't have you bleeding to death before I'm done."

"Just kill me!" the man screamed. "Fucking kill me and get it over with!"

Buddy shook his head. "That would be mercy," he said. "And I don't have any to offer."

"I'm sorry," the man said, whimpering. "I'm sorry about your girl."

"Rachel," Buddy reminded him.

"Rachel," the man corrected. "RACHEL!"

Buddy pulled a can of lighter fluid from a pocket of his fatigue pants and began squirting it on the man's pants. The man yelled and fought, trying in vain to find a way to move himself to safety. Buddy stepped onto the man's limp foot to pin him in place. The man threw his head up and screamed.

"Quit moving now," Buddy said calmly, directing the stream of lighter fluid up and down the man's straining body.

Buddy talked quietly to his dead daughter as he set fire to the sheets that served as curtains. He told her that things would be okay now. When he sprayed the remainder of the lighter fluid onto the sofa and struck fire to it, the flame rose quickly and black smoke billowed against the ceiling.

When his work was done, Buddy stepped out of the front door and stood looking around. His hand was on his gun, ready to use it if he needed to. If any one of the druggies had remained, he was sure that the screams of pain from the burning man would drive them into flight. As those screams filled the air, Buddy let them seep into his body, praying they would fill him and push out the images of his dead Rachel.

Buddy could smell the smoke stronger now, the crackling of the growing fire filling his ears. He stepped from the porch, took the muddy path to the road, and walked away without so much as a look back. When he reached the spot where he had parked his truck, he was not surprised or even angry to find that it was no longer there. The truck had been of little consequence, its only purpose being to get him to the house. Whether or not he got home afterward did not matter to him any more than if he lived or died today. All that mattered was that the man he came after had died and he died hard.

He paused for a moment in the spot the truck had been parked. He realized that he still had his gun in his hand. He holstered it and started walking. He felt like he was walking a foot off the ground, his burden lighter than it had been in days. Some men could go to church and pray away the weight of their transgressions, finding salvation and peace in God. Some men required direct action, only finding peace in a solution that they built themselves, with their own two hands.

Buddy was the latter, a man from a line of men who did not find the world to be a complicated place at all. Most problems had a solution if you had it within yourself to bring it about.

He felt suddenly tired and started his walk home.

7

G ary's House
Richlands, VA

WITH THE DEPARTURE of Gary's neighbor and his extended family, Gary and his clan were left alone in their isolated hilltop neighborhood. Even though the two families were not extremely close, they were neighbors and had been supportive of each other while respecting each other's privacy. With just two families and six homes on the hill, that support had been important on several occasions. They'd supported each other through numerous deaths, weather events, and mechanical problems over the years.

One of the things that Gary had always liked and appreciated about Scott's family was that Scott's wife, Theresa, didn't work outside of the home. Scott was traditional in that he felt it was his wife's job to take care of the house, cook, shop, and shuttle the kids to where they needed to be. Because Theresa didn't work, she was at home all day and able to see if anyone came into their neighborhood that didn't belong there. Having a nosy neighbor was significantly better than having an alarm system. That had always provided them with a feeling of security and comfort. Their neighborhood had once been safe. Gary's family had once been safe. That feeling of safety, was eroding quickly, washing away like sidewalk chalk in a thunderstorm.

After the group finished emptying Will and Sara's house of essentials, they took a break for lunch before starting on Dave and Charlotte's house. Karen and Debra had made a soup of some remaining fresh food that had to be eaten. Gary thought it was delicious, his palate still reeling from the flavorless diet he'd consumed on the trip home. When they finished eating, it was Will and Sara's turn to watch all of the children while Dave, Charlotte, and Gary shuttled critical items from their home to Gary's. This time Gary made sure that several radios were distributed so that each group was able to communicate with the other. Though they were cheap Motorola radios that he had bought on a whim, they did the job.

When Karen and Debra had restored order to the kitchen after the meal, they joined the rest of the group to play with the children.

"With such a large group of babysitters, I don't think you all need me anymore," Will said. "Do you mind if I go check the gate? I want to make sure that Scott closed it on his way out."

"That's a good idea," Debra said. "Just take a radio and your rifle. If there's trouble, let us know."

Will quickly assembled his gear and left. As much as he loved his children, he was not cut out for tending to a larger herd of children. He was anxious to get outside and distract himself with some physical activity.

On his walk to the gate, Will passed Scott's house and the houses Scott's two sons built for their families. As Will passed, he noticed a large note taped to Scott's door. He stood in the road in front of the house staring at it but he couldn't read it across the distance. The house appeared empty and there were no vehicles visible. He decided he had to walk up and see what the note said.

As soon as he got to the base of the porch steps, he could read the sign:

To whom it may concern: My family is safe. We are staying at the church camp. If you are a friend or a loved one, you know where that is. If you do not know where that is, then you have no business here and should get off my property.

Will frowned. He understood that Scott wanted folks to know that he was safe. He did not think it was a good idea, though, to advertise to anyone who might stop by that this house and the two others adjacent to it were empty. Even though it bothered Will to remove something from a neighbor's property, he took the sign down, folded it, and shoved it into his pants pocket.

He turned to walk away, glancing at the doors to the other two empty houses and saw that they each had the same sign on the door. Will removed them, shoving each in his pocket, and hoping that he was doing the right thing.

When he reached the gate, Will felt a little better about removing those signs. Scott had driven through the gate and left it open behind him. While the man was not a bad neighbor, his concern never really extended beyond his family and his church family. If you were not among them, your importance to him was minimal. He could have gotten out of his car and closed the gate behind him as he left. He could have considered that leaving that sign on his door might alert the bad guys that there were fewer people up there now to defend the neighborhood. He didn't.

Will grabbed the red gate and pulled it closed. The gate groaned in protest. A chain and padlock hung from a tall locust post at the edge of the pavement. Will had a key to that padlock on his key ring. He removed the padlock, threaded the chain through the gate, and locked it back. With the gate closed, there was still enough space beyond both sides of the gate for an ATV to drive around and enter the property. The gate was really only in place to keep out cars, so he'd never noticed that it wasn't tied to any fencing. Closing the gate would not stop the dirt bikes and four wheelers that had been harassing them. They'd have to do something about that.

When Will returned to the house, the mower had returned with the last trailer of items from Charlotte and Dave's house. He set his rifle aside and pitched in to help with the unloading and storage of the items. While they worked, Will mentioned his concern over the gate not providing adequate protection from off-road vehicles.

"I think I'm going to walk over to the police station and talk to someone," Gary said. "We shouldn't have to barricade ourselves in up here. I didn't see much in the way of laws being enforced on the way home, but that doesn't mean there's no law enforcement here in our town. I'm going to see what I can find out."

"Want me to go with you?" Will asked.

Gary shook his head. "I want you to keep an eye on everyone here. You did a good job of keeping everyone safe while I was gone and I appreciate that more than I've probably said. I'll just run down there on my own and hopefully be back by dark. It's only about two miles each way."

"If you're sure, Gary," Will said. "I worry about anyone going out there alone."

"I've seen a lot these past few weeks," Gary said. "I can't imagine there's anything my home town can throw at me that I've not already been through."

GARY'S HOME was right at the edge of the town limits. Once he walked off his steep hill and turned left along the road, he was immediately within the boundaries of Richlands, Virginia. Most of the neighborhoods between him and the center of town were older. Mobile homes, aging single-story houses with white aluminum siding, and empty cinderblock buildings were scattered along both sides of the road. Ahead, a convenience store that he'd often relied on for gas and last minute loaves of bread or gallons of milk sat on the right shoulder. The plate glass windows were broken out and a trail of garbage, packaging, and damaged merchandise led from the shattered windows.

This little valley area was heavily populated for a small town. Appalachian towns were that way. There was always a shortage of buildable property, so homes clustered wherever there was decent bottomland. Looking around him, Gary could see hundreds of houses, apartments, and trailers. Despite it being the middle of the afternoon, very few people stirred outside. Some sat on shaded porches rocking in swings, the rhythmic creaking of the chains carrying across the distance.

Gary wondered what these people were doing for cooking. Most of them had grills or could cook on fires outside in the yard, but in a densely-populated area, like this valley, there would be no hiding the fact that you had food to cook. Even the smells of a cookout on a hot summer weekend would carry for long distances and drive the neighbors nuts with hunger. He assumed that now, with some people starting to run out of food, the smell of cooking meat might be like throwing blood in shark-infested waters. If people weren't yet willing to go next door and kill you for your dinner, they would be soon.

Gary could feel eyes on him as he walked the road. He looked toward some of the homes he passed, their fenced yards extending right to the shoulder of the road and their doors no more than thirty feet from him. Sometimes he caught shadowy figures watching him from behind storm doors. At one house, a group of rough-looking men stood in a driveway studying something in the tarp-covered bed of a pickup truck. Gary briefly wondered if it was his generator, but it was too small.

As Gary passed, they stopped speaking and lowered the tarp. They returned his nod with menacing glares that reminded Gary of a dog guarding a bone. He paid them no attention. The trip home had hardened him. Never a man that sought a fight, he would not run from one either. He would have killed the first man among the group that threatened him. As he walked on, the men returned to their conversation, raising the tarp back up and gesturing at some hidden cargo.

Gary was reminded that he was not the same man anymore. While he may look the same to his family, he had been through things. He had changed. They had not seen the extent of those changes and he hoped they wouldn't have to. What would it be like for his daughters to see him kill? He remembered the shocked look his wife and daughter Karen had given him when they saw him rolling the dead man onto the sled.

He walked a little further and approached a shopping center built around a local chain grocery store. From his position on the road he could see the back of the store and saw a compact car parked at the back door, by the loading dock. There was a sign on the side of the car advertising a private security company. Inside the vehicle, Gary could see a man smoking a cigarette. From the bulk around his shoulders, it looked like he was wearing body armor. From the window, a rifle barrel protruded skyward. While it was not pointed in a threatening manner, Gary was sure that it was intentionally displayed. Sometimes the projection of strength and preparedness was all that was required to deter someone with bad intentions.

When the street led him past the front of the same grocery store, Gary could see another private security vehicle parked by the front doors. The plate glass windows in the front of the store had been boarded up with sheets of plywood. Someone had used orange spray-paint to write across the plywood:

SOLD OUT. NO FOOD. CLOSED UNTIL FURTHER NOTICE.

CURIOSITY GOT the best of Gary and he detoured from the street into the parking lot. The grocery store parking lot held a few abandoned vehicles, some neatly parked, and others obviously pushed from the street after they ran out of fuel. Gary walked toward the security guard's car, and the man went on alert. Gary was still fifty feet away when the driver's door swung open and the man crouched behind it, leveling the barrel of an M4 rifle through the open window.

"That's far enough," he said from behind the door.

Gary studied the man. He had the right idea, concealing himself behind the door, but the sheet metal of a Chevy Cobalt offered no ballistic protection at all. Had Gary wanted to shoot him, he could have put .40 caliber bullets through that door all day long without losing any velocity. A better choice would have been for the man to place himself on the other side of the hood with the engine block between them. That would slow or stop a bullet.

"I'm not after food," Gary said.

"Beer's gone too," the man shot back as if he made this speech all day long, every day.

"I'm not after beer," Gary replied.

"Cigarettes?" the man asked. "Because I wish to hell they had some of those. I'd be in there getting a few packs for myself."

"Not cigarettes, either," Gary said. "I just wanted to ask you a few questions, if you don't mind."

"Well, you'd be the first one that showed up here not wanting inside that store," the man said.

"Like I told you, I just want to ask a few questions," Gary said. "I've been out of town and just got back. I was wondering what things have been like here. You're the first person I've run into who seemed like they might know."

Gary was obviously believable because the man rose from behind the car door. Either that, or the man's knees had been killing him from being crouched there.

"You just ask them from there," the man told him, easing the rifle barrel from Gary's direction, but continuing to hold it in a ready position. "I don't mind answering questions but I like my personal space."

"That's not a problem. How long have you been here?" Gary asked.

"Four days," the man said. "After the attacks, the store was pretty much cleaned out. Took a few days for people to figure out the severity of the situation, then they hit the stores like rats on dog food. They had to send cops up here to help keep order. With just one cop per store, it was pretty damn crazy so they called us in. I wasn't here for that part. The store was already closed when I showed up."

"It sold out?" Gary asked.

"That's what they tell me," the man said. "I haven't been in there. I was told that all they had left was non-food items. Spatulas, turkey basters, aluminum foil – that kind of stuff. We're just here to make sure no one wrecks the joint because they're pissed off that there's no food."

"Or beer," Gary remarked.

The man laughed. "Definitely," he said. "Alcoholics and smokers are having one hell of a time right now."

"Do you know if the cops are still working?"

"Some are. I hear their radio chatter. One stops by every day and asks me if anyone has tried to break in. We've been able to keep most folks away. Anyone who lives around here knows that the store got cleaned out, anyway."

Gary nodded. "What about the town itself? Are things pretty calm?"

"The night guy says there's a lot of shit going on after dark," the man said. "Shooting, fighting, all kinds of carrying on."

That didn't surprise Gary. If anything surprised him, it was that the days were any calmer than the nights. "Well, I'll leave you alone. I'm on my way to the police station."

"Good luck with that," the man replied. "I hear there's one cop there guarding the equipment and working the radio. He's locked up tight and armed to the teeth. He probably won't even answer the damn door."

"I would be armed to the teeth too."

"You reporting a crime?" the man asked. "There's not much the police can do for people now."

"No," Gary replied. "I guess I just want to see if the cops are still an option for handling things. We've got a little situation that's going to get out of control pretty fast if something isn't done. I've got some visitors who need a deterrent."

The guard slung his M4 back over his shoulder and lit a cigarette. He leaned back against the car. "You want some advice?"

Gary hesitated a second before replying. "Sure."

"If you got a problem that won't go away, don't involve the cops," the man suggested. "Just do what needs to be done and go on with your life. Make sure that once this mess has all blown over, nothing can be traced back to you. The cops aren't arresting people right now because they can't take care of prisoners. They had to let them all go. They won't be able to help."

"That's an idea," Gary said. "I was hoping there was a better way."

"You probably already know how your situation is going to end anyway, don't you?"

Gary hesitated. "Probably."

"Then why plant a seed in a cop's head? If some worried old lady shows up at the police station next week complaining about her missing lowlife son, do you want the cops to remember the guy who was down there asking for help? No, you don't. You don't want the cops to have any fucking idea what happened to said lowlife. Just keep yourself off their radar. That's the best advice I can give you."

"You might be right," Gary said.

"I am right," the man replied with certainty. "I used to be a cop. I know how cops think."

Though Gary briefly wondered why the man wasn't a cop anymore, it wasn't any of his business. "By the way, what's your name?" he asked. "If you get stuck up here, we could always use someone who knows their way around a weapon."

"Esposito," the man replied. "Steve Esposito. And I hope like all hell that I don't get stuck here."

"Well, I'm Gary. Good luck," Gary said. "I hope you don't either."

"Good luck to you too, buddy," Steve said.

Gary's feet felt heavier as he walked back across the parking lot, stepped through weeds and a small ditch, and rejoined the road. In the short walk back to the road, he'd realized that the security guard was absolutely right about his problem. If one of those guys on the dirt bikes went missing, there were probably dozens of people with reasons to make that happen. Unless there were witnesses, it might be hard for anyone to narrow down who killed anyone.

He turned left, away from town, and began his walk home. He would have to handle this himself.

When Gary, Jim, and Randi had parted ways a few days ago, they had made plans to reconnect by radio at a particular time to make sure everyone made it home safely. Gary's plan had been for everyone to go to a high hilltop near each of their homes and make contact using the good VHF radios they'd taken from the ranger station at Mount Rogers. Gary thought that in a pinch he could probably radio Jim without leaving home. He needed to talk to Jim and see what he thought about his situation, from the lack of security to the lack of any water source.

The high point that Gary had chosen was on Kent's Ridge. It was a hilltop that had a line of sight connection to the valley where Jim lived, which was about twelve miles away as the crow flies. Neither of them had been sure if Randi would be able to connect with them, since she lived in a more mountainous area that could be walled in by rocky ridges, possibly preventing her from getting a signal out.

After a quick dinner, Gary grabbed the same pack he'd carried to town and slung it over his back. "I'll be back in a few hours," he said. "You all keep an eye on things and be careful. I'll radio you before I come through the gate. I'll also pop a green glow stick and hang it off me, in case I can't get you on the radio. If you see green, don't shoot. I don't want to be shot by accident."

His family hugged him and swarmed him with goodbyes. He'd not been home long enough for them to forget what it was like for him to be gone and to not know his fate. The constant worry, the fear that he might not make it home was still fresh. Earlier, planning on a walk to the police station, Gary had not taken a rifle with him for fear of drawing the wrong kind of attention. This time, part of his journey would be on the road and part of it would be through the woods. He would carry the same Glock .40 caliber pistol that had gotten him home, and he would also carry his AR. With the stock retracted, most of the weapon could be hidden in the backpack. If he tossed a jacket over the exposed end, it would be concealed, although not very discreetly. There were times that he wished he'd bought an AR or AK pistol for ease of concealment, but he'd never done it. This was one of the times he wished he had.

It took two hours of strenuous walking to reach the location that he was going to radio from. It was on a large cattle farm with thousands of acres, not on his property. He'd accessed it through a circuitous route that he hoped had allowed him to come in unseen. When he finally got out his radio and established contact, it was a relief to hear Jim's and Randi's voices and know that those two had made it home. Neither of them went into much detail about how the last day of their journey had gone, and Gary was certain there were dozens of stories beneath the surface of their words. Perhaps he would hear them one day.

When Jim asked him how things were at his home, Gary hesitated. While his plan had been only to infer that he was having some doubts about his location and may need to consider moving, the idea of vague allusions went completely out the window. Too much had gone on between them for him not to be honest. He ended up spilling the whole story: the trouble with the masked visitors, his concerns about being able to adequately guard his property, his concerns that his entire plan of being able to bug-in was flawed, and that they may have to bug-out after all.

"There are some empty houses around me, Gary," Jim said. "I think I could talk to the relatives of the people who owned them and see if we might be able to borrow some for a while. I don't think I'd have any problem finding someone willing to do that. At least the house would be looked after while you were living there."

"That might be a good idea," Gary agreed. "I'll need some time to talk to my family, though. I'm not sure this is going to be an easy sell."

"I'm sure it's not," Jim agreed. "Remind them that it's temporary."

"How about we agree to meet up here on the radio in forty-eight hours?" Gary asked.

"Not a problem," Jim said. "I'll be here."

Randi finalized her arrangements to come check on Jim's mother, who'd been pretty sick, and then they all signed off.

Gary had a lot to think about. His family would not be happy about leaving the homes they'd worked so hard to build. While he wasn't happy about that either, he wanted security for his family beyond all things. He continued to beat himself up over his lack of attention to some critical details. The water issue was going to wear on them if the power remained off, as he fully expected it would. Security at his house could possibly be worked out. He could contact some people he knew in town and offer to let them move into his daughters' homes in exchange for helping guard the property, but still there would be no water. It would not be a viable long-term plan.

He also knew enough now to understand that he was too close to town to operate a sustainable property. Further back in the country, there would be a buffer of distance that would keep some folks away. It would be too far for most to walk. How many people were within a one mile radius of where he lived now? He didn't have Google Maps to refer to, but if he imagined the satellite view of his home and drew a circle reaching one mile out from his home he couldn't even guess the number of folks who might live there. There would be thousands. Thousands of folks with no power, no water, no gardens, no livestock, no game, and no prospect for an end to this disaster.

Gary thought of the river passing through the center of town. The town had been built on the headwaters of the Clinch River, renowned as being one of the cleanest rivers in the state, but the water was not clean enough to drink unfiltered. How many people were drinking it now without treating it with bleach, boiling it, or filtering it? The results would be apparent soon.

Without treatment for the chronic diarrhea that would come from drinking untreated river water, folks would become dehydrated and die even faster than the starvation would have killed them. It was a grim prospect indeed.

The light was failing, and Gary hoped he could get home before dark. He didn't want to have to strap a headlight to his head. He imagined it as a target that some unseen reprobate might aim for just out of boredom and because the threat of arrest was non-existent.

Walking toward his home, weaving his way through game trails and cattle pastures, he knew that there was really only one option. He had to convince his family to join forces with Jim. There was also the whole issue of how to get all their stuff to the valley where Jim lived. Gary had outbuildings and a garage full of preparations he'd made. There was food, ammunition, and all kinds of long-term survival gear he'd not even used yet. Some of it hadn't even been opened. He'd been so occupied with his return and getting all the kids under one roof that he'd not had a chance to square away his home for the long haul. At this point, maybe it was best not to even get started if they couldn't stay there.

He thought of his stash of heritage survival seeds. How could he ever plant a garden at his home and guard it? He'd basically need an armed scarecrow stationed in there at all times to keep thieves away. The whole idea of moving made him sick.

However, how could he have known that it would come to this? Just because he'd prepared didn't mean he really expected or wanted anything like this to happen.

When he was halfway home, the sun had settled behind the horizon and Gary walked through the gloaming, picking his steps more carefully. He knew that a truck was really the only way to get their gear moved. They didn't have enough fuel for multiple trips, so it had to be one trip in a large truck. The problem was that he didn't have one and he didn't know anyone that did.

Even if he did know someone, could he just expect that they were going to lend him the truck and the fuel to drive to Jim's? How would he get the truck back? What was the price of fuel now if he were to find someone with fuel to trade? Could it be bought with ammunition or food? Then what kind of hell might rain down on them if the community found out he had food on hand? If people knew he had enough food that he could be trading it off for fuel, would word get out and they instantly become a target?

Within a mile of his home, Gary was far enough along in his thinking that he had come up with the possible location of a truck that could be used. The agency where he and Jim worked had once owned a box truck that was used for moving office furniture and picking up deliveries. It was the size of a large U-Haul or Ryder truck.

If they moved without furniture, they could possibly get all of their gear in it, although he couldn't imagine it was just sitting there with fuel in the tank. He knew where the key was located because he'd borrowed the truck once before. If the key was still there and if he could secure fuel for the trip, this might just be the ticket for them.

Gary was stepping lighter by the time he reached the base of his hill. Figuring out the truck scenario had been a milestone. Now he just had to convince his family to go and hope that Jim could line them up with a home. There was also the matter of securing the truck and getting it back home safely, but that was a problem for tomorrow. For now, Gary was tired and looking forward to getting in bed early, sleeping like a log, and rising in the middle of the night for guard duty.

He started the steep climb toward his home. Even though he'd only been gone a couple of hours, he missed his family. He couldn't believe that he used to be away from them while at work nearly every day without so much as a thought. After his journey home, he'd never take their presence for granted again. As he climbed, he heard the high-pitched whine of two-stroke dirt bike engines. The sound could only be coming from his property.

GARY WAS furious that these idiots on their machines were back at his house again. He dropped his pack, retrieved his rifle from it, and slapped a magazine home. He re-shouldered his pack, chambered a round, and started running up the hill. Though the hill was steep, his conditioning was better than it had been a few weeks ago. Walking hundreds of miles could do that to you.

He could hear the engines winding up, dropping off, then whining again as they accelerated. That told him that whoever was up there was just racing around his property being a jerk. At the top of the hill, he slowed to a walk to regain control of his breathing, sweat pouring from his forehead into his eyes. He raised his shirttail and wiped it from his face.

When he reached the gate, he could see that the grass was beaten down on the shoulder of the driveway where they'd driven around the gate. He had to close that gap somehow. Then an idea struck him and he whipped off his pack. Digging around in the pocket, he came up with a hank of paracord. He stepped into the weeds and tied one end to the thick trunk of a wild cherry tree. He stretched it tight and ran it at chest level back to the gate, tying it high on the gate post. Then he grabbed his pack, ducked under the rope, and ran the rest of the way to his house.

When he came upon the open meadow that served as a common area between all the houses, Gary could see the headlights of three dirt bikes and two ATVs racing around erratically between the houses. There appeared to be no purpose to their behavior other than to create chaos. Gary did not want to kill them – yet – but he did want this to stop. He raised his rifle and fired two quick shots into a distant bank of dirt. The shots got the group's attention and they slowed for a moment, obviously trying to see where the shots were coming from. While they were still, Gary aimed near one of the bikes and pulled the trigger again, hopefully creating the impression that he was ready to kill the riders if he had to.

This spurred them into action. Like a swarm of bees, the group buzzed to life and fell into formation. They began accelerating out of the neighborhood and directly toward Gary.

"Will!" Gary called into his radio. "Can you hear me?"

In a moment, the reply came. "I'm here. Where are you? I don't see a green lightstick."

"I'm near Scott's house," Gary said. "I forgot about the lightstick when I heard the bikes. Come down here. I may need your help."

Gary moved off the road and into the brush while the riders sped past. He did not want to take a chance on getting mowed down. In the dim light he could see exactly what had been described to him before, riders in black with skull masks hiding the lower part of their faces. Regardless of their intentions or their fighting abilities, they definitely presented a menacing sight.

When they had all passed him, he took off running behind them.

He made it less than a dozen steps before he heard the shouts and racing engines that indicated someone had wrecked. He ran up on the scene and saw two bikes wiped out and blocking the narrow trail around the gate, the ATVs trying to get around them. Gary fired a shot into the air as he approached.

This prompted the two ATV drivers to hit the throttle and push their way through the small opening. In the rush, both of them ran over the splayed limbs of one of the downed riders who cursed and cried out. Another rider, who had fallen off his bike, got to his feet and stood his bike up. He was attempting to start it when Gary yelled at him to not move. The rider gave up on trying to start the bike and just jumped onto the seat, crouching and allowing gravity to pull him down the steep driveway. Gary had a perfect shot at his back, but did not feel right about taking it. He knew he probably should, but he couldn't.

The last rider, swept from his bike by the paracord and then run over by his friends, was on his feet now and staggering toward his bike. The clothesline trap had stripped the man's mask off his face and his identity was no longer hidden.

"Don't move," Gary warned. His words did not slow the man. Gary leveled his red dot on the downed bike and fired one shot, then another, into the aluminum engine block. The crankcase shattered, spraying fragments of cast aluminum in all directions. The rider flinched.

"I said don't move," Gary repeated.

This time the rider stopped.

"Turn around."

Gary heard footsteps behind him. "Will? Is that you?"

"I'm here," Will replied.

Gary dug a light out of his pocket and shined it on the man's face just long enough to get a good look at it, then switched the light back off. Gary would have to guess the rider's age at around twenty. Not much more than a boy. Still, the thought of what this man and his friends might have done at Sara's house if she'd not turned the tables on them infuriated him. Perhaps he should kill him and get this over with.

"Did you all steal my generator?" Gary asked.

The young man didn't answer.

"I say we kill him. You think he would have hesitated to kill Sara?" Will spat. "Send a message to the rest of them. Hang his body from a post down by the road."

Gary didn't respond to this. Despite everything, he didn't want to kill another person if he didn't have to. It bothered him. "What's your name?"

There was a burst of gunfire. Rounds hit all around Gary and Will, dropping leaves and small branches on them. They hit the ground, rolling toward the side of the road and landing in the ditch. Gary could no longer see the outline of their captive in the dark. As quickly as it began, the fire subsided.

"That was at least two handguns," Will said. "Sounds like they dumped their magazines on us and took off. It had to be his buddies."

"I want to know who that jerk is," Gary said. "I want to go after him. I want my generator back."

"His name is Wesley," Will said.

Gary reacted with surprise, squinting at Will in the darkness.

"Wesley Molloy," Will said. "His dad is an attorney. They live a mile or so down the road in that big subdivision. They have a McMansion on the hill."

"I can't believe you know him," Gary said, rolling out of the ditch, taking a knee and listening. "I think they're gone."

"We went to school together," Will said. "But we weren't friends. And I have to say that I think you should have killed him."

"I've seen too much killing," Gary said. "Just because people are getting away with killing people now doesn't make it right. I don't want to become that kind of person. I don't want to kill people I don't have to kill."

Will shrugged. "I haven't seen what you've seen, Gary, but I worry that these guys will see this as weakness. They'll be back."

"I hope you're wrong."

"I hope I am too," Will replied.

On the walk back to the house, Gary could not help but dwell on what Will had said.

"Will," he said. "Just so you know, I don't give second chances. I won't hesitate to kill them if they come back."

8

Bluefield, Virginia

AFTER KILLING BOYD, Alice experienced a bout of sheer panic like nothing she'd ever felt before. Despite what she'd been through, despite killing her kidnapper, she paced the kitchen frantically, her heart racing and her mind an unstoppable whirlwind. It was a potent cocktail of the aftereffects of adrenaline and the beginning of realizing that she needed to figure out what to do next. When she finally began to rein herself in and calm down, she knew that she first needed to make sure that there was no one else in the house. While she suspected his mother was dead, she could leave nothing to chance. Boyd may have even had a brother or friend that stayed with him. She had to check.

With the gun still in her shaking hand and pale rays of dying light illuminating her path, Alice walked to the living room, the gun pointed ahead of her. Her breath raced and her heart pounded in her ear like a train bearing down on her. She fought to calm herself.

She'd never felt like this. The floor creaked beneath her feet, each step amplified and increasing her tension.

She found the living room empty. An old sofa, its outdated colors still vivid beneath the protection of a fitted plastic cover, sat in front of a coffee table covered in lace doilies. Alice couldn't imagine how that sofa could be comfortable with that crinkly cover on it. There was a crocheted afghan draped over an old blue recliner. A white Bible sat on the side table. There were pictures covering all the walls, but none of Boyd.

Alice crept toward a hallway where all of the doors were closed. At the first door, she reached for a clear glass knob and turned it, pushing the paneled door open. As soon as she saw the pink tub she pushed the door the rest of the way open. The floor was covered in a pink rug that matched the pink rug around the toilet and the pink furry cover on the toilet lid. Alice shook her head. Her mother was fond of the same fuzzy bathroom accessories. Maybe it was an old lady thing.

With her back to the door, Alice was hit by another wave of sheer panic and spun around, her gun waving wildly. She ran back to the kitchen, confirmed that Boyd was indeed still dead and still where she left him, and then came back to the hallway. The other two rooms were bedrooms. One was obviously the old lady's, the other clearly Boyd's. She even made a quick check of the closets, but there was no one else in the house.

Realizing that it was becoming harder to see, she knew she needed to find a flashlight. She could not handle being trapped in the dark with Boyd's dead body. Neither was leaving immediately an option. She was still wearing the ill-fitting clothing that Boyd had given her and she had no gear for the road. The last thing she remembered from before her kidnapping was that she was in Bluefield, which was roughly an hour from her office *if* you were driving a car, but she had no way of knowing if she was still in Bluefield or not. There were dozens of nearby towns where he could have taken her. She couldn't worry about that now, though. She had to focus on one thing at a time.

Going back to the kitchen, she found a tablecloth and covered Boyd's body with it. She had seen enough of him to last a lifetime. As an afterthought, she checked his pockets and found a lighter, a ring of keys, and a pocket knife with a locking blade. She set the items on the table, after discovering that the ratty dress she was wearing had no pockets. She scanned the countertops and found a flashlight sitting there. She took it, confirmed that it worked, and tried to get a plan together.

She needed clothes first of all. Then she needed something to carry her gear in. She hoped Boyd still had one of the packs they had stolen from the FEMA camp. That would be perfect.

With the flashlight in hand, she went to the old lady's closet and quickly realized that there was nothing in there that she wanted to wear. There was nothing in there even purchased in the last thirty years. Even if they would fit, they were not the kind of clothes you could walk in for days. She couldn't imagined herself hiking home in a polyester pantsuit, a silky blouse, and a scarf tied around her head. She went instead to Boyd's room.

Her earlier visit had simply been a cursory glance to make sure that room was empty. Now she tried to figure out what this room told her about the man. The walls were covered with the kind of posters that you might expect on a teen boy's wall – fast cars with bikini-clad women reclined across them, heavy metal bands, and video games. There was a rack on the wall displaying a collection of cheap samurai swords and martial arts weaponry. That was not a comforting thought to Alice, imagining that Boyd had access to those kind of weapons while she'd been tied in the basement. She thought she was lucky to not end up with a Chinese throwing star sticking out of her forehead.

Shining the light around the room, she hit on one of the black 72-hour backpacks from the FEMA camp.

"Yes!" she said, celebrating any victory at this point.

It was a start. It was a Get Home Bag. The bag was empty but that didn't concern her at this point. She shined the light around the room and realized that, as a man without a job, Boyd had been a creature of comfort and his primary wardrobe was sweat pants, ragged t-shirts, and hoodies. She was pretty certain that despite the difference in their sizes, she could make that work. With drawstring waists and elastic cuffs, sweatpants were not exactly fitted garments and could fit people of all sizes. She shed the dress and pulled on what she hoped was a clean set of black sweatpants that were spilling from a half-open dresser drawer. She put them on with a Black Sabbath shirt she also found in the closet, along with a matching hoodie. The fit wasn't ideal but it was an improvement. Even better, it was a genderless outfit that would blend in easily on the road, both day and night.

She dug around in the dresser and found a pair of socks, taking a spare set for the bag. She pieced together a spare sweat suit and put that in her bag. She found a set of Boyd's tennis shoes and tried them out but they were hopelessly large. She would have to wear her ragged pair from the basement and hope they'd hold up long enough for her to get home, even though one sole was beginning to flap when she walked. If she was lucky there would be a roll of duct tape somewhere she could fix it with.

She pulled out the top drawer of Boyd's dresser and looked for anything useful. It was not what she'd hoped. She found another lighter but that was it. Most of the drawer was filled with empty prescription bottles he'd saved for some reason. She returned to his closet and scanned it for potentially useful items and was again disappointed. There was a boat paddle, a large stick, a pile of shoes, and a few scattered items of clothes.

Before she left, she caught sight of the rack of swords and weapons again. She needed a good knife. Boyd had the sharp hunting knife on his belt, but she wasn't interested in moving his body around to remove the sheath. She examined the rack and spied a Gerber boot knife with a belt clip. That would be perfect. She could clip it inside the sweatpants and wear it without it being visible.

She went back to the living room and looked for another closet. Finding a coat closet, she located a rain coat that must have been one of Boyd's old ones. It was too big for her but it was better than nothing. She crammed it in the bag too. In the old lady's room, Alice found a box of ammunition for the pistol. Several rounds were missing and Alice assumed those missing rounds were the very ones now in the gun. As a mother, Alice couldn't imagine going to a gun store and having to buy a gun and ammunition for the purpose of protecting herself from her own son. That was a hell of a thing to have to deal with in your life.

Alice found no holster for the gun, which made sense if the woman merely carried it around the house and slept with it under her pillow. Alice would just have to carry it in the pocket of her hoodie. It would be easy to get to there. Perhaps the visible weight of it in her pocket would serve as a deterrent and encourage people to keep away from her. She hoped this was the case. On her way out of the room she saw a bottle of ibuprofen sitting on the nightstand and swiped it. Remembering the pain of her previous days on the road, she would appreciate having this when the aching started. However, after her imprisonment in Boyd's basement, she would not complain about resuming her walk home even if her body hurt.

She returned to the kitchen and stared at the tablecloth-covered body once again, making sure that it did not move beneath the cover. In her head, she kept seeing Boyd rise beneath the cover and come after her like some killer in a slasher movie. She would not have been surprised at all. Once she was satisfied that he was still dead, she went through the kitchen looking for anything that might be of use to her. There were still some cans of foods, some stale crackers, and part of a jar of mixed nuts. There was an old jar of applesauce, two cans of deviled ham, and a jar of home canned pickles. Alice threw all of it in the pack, along with a can opener. She took the roll of paper towels from the dispenser and shoved it in her pack, along with a set of utensils.

She opened drawers until she found the junk drawer that every kitchen has. She found more batteries for her flashlight and another cigarette lighter. She even found the roll of duct tape that she'd wondered about earlier. The presence of a small votive candle in the drawer made her think of using candles for light at night if she was holed up in a safe place. She went back to the living room and, sure enough, there was a set on the mantle. She pulled them from the porcelain holders and dropped them into the pack.

She took another glance at Boyd's body and confirmed he hadn't moved.

"Think, think, think," she whispered out loud. "What else do you need?"

Then it came to her. "Water bottle." She started opening cabinets. She found a few small bottles of tonic water under the counter. It wasn't to her liking, but it was better than ditch water. Her stomach had been starting to bother her and she was afraid that the ditch water she'd had was making her sick. That was all she needed.

Despite not wanting to return to the basement, she needed her shoes since she couldn't find any others that fit her. With her flashlight in one hand and the pistol in the other, she descended the stairs to her former cell. By her pile of disgusting clothes, she sat and put her shoes on. When she sat the flashlight down, it rolled slightly and the beam came to rest, shining on the water heater. It gave her an idea. With her shoes on, she crawled to it and tapped it with her knuckles. It sounded full.

She opened the drain valve at the bottom. There was a whistling sound and water started to seep from the valve. Alice quickly turned it off. She remembered seeing some empty Gatorade bottles in the kitchen. She ran up the steps to retrieve them, then returned to the water heater. Carefully tilting each bottle up to the valve, she filled three bottles with the water. After she was done she held the flashlight up to a bottle and examined the contents. The water was clean but had flecks of limestone sediment floating in it. She knew that would settle out over time, and wouldn't harm her if she drank it.

Heading back upstairs, she packed the bottles into her bag and quickly scanned the kitchen, trying to think if there was anything else she needed. She didn't come up with anything. Realizing that the quicker she got on the road, the quicker she'd be home, she shouldered the pack. She checked her pockets and made sure that the gun and flashlight were accessible. Her plan was to walk by moonlight as far as she could so that she wouldn't draw attention, using the light only when absolutely necessary.

She took a last glance at Boyd's body, wondering if she should offer some last dramatic words to the dead psycho who was now glued to the floor by his own congealing blood. She decided that she'd not waste another breath on him.

She went to the back door and glanced through the curtain. She saw nothing out of the ordinary. She opened the door and stepped out on the porch. Looking around, she was hit by the reality of her situation.

"I have no fucking idea where I am," she whispered.

ALICE CAUTIOUSLY MOVED from the backyard to the front, listening for any one of the million things that worried her. Once in front of the house, she could get a rough lay of the land in the moonlight. She was able to make an assumption based on her familiarity with Appalachian towns and guess that the main road would be downhill of where she now found herself.

The street in front of the house extended in both directions and either could be the direction that led out of here. She chose right and began walking. With luck on her side for a change, she soon found that the street joined another. A left turn took her down the hill to an even wider street. Once there, she turned right and soon found herself at a stop sign beside a divided street. That was surely a sign she was moving in the right direction. She studied the street name and it meant nothing to her.

There were houses along the street in both directions. Some had pale glowing lights inside them, probably lanterns or candles. She was deathly afraid of knocking on a door. She didn't want to end up locked in another basement, or worse. She also didn't want to get shot for knocking on a stranger's door under the current circumstances. With her vision telling her nothing, she decided to just stand still and listen for a moment.

After her brain separated and categorized the sounds of the night, she distinctly heard the murmur of conversation. Rather than immediately flipping out and running, which did indeed cross her mind, she continued to listen to the voices and see what she could tell about them. She could soon tell that it was both a man and a woman speaking and that they appeared to be sitting on a nearby porch, although she could not tell which house yet.

She turned slowly, listening for a moment in each direction. She determined that three houses down, in the dark recesses of a front porch, an older couple sat enjoying the cool evening air. At least that's what she assumed they were doing. After thinking it over for a moment, she began walking in their direction. She knew she was headed in the right direction when the conversation halted.

"I got a gun up in here and I ain't a bit afraid to use it," came a cold voice.

Alice froze, trying to figure out what to do next. Had she not been completely lost, she would have just turned and walked away as fast as she could. "My name is Alice," she said. "I'm lost and need some directions."

There was no response, but there was also no movement. She didn't know what she should do, and she had no other options. "Can you help me?"

"Whereabouts you trying to go?" asked a woman's voice.

Alice swallowed hard, not wanting to get into the details of everything that had happened to her over the past few days. She'd be here all night if she tried to tell that story. "I'm just passing through town trying to get to Tazewell and I've taken a wrong turn somewhere."

Tazewell was a town close to her office. She thought it was strategic to choose a nearby town, giving the impression that she had people waiting on her who might come looking for her if she didn't return home.

"How did you get down in here?" the woman asked.

"I was on the highway," Alice said. "There were some bad people and I had to get off the road and hide. Somehow I got turned around and this is where I ended up. This is Bluefield, right?"

"It's Bluefield, all right, and there ain't no shortage of bad people here," the man said. "You need to be careful out there wandering around at night. A girl can end up dead. Or worse."

Alice laughed nervously. "Trust me," she said, "I know all about that." She could make out nothing about these people in the dark. They could be fifty or they could be twenty years older than that.

"You get back on the road," the woman said. "You go right. You walk that way about ten minutes and you'll come to College Avenue. You go right there. That will lead you back to the highway and out of town."

"I can do that," Alice said. "Thanks for your help."

"You be careful out there," the woman said. "It's a lot easier to talk it than to walk it. You keep your eyes open."

"You got a gun?" the man asked.

Alice was hesitant to answer, but decided to be honest. She didn't want to be killed for her gun but she wasn't getting the psycho-vibe from these folks. "Yeah, I do."

"Anyone mess with you," the man said, "you shoot their fucking nuts off."

Alice smiled a smile that no one else could see in the darkness. These folks had no idea what she was capable of. "I'll do that," she said. "I can promise you that."

She turned in the deep grass of their yard and went back to the edge of the road. Once on the solid surface of the pavement, she turned right, just as instructed.

9

The Valley
Russell County, VA

BUDDY HAD BEEN WALKING NEARLY two hours and, strangely, the world was coming back to life around him. Color was gradually returning to his vision. His senses had been completely pummeled by the trauma of his daughter's death and the anger that consumed him. Although he assumed that he had been eating and drinking in the days since her death, he could not recall that he had. He felt lightheaded, and assumed that some of it may have been from not taking in enough food or water.

The road from Macktown to his home traced the bottom of the long, narrow valley. The end closest to Macktown was more populated. At the far end, where his home lay, there were fewer houses. It was a fertile valley and the fields around him contained cattle, corn, and even tobacco patches. He imagined that the men who owned these fields must be working day and night to try to protect their crops and livestock from thieves. He saw men working at the door to a barn. He threw a hand up to wave at them but they didn't wave back. He could not blame them. He felt almost exuberant, freed as he was from the yoke of his obligation. He did what the world required of him and now he could go on about his life and grieve without anger. He could see if he had a life beyond this experience.

A sure sign that he was more present in this world than he had been earlier was his increasing awareness of the condition of his feet. He could tell that the heels of both feet and the tops of several toes were raw and skinless. They burned constantly. The bottom of his feet ached. His feet were now more accustomed to the advances in modern shoe technology that had taken place in the decades since the boots on his feet were made.

He stopped at one point, leaning against a fencepost to see if he could push the dizziness away. The day was hot and the road radiated the heat back at him. He kept his eyes on the ground, breathing deeply and wishing for a cold glass of water. When he raised his eyes, a man near his age stood in the yard of a nearby house, a shotgun levelled at him.

Buddy met the man's eye. "I'm just clearing my head. I ain't walked like this in years."

The man used the barrel of the shotgun to gesture down the road, as if the movement might sweep Buddy from where he stood and push him from this place where he was not wanted.

"Clear it somewhere else," the man said.

"I'm on my way home," Buddy told him. "I live in this valley."

The man took in Buddy's appearance. "Well, you don't live here," the man said. "I don't recognize you, so keep moving."

Buddy thought of the .45 beneath his fatigue jacket. *I have killed two men today and I would have no trouble killing you,* he thought. But that was not true. This man had done nothing to him. Killing him would be wrong. Even killers could have morality. Buddy had learned that from the example his own father set for him.

He straightened up and wiped his hands on his pants legs. His body had become stiffer in the moments of inactivity, his age settling into his bones and muscles. It took more of a push these days to get him going. When he got home, he imagined that he might lay in his porch swing and sleep there for an entire day. Maybe even two. He moved on, the shotgun man continuing to bear him in his sights until he disappeared from view.

For the next mile, he saw no one. Then his ears perked up at the throaty roar of what sounded like exhaust pipes. He'd not seen a moving car all day and he stepped to the shoulder of the road, turning stiffly to look behind him. The move made him lightheaded. The car was loud, not yet visible, and clearly getting closer to him if the V-8 roar was any indication.

In a moment, the heat mirage merged with the oncoming grille of a vehicle. Buddy recognized it as a Plymouth of some sort. The car was hauling ass with no concern for the preservation of fuel. Though surely the driver had to see him, there was no falter of his speed, no decrease in the throttle. On a whim, Buddy stuck out his thumb.

The gesture carried some weight for the driver of the vehicle. The car was nearly upon him when the driver locked up the brakes. In the days before anti-lock brakes, brakes locked when you wanted them to, and that's exactly what happened. The tires squealed and left black trails behind them, the car skidding diagonally in the road, stopping near where Buddy stood. The passenger window was down.

Buddy stooped over, resting his hands on his knees, and saw a man in jeans, a white collarless shirt, a black vest with a pocket watch, and a fedora sitting behind the wheel. It seemed an unusual outfit, of an old style no longer worn. Then Buddy looked down at his own Vietnam fatigues and knew that he was not in a place to judge another man for his fashion choices. They stared at each other.

"What car is this?" Buddy asked.

"It would be a 1973 Plymouth Scamp," the driver replied.

The back glass was shot out and several bullet holes pierced the mustard yellow body panels. "Rough day?"

The driver shrugged. "In a manner of speaking."

"Could a feller catch a ride?"

"Might could," the driver said. He pulled back his vest to reveal a nickel-plated revolver tucked in his waistband. "But the feller better understand he ain't taking this car without a fight."

Buddy drew open his fatigue jacket and revealed his .45 in its shoulder holster. "The feller understands and agrees to keep his pecker in his pants."

The driver smiled. "Get in."

Buddy opened the door and settled into the passenger seat. He sighed. The smell of the vintage car brought back memories of when he'd first returned from Vietnam. In the jungle, he'd forgotten the smell of cars.

"My name is Buddy," he said. "Who do I have the pleasure of riding with?"

"Lloyd," the driver said. "My name is Lloyd."

They barreled through the valley at speeds Buddy had not seen on these types of roads in decades. Lloyd squealed around turns without regard for any creature of God. Had they encountered a man on horseback or bicycle, a stray cow, or just someone walking the road, they would have died a quick and merciful death.

"What brings you to the neighborhood?" Buddy asked. "I see your windshield sticker says you're from Wythe County, assuming this is your car, which would be none of my business."

"It's my car, alright," Lloyd replied. "I'm here to check on my parents and to visit a friend."

"They live in the valley?"

"They do," Lloyd said. "I grew up here and my parents still live here. My friend lives on the far end of the valley."

"I live on the far end of the valley too," Buddy said. "Maybe I know him."

They came around a turn and Lloyd whipped the wheel hard, the vehicle slewing sideways and nearly taking out a row of mailboxes. The vehicle jolted onto a dirt driveway, narrowly missing a deep culvert. Buddy held on to the dashboard with both hands, but was still slung up against the door.

"What brings you to this end of the valley?" Lloyd asked.

"I had to kill a man this morning," Buddy replied without hesitation. "Then my truck was stolen."

Lloyd considered this. "He need killing?"

Buddy nodded. "Most assuredly."

"You use that .45?" Lloyd asked.

"No," Buddy admitted. "I burned him alive."

Lloyd nodded distractedly, his attention drawn to the small brick house that came into view. He slowed, then hit the brakes and slid to a stop in the driveway.

Buddy noticed that the man expertly avoided hitting the other cars in the narrow driveway.

"Looks like you've parked here before," he commented.

"All my life," Lloyd said. He opened his door and looked at Buddy. "I have to go inside. If I leave you here, you promise not to steal my car?"

Buddy nodded. "I promise."

"I'd not take just anyone's word on something like that," Lloyd said. "But you've already told me that you killed a man this morning and how you killed him. You're obviously not prone to lying."

"I actually killed two men today, but one was of no consequence so I failed to mention him. I won't steal your car," Buddy said. "Although I might just close my eyes for a bit. I'm wore out."

Lloyd climbed out of the car and walked across the yard to the back door. He reached onto the top of the porch light for the spare key and used that to let himself in.

Buddy eased himself back in the seat and closed his eyes.

He wasn't sure how long he was out before he felt a nudge at his elbow. He cracked an eyelid and saw Lloyd standing outside his window.

"I need a hand," Lloyd said. "I hate to ask, but do you mind helping me?"

"Of course not," Buddy said. He moved to get out, finding that his body had stiffened while he'd been asleep. Pain shot up his feet and legs when he put weight on them.

Lloyd made an odd sound that may have been a sob and Buddy thought he looked pretty rough. "Everything okay?" he asked.

Lloyd shook his head. "They're dead."

"I'm sorry to hear that, Lloyd," Buddy said. "What happened?"

"I'm not really sure. Best I can tell, Mom accidentally cut herself in the kitchen. She's on blood thinners. It looks like they couldn't stop the bleeding. There's a trail from the kitchen to the bedroom. That's where I found her."

"What about your dad?"

"He couldn't live without Mom," Lloyd said. "Shot himself in the bed beside her."

"What do you need me to do?" Buddy asked.

"I'd like to bury them."

SEVERAL HOURS HAD PASSED before Buddy and Lloyd threw down their shovels beside the filled graves.

"You going to make a marker?" Buddy asked.

"No, I don't think so," Lloyd said. "If things ever get back to normal, I'll have to sell this house. It will never sell if folks know there are two graves in the backyard. Such things used to be common, but folks these days are weird about it."

Buddy nodded but didn't remark on this. It was a very practical and logical consideration in his mind.

"I would like to get a few things from the house," Lloyd said. "In case it gets broken into."

"I don't mind helping," Buddy offered. "I got nowhere else to be."

"I'd appreciate that."

"Make sure you check for any food," Buddy said. "I think it's getting in short supply. You may need everything they've got."

Over the course of another hour, they removed all the guns and ammunition from the house, what food they could find, and several boxes of keepsakes that Lloyd wanted to take with him. It looked like family photos and some other mementos. Several boxes contained Mason jars of various colored liquids.

"That moonshine?" Buddy asked.

Lloyd nodded. "The last of what my grandfather made in his lifetime. My dad never drank it so it just sat in the basement collecting dust. He wouldn't drink it and he wouldn't give it away. Just held onto it for sentimental reasons."

"That why you're taking it?" Buddy asked. "Sentimental reasons?"

"Hell no," Lloyd said. "I'm going to crack open a jar as soon as the last box is in that car."

Buddy smiled. He liked this guy. "What did you do for a living?" Buddy asked. "Before things went to shit."

"I was a barber and a musician," Lloyd replied.

Buddy nodded. "Suits you."

Lloyd locked up his childhood home and pocketed the key. He went to the open trunk and stood looking into it while Buddy folded his stiff frame into the car.

"I've got blackberry, peach, and plain old clear," Lloyd called. "Do you have a preference?"

Buddy considered this. "I've always been partial to blackberry."

"Blackberry it is," Lloyd said, shutting the trunk and taking the driver's seat with a jar in hand.

He stared out at the fresh graves while he unscrewed the ring and popped the lid with his fingernail. He held his nose over the jar and inhaled. With the smell of that liquor came a flood of memories. Lloyd recalled his grandparents and the thousands of stories they'd shared over the years. He had loved them. He thought of his parents and their life together in this house. He thought of his childhood and how quickly it had all passed to bring him to this point. It was as if this jar held the distillation of an entire lineage. Not just his lifetime, but several lifetimes.

Lloyd brought his lips to the edge and drank deeply. Much in the way that Buddy had brought resolution to a chapter of his life by killing a man that morning, Lloyd also turned the page to a new chapter of his own life by opening a jar that his father had held for most of his life but refused to drink.

"Whereabouts does your friend live exactly?" Buddy asked.

Lloyd finished his drink and passed the jar to Buddy. "About a mile and a half past that little white church. Fellow named Jim Powell. Been a friend of mine all my life."

"Then we're going to the same neighborhood," Buddy said. "I know Jim. We probably live within a mile or less of each other."

"Best have you a drink of that before I pull out," Lloyd said. "My driving don't mix with drinking. You'll spill it."

Buddy took a sip. A smile spread across his lips. "Sweet nectar of the Gods," he whispered. "That's good shit. Takes me back."

"Me too," Lloyd said. "Me too."

10

C laypool Hill, VA

A WEARY ALICE crouched behind a guardrail at the crowded intersection of Route 19 and Route 460. Since leaving Boyd's, she'd walked forty miles in two exhausting days. Her feet throbbed with each step. They throbbed even worse when she stopped to rest and she could feel the blood pulsing in them as if they were about to explode. Over the last two hours, a sharp pain had emerged in the side of her knee and nearly took her breath at times, but she would not slow down. She limped on.

Her stomach did slow her down, though. Frequent intestinal cramps and diarrhea had plagued her for these two days. She knew it traced back to drinking ditch water. She tried to stay hydrated, but all food and liquid passed right through her. Though she was miserable, she had no time for it.

Her initial plan had been to walk out of the Bluefield area in the same manner as she entered it, keeping to the shoulder of the road, hiding when she approached other people, although she found that her experiences had changed her in ways she had not expected. That first night, she kept walking until she was out of the town of Bluefield and found a place to hole up on the side of the road. She awoke early and started walking immediately, eating on the road.

When she met her first group of travelers, she waited for the panic to well up within her and urge her into hiding. It never came. Instead, she drew her pistol and held it in her hand as she and the group passed each other. Whether it was the gun, her demeanor, or the look in her eyes she didn't know, but the group did not speak to her. They looked at her, then averted their eyes, pausing all conversation until she passed.

Most did not even have weapons, or concealed them if they did. In more populated areas along the highway, where houses lined both sides of the road, some people had attempted to speak to her despite her icy demeanor. They appeared harmless, but she took no chances. She spoke to no one and carried her gun openly at all times now.

She had learned the value of casting a threatening presence into the world and making people shy from her path. She had a cousin, prone to violence and drunkenness, who had been such a man. Folks said of him that Heaven wouldn't take him and the devil was too scared to let him into Hell. That was what Alice tried to be in her mind. A wraith so scarred and with a soul so blackened that a glimpse of her eyes froze the questions in the very mouth of the questioner and they let her pass without bother.

In a remote section near a golf course, a man on a motorized scooter offered her a ride. Had he not been drunk, he would have taken one look at her and kept moving, just as everyone else did. She considered his offer, as the ride would have knocked at least three hours' walking from her trip, but she couldn't make herself do it.

"Got this moped when I got my fourth DUI," the man told her. "You don't need a license and it gets fifty miles to a gallon. Who's having the last laugh now?"

He sped off after she declined a second time with a pang of regret. What would she do if he sped off the highway toward some unknown destination? At forty-five miles per hour she couldn't exactly jump off and she couldn't kill him while he was driving or they'd wreck. She just couldn't take the chance and put her fate in someone else's hands. She could not end up caged in someone's basement again, or worse.

She saw the roadblock at Claypool Hill from a good distance. She approached in cover and hid to observe it for a while. A few folks on bicycles and two men on horseback passed through the checkpoint. They weren't delayed for long and there was no overt hostility from the men working the checkpoint. Even though it looked safe, she still opted to go around it.

She cut up into a subdivision of houses and gave the intersection a wide berth. Sticking to the paved road through the subdivision, she saw curtains move and folks watching from dim interiors. A man with a shotgun stood by a barbecue grill, tending a small fire. As she watched, he slung a long-tailed carcass onto the grill. It could only have been a cat. It reminded her that she'd not eaten since midday, but it would have to wait. She would not stop this close to her destination.

The subdivision road crossed the highway that went into the town of Richlands. That was not the direction that Alice needed to go so she crossed the road and entered a cemetery. It was late and the sun was setting, but the cemetery was more peaceful than gloomy. It was one of the few places she'd been recently that seemed completely unthreatening, even though it was becoming overgrown without daily mowing and maintenance. It was almost like a park.

At one point, she came upon a fresh grave with a plywood marker. There were roses scattered across the heaped mound of dirt. The date on the board, written with a black marker, indicated a date of death somewhere around the start of this whole event. She was glad to know that some rituals were intact. Someone had cared enough to bury this person in a proper cemetery with a marker and flowers.

Perhaps there was hope for the world after all.

At the edge of the cemetery, she cut across a vacant lot then down a steep hill to a grassy embankment where she crouched and slid down to a ditch. She was back alongside the highway now, safely past the roadblock. Her office was just a couple of miles ahead of her. It felt like years since she'd left on that work trip and gone to Richmond. A lot had happened since then.

There was no way she'd make it to the office before dark, but there was also no way she was spending another night on the road. She had a flashlight and some spare batteries. She'd just have to be careful and stay on her guard. She adjusted her pack, tightened the belt, and started walking briskly, taking the longest strides she could. The pain in her knee nearly brought tears to her eyes and she tried to distract herself by remembering personal stories about the landmarks along the way.

She passed the bowling alley where she'd once had a birthday party for her son. When she and her husband first met, they went on several dates there. A few minutes later, she caught sight of a cinderblock video store where she'd once worked part-time renting VHS movies. She tried to recall some of the movies that had been new releases when she'd worked there, and couldn't recall a single one. She did remember that the best part of the job was that she could take home a movie or two every night for free if she wanted. That was a big deal to her then. People always wanted to hang out at her apartment because of the free movies.

Ten minutes later there was another building that had once been a gun store but now sat empty. Then a pawn shop, an ice cream shop, a camper store. She kept the challenge going in her head for as long as she could, but for the last two miles there were just cattle pastures on both sides of the road – no landmarks, no buildings, no associated memories. The only houses were set far back from the road. It was dark enough now that she could only see shapes. The road was easy enough to follow, its surface catching a little moonlight, so she walked without using her light. She carried it in her left hand, ready for use. In her right she carried the pistol and it was ready too.

Before she came to her office complex, she passed a large church. There was a steel building that the church used as a gym. People were gathered there in the parking lot. There was a fire going in a steel drum and several Coleman lanterns hanging around the entrance to the building. It looked like they were operating a shelter of some sort. Although she knew several folks who attended that church, she was by this point so alienated from the company of strangers that she could not see herself approaching them, even for a hot meal or a cot. Without her light, no one saw her and she passed in welcome obscurity.

Past the church, she turned left onto a street that ran between her office complex and the local community college. Beyond the college, there was also a National Guard armory. At the armory, she could see some outdoor fires going, with the vague shape of men standing around them. A dull glow came from the high windows of the armory building and she wondered if it might also be some sort of shelter. Again, she did not trust people enough to seek their company or assistance. She would go to her own building and see what she could find.

She first passed the darkened clinic buildings, their one-story profiles easily recognizable. From the way that reflecting firelight from the armory varied from window to window, she could tell that these buildings had been broken into and vandalized. She stopped and listened very carefully. In the distance, she could hear the voices of the armory men telling stories and laughing around the fire. From her buildings, she heard nothing.

Her office was in a two-story building. The upper stories were not accessible except by access controlled steel doors or an elevator. With no power, the elevator should have kept folks out of the upper stories. Once the power went out, the steel doors to the second floor would go into fail-secure mode and lock down and could only be opened at that point by using a key.

Alice passed her blue Honda Accord in the parking lot. It was less than two years old and was one of the nicer cars she'd ever owned. It was one of the few cars in the parking lot and she could guess by the reek of fuel that someone had either siphoned the gas from it or punctured the gas tank. She walked around the car and found the windows intact. It almost surprised her. She sadly noted that it did rest on four flat tires.

From the landscaping around the parking lot, she picked up a retaining wall stone about the size of a large brick. With both hands, she threw it through the driver's window of her Honda. Concerned now that the noise might draw the wrong kind of attention, she used her flashlight and quickly located the large ring of keys in the center console. Because Human Resources sometimes required more than eight hours of work a day, she was often in the building late at night. She kept a key to every door she used because she'd been there during a power failure one night and had worried that she might become trapped in the building. The maintenance staff had assured her that she could not be, but she felt better having the keys anyway.

She figured that she might as well use the light now because the noise of the breaking car window would certainly have gotten the attention of anyone in the vicinity anyway. Shining it discreetly at her feet, Alice walked around the front of the building. Once there, she was shocked to see the destruction that awaited her. The glass entry doors had been shattered. Shining her light through them, she saw piles of furniture, scattered papers, and knew that the office had been trashed.

"Please let the upper floors be safe," she whispered. "I can't go any further tonight."

She'd been in the building many times at night and it had never bothered her. In this wrecked state it felt different. The building felt like the scene of violence. It made her feel as if there were people in there waiting to spring on her and do violence to her, just as they'd done to the building. She found herself panicking.

Settle down, she thought. *Get control of yourself.*

She picked up her pace and walked through the hallways to the battered steel door that led to the stairwell. She pushed on it and found it solid. Battered or not, it had appeared to hold. She hoped the lock had not been beaten to the point that her key would not open it. She flipped through her chain of keys until she found the right one and slipped it inside. She turned it and her heart surged when the door unlocked.

Thank God.

She played her light around inside the stairwell and saw nothing out of the ordinary, stepped inside quickly, and the steel door locked behind her. Holding both the gun and light, she took the steps. She could see nothing that indicated anyone had been up this way since the building closed on the last day of business.

When the steps took a right turn, she shined her light around anxiously, heart racing. Still, she could see nothing alarming. In a moment she was at the top of the steps and facing another steel door just like the one she'd entered in the downstairs hallway. Since the fire code did not allow stairwell doors to lock from the inside, Alice did not need a key to exit the stairwell on the second floor. She felt a great apprehension, wondering if people could be up there waiting on her, ready to kill her for entering space they'd claimed as their own.

She turned the lock gently, hearing the click that sounded way too loud in the silence of the building. She pulled the door open slowly, her heart wrenching when the hinges groaned. She'd never noticed before that they made so much noise. She played the light into the hallway, hoping that no one would be standing there waiting on her like in some slasher movie. She knew that her heart would stop instantly. Thankfully, there was no one there, but what she saw made her freeze in her tracks.

On the wall directly across from her, someone had used a permanent marker to leave a message: JIM, RANDI, AND GARY MADE IT THIS FAR. THERE'S FOOD AND WATER IN OFFICE 17.

Alice's knees weakened from relief and the onrush of emotions. She sagged against the wall, her head resting on the flat white paint. Not only had the others made it back, but there was food and water. She also had to think that, as much as she and Jim fought sometimes, he'd left this message for her, hoping she'd make it back.

Still not convinced she was alone, Alice made a complete circuit of the upper floor of the building, checking every office, every closet, every restroom, and every other place she could imagine someone fitting into. There was no one there. Except for the minor indications that someone had been here – most likely Jim, Randi, and Gary – things were as tidy as they always were.

Alice ended her search at Office 17. She opened the door and shined her light inside. On the desk were several unopened bottles of water, some crackers, and a few plastic lunch-sized tubs of Campbell's soup. In a desk chair, a couple of fleece blankets were folded and stacked. On the desk blotter was a large scented candle in a jar. Beside it was a cigarette lighter and a note written on a sheet of copy paper.

GUESS YOU MISSED A CANDLE IN YOUR FIRE INSPECTIONS, ALICE. GOOD THING YOU DID.

She laughed for the first time in a long time. She closed the office door, locked it behind her, and propped her flashlight on the desk. She lit the candle and it threw a warm glow in the windowless office. She collapsed in the desk chair and felt like she could cry. The relief of simply being back in familiar territory was overwhelming. She thought of going to her own office, but it was on an outside wall and she did not want the glow of the candle drawing attention to her office window. She would stay here. She would eat and drink all that her exhaustion would allow her, then she could prop her feet up and sleep.

She would have a long walk tomorrow, but she hoped it would take her home to her family.

11

G ary's House
Richlands, VA

GARY LOADED the car with his backpack and his radio. He had several AR and M4 variations that he'd bought over the years. He grabbed a Bushmaster from the gun safe.

"I've never seen that one before," Will commented.

"It's special," Gary said. "Let's just leave it at that."

He had a half-dozen spare mags, a headlamp, and a few other pieces of gear, all of it concealed in his pack. The rifle itself would be hidden beneath a blanket in the passenger seat of the car, easily accessible if things went to shit. On his belt, carried open and accessible, Gary had his Glock with two spare mags. He had two more full magazines in a pouch on the outside of his pack.

His first stop was the home of Wesley Molloy, the young man he'd apprehended on his property the night before. It seemed a little farfetched, but he wanted to see if the punk still had his generator. He wasn't sure if he would actually kill someone to get it back, but he wasn't sure that he wouldn't. It wasn't like he could go out and buy another one.

The subdivision the Molloys lived in was one of the largest in the area. If you were a coal executive or a physician, but not rich enough to own an estate, this was where you lived. It was also where you lived if you had aspirations of wealth, just so you could claim you lived there. The neighborhood certainly had the largest homes in the little coal town. It wasn't too far from Gary's home and he reached the entrance after less than five minutes of driving. It was uneventful except for having to dodge a downed tree and a few abandoned vehicles that hadn't been pulled from the roadway. With few cars moving, the Department of Transportation had no plans to keep the road clear.

Gary was surprised he was able to drive right into the subdivision. There was no guard, no blocked entrance, nothing. Had he lived here, he would have made some type of effort at trying to restrict entry into the neighborhood. Even a rudimentary gate made from a downed tree would send a message that people who didn't belong there should keep moving. It said a lot about these people that they weren't working together. Maybe all these people had left and abandoned their houses just like he was planning on doing with his.

Will had been able to tell him exactly where to find the house he was looking for. It was a house he'd noticed before, both due to its size and pretension, but he never knew who lived there. There were no other cars moving in the subdivision. Unlike when he visited town yesterday, he didn't even feel like he was being watched here. Were they all gone? Dead? Or just apathetic and resigned to some dire fate? No children played and no one worked outside. He would not have been surprised to see a tumbleweed blow past. The place had that kind of feel.

The farther he got off the main road, the more expensive the houses appeared to be. They were larger, with more of the architectural features and high end materials that drove the price up. The vehicles in the driveways were more expensive too. In the end, however, a Hummer or Cadillac Escalade with no gas was no more useful than a Dodge Neon with no gas. A dead car was a dead car.

Gary turned into what he thought was the Molloys' driveway and parked behind a half-dozen vehicles. There was a Mercedes SUV, a Mini Cooper, and a Lexus. There was a BMW with all kinds of knick-knacks hanging from the rearview mirror. One of them was a graduation tassel. There was a customized Honda with low-profile tires on expensive wheels and an aftermarket exhaust. Gary assumed this belonged to the boy he'd dealt with last night. It seemed like just the kind of vehicle he would drive.

Past the vehicles, Gary approached the four-car garage. The house was an enormous brick monstrosity devoid of style. It was built for size more than anything else. One look at the sealed black asphalt of the driveway told Gary that several dirt bikes and ATVs with muddy tires had been using this garage. To his right was a sidewalk that led to a covered entry. Gary followed the sidewalk beneath several windows but saw no movement in those windows. He walked between two brick columns with iron horse heads upon them, climbed six cast limestone steps, and paused on the porch.

He listened carefully, hearing no steps, no voices, not even a shotgun racking a shell into the chamber. That he could hear nothing inside the house was not entirely surprising. A newer brick house with proper insulation could mask a lot of noise, including that of cocking weapons. He thought it best to maintain vigilance. He took a step and stopped in front of the door. It had looked like wood from a distance but he could now see that it was fiberglass. He knocked on the door, then stepped to the side. He hoped that someone firing through the door would not be able to hit him this way.

No one came. No one fired.

He knocked again and put his ear to the door. It made him nervous to do that, but he was determined to find his generator. Still, he could hear nothing inside the house. To one side of the door was a sidelight, a tall, narrow pane of glass that allowed natural light into the entry of the home. Gary approached the sidelight, boldly pressed his face against it, and cupped his eyes. With the design of the house, he could see straight through it to the backyard. There was a foyer, and beyond that a great room with an enormous glass wall that looked out onto a wide deck.

Gary knocked again, conscious that he didn't belong in this neighborhood and his knocking could be drawing attention. There were several houses that had a clear of line of fire to his position. Someone could shoot at him thinking he was a thief or a looter. Someone could attack him for his car or the fuel in the tank.

He went back to the sidelight and stared through again. It almost looked like there were people sitting on the couch in the great room watching television, but Gary couldn't tell for sure. It was always hard to look from a sunny location into the darkened interior of a house, even with your eyes shaded. He could just as easily been looking at a stack of puffy sofa pillows.

Wondering if he might be able to see better with binoculars, Gary went back to his vehicle and retrieved a cheap set from his pack. Back at the door, Gary knocked one more time before moving back to the sidelight and pressing the binoculars against the glass. The field of view was so narrow that only a small section of the room was visible through the lenses. He had to angle them in different directions all over the room before orienting himself and finding the shapes on the sofa. When he did, he jerked violently backward and gasped as his view was filled with the bloated face of a dead woman, her head misshapen and nearly obscured by a cloud of flies.

Recovering from the shock, Gary put the binoculars back to his eyes and saw that she was sitting beside another corpse, that of a man, presumably her husband. The man's face was also deformed both through bloating and through the possible gunshot wound that took a chunk of his forehead out. His face was also crusted with a thick mass of flies. In his lap, Gary could see a large revolver, the trigger finger still loosely threaded through the trigger guard, where it had likely fallen after the fatal shot.

They had killed themselves. At least the man had killed himself. Maybe he had killed his wife or maybe she had killed herself too. He wondered why. One thing about the current situation of the world was that it shook up the social strata. People who had valuable skills in the old world might not find themselves so valuable when the rules changed. Perhaps they couldn't stand the idea that they were just going to be like everyone else, struggling for food, fuel, and resources just to stay alive.

Gary decided that he had no interest in going inside. He wasn't sure that his generator was even in there, and if it was, they could have it. He had better things to do than risk his life in that stinking house.

GARY LIVED eight miles from his office and it normally took him ten to fifteen minutes to get there, as long as he didn't get behind a school bus. The first half of the trip was on a winding two-lane mountain road. The last half was on a four-lane highway. The two-lane road didn't have any shoulders for vehicles to pull off on if they ran out of fuel, so drivers had coasted as far as they could get, then abandoned their vehicles where they sat. In some places, it created traffic jams that had been difficult to get around. One had been impassible until Gary released the emergency brakes on several vehicles, put them in neutral, and let them roll over an embankment. The only houses in sight had shown no signs of life so Gary hoped that he didn't draw any undue attention from his actions. In better times, vehicles crashing over hillsides drew a crowd.

The truck he hoped to return in was bigger than the Nissan he was driving now. If he didn't create a return lane of sufficient size, he had no hope of getting back. It was still early in the day and he hoped that there wouldn't be many people out walking or stirring about. He didn't want to have any confrontations or have to turn down any hitchhikers needing rides. He just wanted a smooth day for a change. He couldn't remember the last one he'd had. That was kind of funny when he thought about it. Most of his life had been fairly uneventful, even boring at times. Now, he'd give anything for a boring day.

When he reached the four-lane road, he was pleased to find it clear. There were vehicles on the side of the road that appeared to have run out of fuel and many of them showed signs of impact. He knew that both the state police and the National Guard had vehicles capable of clearing highways under these circumstances. It looked like such a vehicle, or a piece of heavy construction equipment, had been used to clear the road.

This section of highway was relatively unpopulated, and he saw absolutely no one for the remainder of his drive. When he turned off the main road and onto the campus of his employer, he was shocked by the condition of the buildings. All of them appeared to have suffered damage. The oldest building, a single-story clinic, had windows broken out and showed signs of looting. He wasn't surprised since that building had stored medications. Gary also thought that he may have seen a body lying near the building but he didn't investigate. Bodies were becoming a common sight and he didn't want to see any more dead people than he'd already seen.

The maintenance shop was at the rear of the ten-acre complex. As Gary drove by the two-story administration building that had housed his office, he had a thought. Prior to leaving on his ill-fated trip, he had ordered some ammunition from an online retailer. He was planning on taking a tactical shooting class and there was a requirement to bring one thousand rounds of your preferred caliber. Gary had ordered one thousand rounds of target quality ammo for his .40 caliber Glock.

The box was supposed to arrive the day he left. When he got a package at work, someone usually took it up to his office and left it outside the door. If they did, he might have a thousand rounds of very useful ammunition sitting up there waiting for him. It all depended on whether the ammo had arrived on time, if someone delivered it up to his office, and if no looter or vandal had beat him to it.

He parked his car on the far side of the building out of the view of anyone who might be passing by. He pulled the headlamp from his pack, strapped it on, and slung the pack over his shoulders. He probably didn't need it, but he didn't want to leave it there to tempt someone to break into the car. Staring at his blanket-covered AR rifle, he realized that its camouflage was pretty inadequate, so he took it as well. Not knowing how he was going to carry the ammo with all this crap on him, he locked the car and headed for the front door.

It turned out that Gary didn't need his keys for the front door. The full-length glass had been shattered and he merely stepped through the aluminum frame, his feet crunching on the pellets of tempered glass that littered the carpeted entry. The noise was loud in the quiet building and Gary suddenly felt very vulnerable. He switched on his headlamp and took a look around. Not only was the building vandalized, it looked like people had been hanging around in there. There were food wrappers, empty bottles, and what looked like used toilet paper. There was a charred section of carpet that looked as if someone may even have tried to build a campfire or cooking fire in the middle of the lobby.

Around the corner to the left was the area where packages were usually dropped off by UPS or FedEx. Of course there was nothing there. Anything that had been there had most certainly been stolen by this time. Gary turned around and headed deeper into the interior of the building, hoping the steel security had not been breached.

The back hallways received very little natural light. There were no windows onto the hallway itself and the only light came in through open offices. Several office doors were open, probably not locked to begin with. Other wooden office doors showed signs of attempted entry, the wood veneer surfaces scarred and splintered. There were office chairs in the hallway, as well as smashed computers. In one office, a torso dummy used to teach CPR was propped up in an office chair, wearing lipstick and holding a phone receiver to his ear. Reams of copy paper were opened and scattered, carpeting the debris-filled floor. A bathroom door was wedged open and Gary shined his light inside. All the sinks had been smashed and the doors torn from the toilet stalls. Someone had expended a lot of energy wrecking the building.

Thankfully, the steel door leading to the stairwell was battered but not breached. Scratches around the jamb indicated that someone may have tried to get an instrument in there to pry it open, but had not succeeded. Gary slung his rifle over his shoulder, hoping that the cluttered floor would give him ample warning if someone approached him from behind while he was digging for his keys.

He was pleased that the lock worked just as it was supposed to. He turned the key slowly so the throw of the bolt did not echo in the open stairwell. Then he pushed gently and the door swung open. He slipped inside, closing the door behind him.

He shined his light around, making sure that no one was in the dark stairwell with him. He took the stairs one at time, stepping softly and trying to keep the noise down. It did not look like anyone had accessed the upper floors, but that could be intentional. Someone could have picked the lock or used a ladder to find an open window and was living up there. He didn't want any surprises.

When he reached the top landing, he paused and listened. He couldn't hear anything at all. He placed his ear against the door and listened. He slung his rifle over his shoulder and un-holstered the Glock. It would be easier to use than the rifle if someone was waiting on him on the other side of the door.

He turned the handle to open the door and it was a lot louder than he would have liked. In the silent building, it sounded as loud as knocking over a stack of cans. With the door unlatched, he faced a dilemma: make a rapid entry while he wielded his pistol, or gently ooze inside as stealthily as possible. He chose curtain number one, yanking the door open and holding his pistol at the ready.

The first thing he noticed was the message written on the wall in marker, advising that he, Jim, and Randi had made it this far and that there was food in one of the offices. The second thing he noticed was the frightened eyes of Alice staring at him over the shaking barrel of a pistol. He could see the look of panic in her eyes, knowing instantly that she recognized him and did not want to shoot him, but also knowing that in her terror she could not stop herself from pulling the trigger. Gary threw himself to the side, back into the stairwell, just as the gun went off.

Gary managed to get his body out of the way of the shot, but the steel door was still easing shut on its hydraulic closer. The angle of the door deflected the slug into the stairwell. As Gary fell, he heard the round sing over his head, then ricochet once, twice, three times, before he was done falling. He had no idea where the round ended up but a lack of searing pain told him that it had not lodged itself into his flesh.

"Oh my God, Gary!" Alice cried, her voice shrill with panic. "OH MY GOD!"

She burst into the stairwell after him, gun in hand.

"It's okay, Alice. I'm not hit," Gary gasped. He lay on his back, stunned from the hard fall. He held out his hand. "Just hand me the gun."

His request snapped her back to reality and she calmly declined, tucking the revolver into the waistband of her pants. "I'll hang onto it. I think I'm okay now."

She dropped to her knees and threw her arms around Gary, hugging him tightly. "I'm sorry I shot at you," she said. "I was just getting ready to leave for home and I saw the doorknob turning right in front of me. I panicked."

Gary picked up his dislodged headlamp where it lay on the concrete floor. He struggled to his feet, his pack and rifle still strapped to him but hanging awkwardly to the side. "It's okay," he said. "Let's get out of here and into some light."

He shined his light around and found his Glock. It had tumbled down ten stairs to the first landing. He holstered the pistol, then followed Alice out of the stairwell. He gestured at the writing on the wall.

"I probably would have reacted quicker, but I was distracted by that message," he said.

"That message really lifted my spirits when I came through that door," Alice said. "I knew that you guys had made it this far and I knew where to find some food."

"Jim and Randi said they were going to spend the night here," Gary said. "I parted ways with them at Claypool Hill, heading toward my own house."

"So they made it home?" Alice asked. Then she frowned. "I guess you don't know with the phones out, do you?"

"I do know," he said. "We've talked by radio. Everyone has their own set of problems to deal with, but everyone is home."

"Except for me," Alice said.

"Is Rebecca still at the camp?" Gary asked. "I thought you guys were heading for the camp together."

"The camp was a joke," Alice said. "They had no real plans for getting us home. They were just trying to win political points by getting us off the roads and out of the hair of local cops. Rebecca and I ended up trying to make a run for it. She was murdered on the way home."

Gary was shocked, his mouth dropping open in disbelief. "Murdered?"

She nodded. "It's too long a story for now, but the road home was brutal. I've kicked myself every day for not leaving with you guys."

Gary leaned forward and hugged Alice again. "I'm sorry," he said. "We would never have left you guys if we'd known."

Alice patted him on the back. "That's okay, Gary. You couldn't have convinced us to have acted any differently back at that hotel. We really thought you guys were crazy. It didn't take me but a couple of days in that FEMA camp to figure out that you guys made the right decision."

Gary glanced at a nearby window, noticing that it was probably close to noon now and he needed to get a move on. "Why such a late start?" he asked. "With this being your last day, I would think you'd be hauling butt down the road at first light."

"The mind is willing but the body is weak," Alice said with a fragile smile. "I've been having stomach issues since I had to drink some questionable water out of a ditch."

"You might have picked up Giardia," Gary said. "I've got meds at home that will treat that. It takes an antibiotic."

"Then the heel came off my shoe yesterday," Alice said. "I've taped it back on but it keeps coming loose. Now I've got this enormous blister on the bottom of my foot and each step is excruciating. I know I'll make it, but it's going to hurt like hell."

Gary didn't know what to say. He could tell that Alice needed help, but so did his family. Perhaps if Alice was willing, he could help both of them.

"I need to get moving, Alice," Gary said. "I'm going to get my family out of town. The place we're living is not really set up for long-term survival. We're too close to town and I just don't think we can secure the location."

"Were you going to move here?" Alice asked.

"No. We're going to join forces with Jim. He says there's a house we can use near where he lives. It's far enough out in the country that I think it will cut down on people wandering by and we can also help each other out if there's any trouble."

Alice nodded, taking it all in. "So why are you here?"

Gary smiled awkwardly. "Basically, I'm here to steal a truck."

"I'm still Human Resources," Alice said. "I might have to terminate you for admitting something like that."

Gary got a panicked look in his eyes for a moment before realizing that Alice was teasing him. "If you're willing to hang out with me and my family for a night, I'll drive you to Russell County tomorrow and see what we can do about getting you home. I can also hook you up with some meds to get those stomach issues under control."

It didn't take Alice long to think it over. "As much as I miss my family, I'm just not sure I can do another twenty miles on foot today. That would be great. Thank you."

"Follow me," Gary said. "We've got work to do."

GARY STARTED in Jim's office, using his master key to open the office door. Since one of Jim's duties was overseeing the agency's properties, he had hundreds, if not thousands, of keys to deal with. He managed this by storing them in a carefully organized key cabinet in his office.

One section of the cabinet held keys to the various maintenance vehicles and equipment that the agency owned. After flipping through numerous white key tags, Gary found one labeled *Box Truck*.

After more scouring of the box he came up with a spare key to the maintenance shop. He dropped those in his pocket, along with a key to the padlock on the steel Conex box that they used for storing items that didn't fit into their shop building. The Conex boxes were very hard to break into, with welded shields over the padlock points that kept the locks from being opened with bolt cutters.

When Gary finally had all of the keys in his pocket that he thought he'd need, he headed toward the stairwell. Then he realized he was forgetting something. "Uh oh," he said, stopping in his tracks.

"What is it?" Alice asked.

"I forgot I wanted to check my office for a package," he said. "Wait here."

Gary trotted down the hall, his rifle and pack noisily jostling on his back. When he turned down the alcove where his office was located, he saw a compact box about a foot tall. He approached it and tapped it with his foot. It didn't budge.

"Yes!" He leaned over and picked up the heavy box, heading down the hallway with it.

He and Alice carefully made it to the Nissan, making sure that no one was around. Gary's first stop was to go behind the maintenance shop and make sure that the truck had not been damaged. He found it exactly where it was supposed to be. The vehicle was used so little that the white cargo box was starting to turn green from algae. An initial inspection revealed no flat tires and no broken windows. That was encouraging.

Gary crouched and sniffed. No fuel smell. He looked beneath the tank and saw no disappointing fuel stains. It appeared that the truck was unmolested. Although it was sitting out here in the open, the parking lot behind the maintenance shop was so out of the way it wasn't likely anyone would see the vehicle unless they knew where to look.

Gary unlocked the door and climbed in. The truck was old with torn vinyl seats, a cracked dashboard, and that smell that only a thirty year old truck has. He turned the key and the fuel gauge ran up to a little less than half of a tank. He wasn't sure if that was enough or not, but it was enough that he would certainly try to make it. He hoped he could find more fuel in the maintenance shop. On a whim, he turned the key, just wanting to feel out the engine and see if it was going to cooperate or not. It turned over a little sluggishly. It didn't start and he chose not to push his luck in case the battery was weak. He would just have to see if he could find some booster cables in the maintenance shop.

The maintenance shop was set off toward the back of the agency's property. Shop buildings tended to accumulate lots of clutter around them and become eyesores, so it was best to put them in places where they didn't attract a lot of attention. It was surrounded by tall pines that screened it from the rest of the property. This also may have helped in keeping the nondescript building from being broken into. Gary stood in front of the building and surveyed the area, seeing no indication that the building had been ransacked.

"This was probably the most useful building on the entire property," Alice said. "But people chose to break into the buildings with drugs first. That tells you a lot about people."

"What it tells me is that the kind of people who would know how to make use of tools aren't out breaking into buildings," Gary replied. "Only the lowlifes."

Gary knew that the maintenance staff changed the lock on this building on a regular basis because a lot of people had access to it. He hoped the key he'd taken was the most current key. He was very pleased when the key he'd taken from Jim's office opened the lock. He pulled a flashlight from his pack and swung the door open and peered into the windowless cavern of the metal building. "Do you have a flashlight?" he asked.

Alice nodded and pulled one from her back pocket.

"We're looking for a couple of things. We need any fuel cans, full or empty. I also need either booster cables or one of those rechargeable boosting boxes. As far as I know, that's all I'm looking for.

"Got it," Alice said.

Gary clicked his light on and they went inside. The building was about sixty feet wide and twice that long. It was lined with shelves full of maintenance supplies and had a workshop area at one end. As soon as they were through the door, Gary flashed his light around the room and saw a yellow steel cabinet that said FLAMMABLE on the front in bold red letters.

"There," he said. "That should have the fuel cans in it."

Fortunately, the cabinet was unlocked. When they opened the door, they found the cabinet to be about half-full of red steel gas cans with a few yellow cans for diesel. Gary pulled all of the cans from the cabinet and set them on the floor. Some were full, some were less than full, but all had some level of fuel in them.

"This is great," Gary said. "This will definitely get us to Jim's and give you enough to get home."

Alice couldn't even think about that now. She had to focus on one step at a time. It was the only way she could keep her emotions in check. "What else did you need?" she asked.

"One of those rechargeable battery booster boxes. I know they have a couple of them. They have a handle on top and booster cables built onto the side of them. They use them for jump-starting cars when the batteries are dead."

Alice started off on her own, shining her light around the walls and floor of the crowded building. In a few minutes she called out to Gary. "Is this it?"

Gary left the gas cans and went around the end of a shelving unit. In the beam of Alice's light, Gary could see an industrial battery charger, but it was not what he was looking for.

"That's not it. That will boost a battery if you can plug it into electricity but not if there's no power."

He stood there with her and they both ambled around with their lights.

"These guys have a lot of crap," Alice remarked.

"Yes!" Gary said.

"You find it?"

"No," Gary said. "I did find a generator, though. Mine got stolen from my house. That's part of the reason we're leaving. We're too close to town and we're having a constant security problem."

"So you're going to take it?" Alice said. There was something in her tone again, something wanting him to clarify that he was borrowing and not stealing.

"Yes, I'm taking it," Gary said. "I'll bring it back after this is all over. I promise."

"And the gas?"

"I'll refill the cans and bring them back," Gary said. "Happy?"

"Yes," she replied. "I can help you borrow but I won't help you steal."

"Fair enough."

They looked for another fifteen minutes and couldn't find the booster box.

"It could be on one of the maintenance trucks or they could have lent it to someone," Gary said. "It could be anywhere."

"If you've got the generator to provide electrical power, can you use the other one? The one I found earlier?" Alice asked.

Gary mulled it over. "I think so," he said. "That's a good idea."

"This place is making me a little nervous," she said. "What do we need to do to get out of here?"

"I need to get that big truck started first, then we can see about getting things loaded," Gary said. "I'm not sure I can roll that generator across gravel, but if I can get it close to the back door of this building we can run extension cords to that charger unit and boost the battery."

"Then let's do it and get out of here," Alice urged.

They got everything in place first, with the charger outside and connected to the battery, then located a one hundred foot extension cord on a wall hook and ran it out to the charger. Last, because of fear of the noise drawing attention, they started the generator. As soon as it was running, Gary jumped in the truck and turned the key. The engine turned with more power, but it still didn't crank.

"Darn it," he mumbled. "What's wrong with this truck?"

"Is it diesel?" Alice asked.

"I have no idea," Gary said. "How do I tell?"

"Some of them say DIESEL ONLY on the dash," Alice said. "Or they say it by the fuel cap."

Gary stared at the dash and, sure enough, there were small white letters by the fuel gauge that said DIESEL ONLY. "It *is* diesel!" he yelled out.

"You may have to use starting fluid," Alice called back. "My dad was a farmer. On the old diesel tractors my dad had to use starting fluid."

Gary threw his hands up in frustration. He didn't have any idea where to start looking for starter fluid and he was getting nervous about the sound of the generator. "Where did your dad keep his?"

Alice came to the door of the tall truck and pointed behind the seat. "Back there," she said. "That's where he would have kept his."

Gary stepped out onto the running board and flipped the seat forward. He grabbed a yellow spray can and read the label. "I'll be darned," he said. "This is it."

Gary jumped out of the door and ran back to the fuel filler tube to remove the cap.

"What are you doing?" Alice asked.

Gary stopped. "You don't add it to the tank?"

"Give me that," she said, extending her hand. "And you get in the truck."

Alice took the can and went around the front of the truck. She found the hood release and popped it. Due to her height, she had some trouble climbing onto the bumper of the truck, and then some trouble staying there once she got up there. She leaned forward and unscrewed the breather cover.

"I'm going to spray this into the engine!" she yelled. "When I tell you to start cranking, you turn the key and don't let up until it catches. Got it?"

"Got it!" Alice shook the can, crossed her fingers, and sprayed a long burst of the ether spray into the intake. "Crank it!"

Gary turned the key. The engine turned, then surged, but didn't catch. Alice sprayed another burst. The engine almost caught that time. Again, she hit it with the spray. Finally, the engine hit, surging loudly and pouring a burst of blue smoke from the exhaust. Alice replaced the air filter cover and slid down from the bumper.

They worked furiously to disconnect their cords and the charger. Gary threw it all into the back of the truck. They locked the back door to the shop and Alice walked through to the front while Gary drove the truck around to the front door. As he drove, he scanned the parking lots and roads of the property for any indication that their activities were being watched but he saw nothing.

When he whipped around the front of the building, he backed up as close to the shop door as he could, then locked the brake. He decided to let the engine run rather than take a chance on it not starting again. He jumped out of the truck and walked to the back to begin loading fuel cans into the truck. That's when it hit him how high the box bed of the truck was off the ground.

"I'm not sure how I'm going to get that generator in there," Gary said. "Does this truck have a ramp?" He looked above the rear bumper and saw no sign of a ramp.

"There's a forklift," Alice said. "Can you drive it?"

Gary looked frustrated. "No," he said. "Not sure that I can. Never tried."

"Let me take a look at it while you load the gas," Alice said. She disappeared back into the dark shop.

The forklift was in a dark corner close to a wall-mounted charger. It was a battery-powered forklift and she hoped they'd left it charged. She wasn't sure how they worked, but she'd run a tractor on her dad's farm and it might be close to that.

She found a key in the ignition and turned it. There was beeping and a series of diagnostic lights flashed on the dashboard. She found that forward and reverse were controlled by a shuttle lever on the steering column, just like her dad's tractor. A series of three levers controlled the fork operation and all were clearly marked. She pulled one and it tipped the forks forward. She tried another and it raised the forks.

"Simple enough," she said. She flipped the lever into reverse and hit the throttle.

Nothing happened.

She stared at the dash and saw a brake light illuminated. She examined the control panel and found a lever that could be the brake, although the markings were worn off. She flipped the lever down and the light on the dash went off. Then she hit the throttle again. This time the forklift shot backward uncontrollably and smashed into a refrigerator before she could get her foot on the brake.

"Shit!"

Gary came flying through the door. "You okay?"

Refrigerant gas hissed from the wall of the crushed refrigerator and she could hear crushed soft drinks spewing from around the mangled door. "I'm fine," she said. "Just getting the hang of it."

Gary nodded suspiciously and gave her a wide berth.

"See if you can get that garage door open and we'll get out of here," she said.

With no power, Gary had to use the emergency door release and muscle the door up. At ten feet tall, the door was heavy and that took some effort. Once he had it up, he wheeled the generator onto the forks of the forklift and Alice placed it in the truck with surprising deftness.

"Got the hang of that, I see," he said.

"There's a steep learning curve," Alice said, glancing at the destroyed refrigerator. "Good thing you were outside."

"No kidding."

"Do we have everything?"

Gary went over the list in his head. They had the battery charger, the cord, the generator, and all of the cans of fuel. "That's it."

"Then let's lock this building back up and get out of here," she said. "I'm getting paranoid."

When they locked up the building, Gary dug the keys to the Nissan from his pocket and tossed them to Alice.

"What?" she asked. "I'm not riding with you?"

"Let's take the car," he said. "We'll gas it up at the house and you can use it to get home after we get to Jim's."

Alice nodded. "Okay. I'll follow you."

"We don't stop for anything," he said. "If people wave, if they get in the road, if they point guns, whatever, we keep going. You got it?"

"Understood," Alice said.

12

T he Valley
Jim's House

ALTHOUGH FAR FROM having returned to normal, life at Jim's house was at least peaceful at the moment. Having dealt with the criminal Charlie Rakes and his family, Jim had moved everyone back into the family's home and out of the cave. The cave had served exactly the purpose he'd built it for, providing his family with a secure, fortified location in which to hide out during an emergency. The only downside had been that his mother had contracted a respiratory infection from the damp conditions. Fortunately, with Randi's nursing assistance, she was on the mend and improving daily.

Jim was utterly impressed with how well his family had done in his absence. He couldn't have been more proud of them. His wife had followed his instructions to the letter. Not only that, but his son Pete had developed a mature survival mindset in his father's absence that allowed him to go beyond Jim's instructions. He'd set up an observation post based on a discussion that he and Jim had once had.

Jim had simply mentioned off-hand that a particular rise would be a good place to install a lookout. Pete recalled that and practically built his own sniper hide on top of a hill on their property so he could keep an eye out for anything that might threaten their family. While his daughter Ariel seemed to be the same playful, fun child he'd left, Pete had become a serious young man.

Jim still found that there was lots of work to be done. Despite having left his family with a notebook of instructions, there were a ton of projects he'd always wanted to do but never started. There were also supplies he'd purchased that had never made it to the notebooks. He knew he had a mountain of work ahead of him and that it would take a lot to get his place to where he wanted it. He had no idea how long this disaster would continue, and wanted to have options. He'd prepared for this. He did not want his family to suffer any more than they had to. They had food, water, and heat. If they could maintain security, this could be a situation with long-term sustainability.

In his last radio communication with Gary and Randi, Gary had indicated that he was having some trouble at his place. Jim was not surprised. Although Gary had a basic level of privacy at his home, he was still way too close to town. It was not a defensible or sustainable location. If Gary had previously developed a decent-sized survival group with a plan to hole-up at Gary's house if the shit hit the fan, they might have had half a chance. He would have at least had enough people to maintain perimeter security. Without a group, it was just one large family trying to fight off hundreds of hungry families. It was a family that would eventually be brought down by the coyotes nipping at their heels. It was inevitable.

Although Jim did not have a group, his location was more secure than Gary's. They were physically distant from the local population centers. That was a huge matter when people were reduced to walking as their primary means of transportation. What people were living back there tended to be producers of food rather than just consumers. That significantly affected the stability of a community.

If it hadn't been for the rogues in the trailer park and that Charlie Rakes character, their location would have been ideal. Jim assumed there was no perfect location, at least within the reach of normal people with normal financial means. However, he had always been such a hermit that the idea of a mutual support network had been irritating to him. He didn't want to need people. He didn't want to be bothered by people. At least that was the way he'd always thought before. He understood now that he would benefit from having a network of people close by. People he could depend on.

That was why he'd quickly told Gary that there might be some options nearby in the valley if Gary wanted to move his family. Jim knew it would be a difficult move. He couldn't imagine having to pick up everything and move, but these were difficult times that sometimes required desperate measures. If you had to move to keep your family safe, then you did it. No question. The family was the first priority. A house could be rebuilt. A family could not.

Based on what he'd seen, and what his wife Ellen had told him, Jim knew there were several empty houses near them. A lot of them had been burned down since the lowlife Charlie Rakes apparently had a thing for pyromania and couldn't resist burning down nearly every house he stepped inside. Some of those had dead bodies in them that would have to be dealt with. A house that sat for weeks in the summer with a dead body in it may never be habitable again. He wasn't sure what would be done with those. They'd probably have to be burned down anyway, giving the late Charlie Rakes the last laugh.

There were some families left but Jim didn't know how many yet. He'd seen activity at the Wimmer house up the road and knew that the old man's extended family had probably come home to look after him. They were a tight group and there were a lot of them. They would be a good asset for keeping the community safe. There was also Buddy Baisden up the road, but no one had seen much of him since this whole mess started. Jim didn't know him well but he seemed to be a decent guy. Ellen said that his daughter had died a day or two before this whole mess started.

While Jim wanted to visit those families and see how they were doing, he needed to go into town first. The best house for Gary's family would be that of his old friend Henry. This was also the house that Charlie Rakes had taken as his own. Charlie had killed Henry, his wife, and their son David before Jim put a bullet in his head. He needed to check with David's wife and make sure she knew her husband and his parents were dead. Jim had buried them on their farm the day after he got back. He needed to see if David's wife needed anything from the house or if she had any objection to Gary moving his family in on a temporary basis.

Tomorrow he planned to ride his mountain bike into town to visit David's wife, if he could find her. He knew where she lived, but there was no guarantee that she was still there. She may have gone to live with another family or relative when David didn't come back. It was less than five miles and he was determined to save fuel for emergencies. He had a 500 gallon tank in the barn with off-road diesel in it for the tractors and excavator. It wasn't full but there was enough to refill his truck several times over; however, he didn't want to waste it on a five mile trip into town. He'd ridden his bike a lot farther when he was in a lot worse shape. After walking from Richmond, a bike ride into town would be a breeze.

For today, there were projects that needed done. Jim had spent most of the day with Pete and Pops fine-tuning the perimeter alarms they had attempted to install in Jim's absence. Home improvement stores often sold what they referred to as "driveway alarms." They detected cars coming up the driveway and signaled an alarm in the house, usually a strobe or a chime. There was a home improvement store near Jim's office and they frequently changed what brand of driveway alarm they were selling. Every time they changed brands, they put the old brand on clearance. When they did, Jim stocked up.

He always purchased them with the same use in mind. He would install them as perimeter alarms in an emergency. He'd left instructions in the notebook and Pete and Pops had tried to install them, but Jim wanted to revamp their installation. He installed several on the driveway at different intervals. He also installed them at choke points around the house, such as between outbuildings, between his shop building and the barn, between the dairy and the tractor shed. The only ones he'd leave on during the day were on the driveway. At night, he'd turn them all on, with the sensitivity adjusted so they'd pick up a person but not an animal.

That was another thing he intended to fix as soon as possible. His parents had brought their Schnauzer with them but she was far from being a guard dog, unless you were needing your lap guarded. His family had lost both of their dogs the previous winter due to old age and it had been hard for them. They'd been reluctant to replace them, as if it were disrespectful to the memory of their faithful pets. Now they absolutely had to. Dogs were the best security a homestead could have and they needed dogs in place as soon as possible. He hoped he could find a neighbor or someone in town with dogs that they couldn't feed or care for. He'd offer to take them off their hands.

Jim had also bought a lot of solar motion lights over the years. He hated having to run electricity to all of the places where he felt needed security lights. He'd been overjoyed when the solar versions of these lights came onto the market. As the price came down, he bought more and more of them. The units he preferred required nothing but a solid place to mount them. They were very simple. They had a solar cell that charged an internal battery. There were a few switches to adjust the sensitivity and the length of time that the light stayed on. That was it. On his property, they were not only mounted on buildings but in conveniently-located trees.

The family did not have a huge garden but they did raise a lot of foods they liked to eat. They usually had corn, tomatoes, peppers, potatoes, carrots, and squash. The garden had been neglected in Jim's absence but he couldn't hold that against his family. It wasn't like they didn't have other things to do. Jim's father had taken a recent interest in the garden and was trying to get it back in order during the cooler parts of the day. Jim had broken into his stock of vacuum-sealed emergency seeds. They were all heirloom varieties which would produce viable seeds that could be dried and planted the next year.

He had seeds for cold weather crops that could be grown in the fall that would supplement their food stores. They didn't grow those particular crops on a regular basis but with no grocery stores available, the food would be useful for their own diets or as a trade item. It wasn't about having what you preferred to eat, it was about having anything at *all* to eat.

Jim, Pops, and Pete had taken a water break from their perimeter alarm project and were sitting on the front steps when they heard a loud vehicle exhaust. Times being what they were, everyone on the steps paid attention as a distant vehicle became visible on the road. When it stopped at Jim's gate, the people on the porch went into high alert.

"Pete, hand me my rifle," Jim said.

"Do I need mine?"

Jim shook his head. "Just mine," he said. "You stay here with Pops. I'll take a radio and if I need you, I'll call."

That may not have been the answer Pete wanted, but he knew this was not the time to argue. He went into the house and returned with Jim's M4 and a pouch with two spare mags. Jim took the rifle and the mags and jogged to his truck. He drew back on the charging handle and chambered a round before he entered the vehicle. He started the engine, backed out of his parking place, and sped off down the driveway while Pops and Pete watched anxiously from the porch.

Driving down the driveway, Jim was forced to weave around the barriers that his family had put in place while he was walking home. They didn't block the driveway completely, but they made it impossible to charge up the driveway at any more than about ten miles per hour. As Jim neared the gate, he recognized the oddly-dressed man standing at his gate and slowed down. He picked up his radio.

"It's Lloyd," Jim said into the radio. "It's just Lloyd. He made it. I'm going to let him through the gate."

"Roger that," Pete said. "I like Lloyd. I'm glad he's here."

Jim chuckled. "I'll let him know."

Jim jumped out of the driver's seat. "You're alive!" he said. "Good to see you." He strode to the gate and unlocked it, pulling it toward him and letting it swing open. He hugged his friend.

"You had doubts about my fate?" Lloyd asked.

"Not really. Well, maybe. You did have a cop at gunpoint. Sometimes that ends badly." Jim saw that there was a second person in the car at that point. "Is that Masa?"

Lloyd shook his head. "No, Masa decided to stay with some hippie friends on their farm outside of town. It's practically a commune. He thought this trip might be too risky for his delicate disposition," he said. "This guy is a neighbor of yours. He says his name is Buddy Baisden. I picked him up hitchhiking."

Jim wasn't quite sure what to make of seeing this pair traveling together. Seeing those two worlds meet was odd. "Well, you all come in and I'll lock this gate back. Did you check on your parents? I was planning on heading down there tomorrow."

Lloyd shrugged. "Let's talk about that at the house." Something in the way he said it already told Jim that what he found wasn't good.

Jim pushed the gate open and let Lloyd drive through. He locked it back, then headed back to his own vehicle. He backed into a three-point turn and led Lloyd and his Scamp up to the house. As they approached, Jim could see that the whole family had come to the porch. He figured that Pete must have told them all that Lloyd was here. They all knew the story of how Lloyd had helped get Jim home.

Jim's parents had watched Lloyd grow up too, since he was inseparable from their own son. They were glad to see him alive, particularly since they knew his role in helping support Jim in his journey home. Everyone knew that the last time Jim had seen his best friend, he'd been holding an angry cop at gunpoint. Everyone wanted to know how that ended.

When they arrived at the house, Jim parked his truck and Lloyd rolled in behind him. Everyone spilled from the porch and came down to the yard. Jim's parents hugged Lloyd and thanked him for helping Jim. Ellen hugged him too. Pete, who had always idolized Lloyd for his taste in old cars, shook his hand. The aloof Ariel waved halfheartedly. It took a lot to impress her.

Buddy got out of the car and stood back from the group. While Lloyd was hugging and shaking hands, Jim approached Buddy and extended his hand. He thought it odd that Buddy was dressed in vintage army fatigues but he said nothing about it.

"Buddy, how you doing?" Buddy shook Jim's hand.

"I'm okay, I guess. Haven't seen you in a while. How you been?"

"Just got home," Jim replied. "Had to walk back from Richmond. It was a long, hard trip."

Buddy smiled. "I'll bet. I heard a little about it from your friend, Lloyd."

"How did you two meet up anyway?"

"I was hitchhiking," Buddy said. "I had some business in Mack-town and my truck got stolen."

Jim nodded. "It's a dangerous world right now."

"Jim," Ellen called. "We're getting ready to eat. There's plenty for company. Let's head back into the house before it gets cold."

"Buddy, you heard the woman," Jim said.

Buddy shook his head. "No, really, that's okay. I'm just going to walk back up the road to my house, I reckon. I'll be fine."

"I don't reckon," Jim said. "You can eat with us. The food is fixed already. I've been wanting to get up with all the neighbors anyway and this will save me a trip."

Buddy worked it over in his head, then conceded. Maybe part of getting on with his new life was making some new acquaintances.

"Okay," he said. "I appreciate the hospitality."

"So what happened with you and the cop?" Pete asked Lloyd after everyone was seated with a plate of food. It was the unasked question on everyone's mind.

"You'll probably find it a little disappointing," Lloyd said. "You know I'm a storyteller so I spent my whole drive over trying to think of some way to embellish the story and make it more interesting. I couldn't come up with anything, so I'll tell you the truth. I made him get in the trunk of his car and I locked him in there."

"Don't newer cars have those emergency releases inside them?" Jim asked.

"I've never owned a newer car, so I don't know. That '73 model out there is one of the newest I've ever owned," Lloyd said. "But I had heard that, so to make sure he couldn't get out, I took one of those heavy cargo straps and ratcheted the trunk lid down. I figured it would keep him for a little while, until someone heard him hollering and let him out. The highlight was when he complained that he'd suffocate so I offered to shoot a few air holes in the trunk. He declined my offer."

Pete, always amused with Lloyd, thought this was hilarious and cackled.

"After that, Masa and I had to come up with a plan pretty quick. We loaded all my good instruments and some of my guns into my old truck and he drove them out to a friend's farm where he planned on staying for a while. It's nothing but a bunch of hippies and Masa likes hanging out with them because they go skinny-dipping all the time. I wanted to check on my parents, so I gassed up the old Scamp and burned up the back roads to get over here."

"Any trouble with that plan?" Jim asked. "I remember telling you I didn't think that would work."

"I ran into plenty of trouble," Lloyd said. "Did you see all the bullet holes?"

"Were those from the good guys or the bad guys?" Ellen asked.

"Anyone shooting at me is a bad guy," Lloyd said. "I don't care who they work for or what uniform they're wearing."

"I told you that the run and gun approach might be harder than you expected," Jim said.

"It was a hell of a lot harder than I expected. I made it two exits down the interstate before I had to get off it. I had the Army and a state trooper both chasing me. Fortunately, the Army was too slow and the trooper couldn't drive worth a lick."

Lloyd paused for a bite. "All the back roads were full of wrecks or blocked by wacked out rednecks who'd decided they were highwaymen. Took me three days to get back home that way. I ended up having to take that old dirt road that runs from Atkins to Burke's Garden."

"We came through near there," Jim said. "We got off the Appalachian Trail there."

"That place creeps me out," Lloyd said. "All those Amish running around like Children of the Corn."

"They were nice to us," Jim said. "Gave us food and water."

"Guess you didn't blow by them at seventy-five miles-per-hour and scare the Cocoa Puffs out of them, did you?" Lloyd asked.

"Uh, not on foot, I didn't," Jim replied.

"What about your parents?" Jim's mother asked. "Did you stop by your house yet?"

Lloyd grew quiet and set down his fork. He was looking for the words when Buddy interjected.

"They didn't make it," Buddy said quietly. "We stopped by there just after Lloyd here picked me up on the road."

"I feel awful," Jim said. "If I'd gotten by there sooner, maybe I could have done something."

"No one could have done anything," Lloyd said. "It looked like some kind of accident. It must have happened several days ago." He left it at that.

There was an uncomfortable silence. While they were just two deaths out of many, they were important people to Lloyd. Life could seem cheap in a disaster, but not the lives of the people that meant something to you. They still mattered. It still hurt.

"So what were you wanting to talk to me about?" Buddy asked Jim, changing the subject. "You said you were trying to get around to all of the neighbors?"

"I don't guess anything in particular," Jim said. "I wanted to check in with everyone and see who was alive and if they were doing okay. I was going to talk to folks about using a common radio channel if they have walkie-talkies so we would all have a way to communicate if we need to. I doubt the trouble is over and I want to make sure we all have backup if we need it."

Buddy nodded. "Sounds like a good plan. Not sure if I have any walkie-talkies, though."

"We have plenty," Jim said. "I'll send you home with one."

"Speaking of home, I was wondering about staying with you guys," Lloyd said. "After what happened at my parents' house, I'm not sure I want to stay there. It looks like you all have a full house, though."

"We can make room," Jim said. "I wouldn't turn you away." At the same time, he knew that they *were* overcrowded. Jim wasn't a people person and he preferred having a little extra space if he had the option. He loved his family but he needed space to think sometimes.

"He could stay with me," Buddy offered. "I've got plenty of room and it's...it's just me up there."

"I'm sorry," Jim said, recalling what Ellen had said about Buddy's daughter. "I was gone when your daughter died. Sorry to hear about it."

Buddy waved him off. "It's done now. It's taken care of."

It sounded like an odd comment to Jim. He wasn't sure how the death of a loved one was ever *taken care of,* but as long as the man was at peace with it, it wasn't for Jim to question. Everyone had their own way of dealing with loss.

"You sure you got room for me?" Lloyd asked.

"There's plenty of room," Buddy said. "I'm a little behind on my housekeeping. We'll have to do a little work to get things in order but it won't be a problem."

"I brought my own food, liquor and guns," Lloyd said. "I'll try not to be a burden."

"And he provides comic relief," Jim added.

Buddy laughed. "I could use some of that."

"Then it's settled," Lloyd said.

13

—————

K ent's Ridge Road
Outside of Richlands, VA

GARY LIKED to think he was a student of the power of positive thinking, and managed to convince himself that the drive home would go smoothly as long as he kept telling himself that. He developed an affirmation and started repeating it aloud.

"We're going to be fine," he said. "We won't encounter any trouble." He even forced a little smile. He felt like Obi Wan Kenobi telling the Imperial Troopers that these were not the droids they were looking for.

He started repeating this mantra as soon as he pulled the truck out of his old office complex and onto the four-lane highway. The road was clear ahead of him. He checked his mirror and saw that Alice was right behind him. That was a good start.

"We're going to be fine," he repeated. "We won't encounter any trouble."

The highway remained as empty as it had been on his way in

earlier. He saw no cars and no people moving around. The world was quiet, just the way he wanted it.

"We're going to be fine," he said. "We won't encounter any trouble."

He was able to get the truck up to nearly fifty miles per hour on the smooth road. It didn't drive well, and he was afraid to go any faster than that. The alignment was off and he constantly had to work the steering wheel to keep it moving in the right direction. Scoring the truck was a big accomplishment. His plan was coming together. If they could get this truck loaded in the next day or two and get on the road, they would be at Jim's place in no time.

"We're going to be fine," he said. "We won't encounter any trouble."

About five minutes after leaving the office, he crossed the bridge over the Little River and prepared to turn left onto Kent's Ridge Road. There used to be a traffic light there. Not only was it now useless without power, but someone had been shooting at it for entertainment. It looked like a sad yellow piñata.

Gary looked up the road to make sure there were no vehicles headed in his direction. His attention was so focused on the oncoming lane that he didn't notice that several fence posts had been thrown out into the intersection, completely blocking the road. Gary had to slam on the brakes to stop in time. They whined in protest and the truck shuddered to a stop. While the fence posts weren't huge, he wasn't sure he could drive over them. He didn't want to take a chance of damaging the vehicle. A punctured oil pan or damaged brake line could delay, if not derail, his entire plan.

The squeal of tires behind him indicated that neither had Alice seen the obstruction. There was no impact; she'd somehow managed to stop in time. Gary's window was down and he followed the sound of laughter to the guardrail. There sat five scruffy men, nearly hidden in the shade of overhanging branches. Judging by their amusement, they were the source of the fence posts.

"Darn it," Gary said under his breath. So much for the stupid affirmation.

One of the men stood and hitched his pants. He was tall and thin with a wispy beard. He wore a wife beater tank top and torn jeans. His lip puffed out from tobacco he'd managed to find somewhere. He spat as he strolled toward Gary's truck. He'd clearly come upon this piece of highway sometime in the last couple of hours and decided that it was his.

Gary's rifle was in the seat beside him. Without making any obvious movements, he pulled it over into his lap and got hands where they needed to be. He glanced down, confirming there was a round in the chamber. Red dot on, safety off. Then, as casually as he could, he unholstered his Glock and held it across his lap as well.

"You were about to run over my fucking fence posts," the man said as he walked toward Gary's truck. "You mess up my roadblock and I'm liable to get pissed off."

His buddies laughed. He turned around and grinned at them, enjoying playing the badass. In his peripheral vision, Gary saw a bottle moving between the hands of the men on the guardrail. A man raised it to his lips and drank from it.

Gary was not playing this game. "You need to move that," he said, his voice flat and firm, with no room for misinterpretation.

As much as he didn't want to kill anyone else, he and Alice were outnumbered here and he wasn't sure he could count on her. He'd never seen her perform under this kind of pressure. From everything he knew, she preferred to mediate rather than fight. Sure she'd shot at him back in the stairwell but that was out of fear. It didn't mean she was up for this.

The man frowned at Gary, displeased with the reaction he'd received. "Look at you, giving all the damn orders and telling me what to do. I don't like the way you're talking to me. The toll just went up." He turned back to his friends. "How much is the toll now, boys?"

"What they got?" one of the men replied.

"Toll?" Gary said. "I'm heading home. I live on this road. I'm not paying you any toll."

"Then you're not using *my* fucking road," the man said with finality.

"It's not your road and I'm not turning back."

"I didn't say that leaving was an option," the man replied, staring Gary hard in the eye.

"He's got a woman behind him," came a voice from the guardrail. "You all can have what's in the damn truck. I want the woman."

The rest of the men laughed. The man got up and started walking confidently toward Alice's car, smoothing his hair down and grinning at his friends.

"What's in the truck?" the man outside of Gary's window asked, pulling Gary's attention back.

He was closer now. He'd moved at least two steps closer while Gary had been watching the man on the guardrail. The other man, the one approaching Alice, was past Gary now and heading behind the truck. Gary could not watch him without taking his eyes off the man beside him and he was sure that was a bad idea. He could not let this man get the jump on him.

Behind him, he could hear Romeo talking to Alice through her window. A quick glance at the side mirror showed the man leaning over to rest his arms in Alice's open window. Gary turned his eyes back to the man outside his own window. He'd moved another step forward. If he leaned forward, he could touch the handle of Gary's door.

"Get out of there and open the back of this truck before I pull you out of there," the man ordered. "I want to see what you're hauling."

Gary tried to think. The other men remained on the guardrail, laughing at the romantic gestures of their partner. This was obviously the most fun they'd had all day.

"Get out *now!*" the man repeated to Gary. He was getting agitated. This was going south. Gary sensed that there was no salvaging the situation.

There was the sudden pop of a gunshot from behind the truck. The man beside Gary turned in surprise and reached for his waistband. There was no time to think. Gary quickly raised his Glock over the door frame and shot the man twice through the open window, double-tapping him right through the heart. He fell over backward, a red stain spreading on his dirty white shirt. Instead of sticking his head out the window to check the situation behind him, Gary glanced at his mirror first and saw that Romeo had fallen and was writhing in the road, holding his abdomen. Alice must have shot him through the car door.

"YOU BITCH!" he screamed.

Alice leaned out the window and put another round in him, silencing him.

Gary checked the guardrail and saw that the men there had taken cover behind it. He could see them crouching there, the tops of their heads exposed, their knees showing below it. Gary was not sure if they were a threat yet. He could not see a gun, but it was safest to assume everyone was armed.

"Are you okay?" he yelled to Alice.

"Yes!" Alice said. "I'm okay."

"We have to clear the road," he said. "I'll need your help."

Gary made sure the emergency brake was set and threw open his door. He holstered his Glock and grabbed the Bushmaster AR, slid out of the seat, dropped off the running board, and glanced down at the man he'd shot. He was dead. Eyes wide open, blood pooling beneath him. Moving his eyes back to the guardrail, Gary saw a handgun being leveled in their direction.

"Gun!" he screamed. "Get down!"

Gary spun, dropped to a knee, and aimed at the guardrail. They obviously didn't understand that a guardrail would not stop high-velocity rifle rounds. Instead of squeezing the trigger, Gary pushed slightly forward on the handguard, activating his little surprise, Slide Fire stock, and opening the gates of Hell on his attackers. The specially-equipped Bushmaster sprayed rounds at the guardrail at a rate of around 900 rounds per minute. Although he hadn't practiced with the stock a lot, Gary found it very controllable and kept his fire just where he wanted it. It didn't take long for the guardrail to look like a section of punched tickertape.

In seconds, he'd blown through his 30-round mag and ran dry. Oily smoke rose from the hot barrel. In a practiced gesture, he ejected the empty, jammed a full one home, and released the bolt. He looked through his red dot and saw no movement. He didn't know if he'd hit anyone or just driven them down over the bank. It didn't really matter. Without lowering his rifle, he felt for the empty mag on the ground and shoved it into the cargo pocket of his pants.

"Can you get those fence posts out of the road while I cover us?" Gary asked.

Alice's door opened hesitantly, then she ran by him.

The posts were heavy, pressure-treated lumber. Alice struggled to try and lift one, quickly realizing that it was easier to roll them. It still took her several minutes. Gary kept watch on the guardrail while she cleared their path. He neither heard a sound nor saw any movement. Watching Alice work, the husband and father in him became concerned for how she was dealing with what just happened.

"You know that guy didn't leave you any choice," Gary said. "You did what you had to do. It'll be okay."

She didn't respond. Gary tried again, worried that she might go into shock from the trauma of what she'd done. It was in his nature to be consoling. He had no idea what she'd been through with Boyd, though. No idea how she'd changed.

"It can be hard to deal with taking your first life," he continued. "You just have to remember that the rules are different now and those guys left us no choice. It's not like we could have called the cops."

She rolled the last post clear of their path and started back toward him, brushing her hands off on her pants. She stopped right in front of him and looked him hard in the eye.

"He's *not* the first man I killed, Gary," she said. "The first one I had to stab. Then I had to fight him off while he bled all over me. Finally, I crushed his skull with a cast iron skillet. Because I wanted to be sure he was dead, I still shot him in the fucking face. So I'm okay with what I just did. Trust me."

Gary had no response at first, finally stammering, "I-I'm g-glad you're okay."

Alice was already walking back to the car. "By the way, not that

I'm complaining, but I thought machine guns were illegal," she said over her shoulder. "Where the hell did you get that thing?"

"It's not full auto," he said. "It's called bump fire."

"That doesn't tell me anything."

"I'll explain later," Gary said, his eyes still monitoring their surroundings. "We need to get out of here. You good to drive?"

She raised an eyebrow at him, giving him a look that told him he needed to quit asking about her state of mind.

"Once you're in your vehicle, I'll get in mine," he said. "Hopefully, it will be smooth sailing from here." It occurred to him that the statement sounded a lot like the useless affirmation he'd been repeating before they ran into this mess. So much for the power of positive thinking.

When he heard Alice's car door shut and the Nissan start, Gary climbed into the truck and eased onto the two-lane road. He kept his rifle leveled out the window until he was sure they were not going to take any more fire. As his own adrenaline started to burn off, he grasped the steering wheel tightly in both hands and took deep breaths.

By the time that Gary reached the bottom of his driveway, his emotions were a mixed bag. He was still a little shaky from the encounter on the road but he had things to be grateful for too. He'd made it back to the house with the truck and he'd found Alice alive. He stopped the truck at the base of his driveway and got out, walking back to the Nissan.

"There's a gate near the top of the hill. I have to stop and open it. Once I drive through, I'm going to stop, let you drive through, and then I'll lock it back. Okay?"

Alice nodded. "Got it."

Gary continued looking at her. "You okay?" he asked.

"I thought we'd gone over this?" she replied, giving him that raised eyebrow again.

Gary nodded and returned to his truck. He let the brake off and started up the steep hill. It was the largest vehicle he'd ever driven up the narrow road and it felt awkward, but he had no trouble. When he got to the gate, he killed the engine, put it in park, and applied the parking brake. It was a very steep hill and he was afraid the truck might roll away.

He quickly unlocked and opened the gate, then returned to his truck. He pulled up far enough that Alice could pass through behind him, then got back out to close and re-lock the gate. He jogged back to the truck and drove slowly up the remainder of the hill.

He pulled his radio from its pouch and confirmed the channel. "Honey, I'm home," Gary said. It was a weak attempt at humor but he needed any levity he could get at this point.

Will, not surprisingly, was the first to respond. "Sounds like you found what you were looking for. I hear a truck."

"I did," Gary said. "And more. I've got someone with me."

When Gary got close to the house, his family was crowding into the doorway to see who was with him. Will and Dave came out with rifles. Will had a set of binoculars and was scanning the perimeter of the property for any unwelcome guests. When he didn't find anything alarming, he waved everyone out.

Gary pulled past the house, then threw it in reverse and backed up the driveway, getting as close to the garage as he could. Once he had the truck parked, Alice pulled in and parked in front of him.

Gary hopped out of the truck and Debra came and hugged him tightly. "I don't like you going places alone," she said.

Alice got out of the car and approached the group.

"Who's that, Mommy?" Lana asked her mother.

"That's someone Papaw works with," Debra interjected. She walked over and hugged Alice. "How did this happen? Where did he find you?"

Alice smiled. "I haven't made it home yet. I'm sure Gary told you that we split up on the way home. The government's promises didn't pan out, so we ended up having to head out on our own. I just made it back to the office last night and Gary found me there. He offered to help me get home."

"We?" Debra asked, looking toward the car to see if someone else was in there.

"Rebecca started out with me," Alice said. "She didn't make it. She was murdered."

Debra was clearly shocked, raising her hand to cover her gaping mouth. "I'm so sorry."

"It's okay," Alice said. "I just feel lucky to have made it this far. It's bad out there, and worse if you're by yourself."

"Are you hungry?"

"I am," Alice admitted hesitantly. "But I don't want to take your food. I know it's hard to come by."

"It'll be okay, Alice," Gary said. "We're in good shape for now."

"If you insist," Alice said. "I would also like to clean up a little if I could."

"There's no running water, but I can set you up with a pot of warm water and a towel," Karen offered.

"That sounds heavenly," Alice said. "You don't want to know how long it's been since I had a shower."

Karen led her off, while Debra headed to the kitchen. Everyone except for Will, Dave, and Gary followed her.

"Any trouble?" Will asked when the others were gone.

"Getting the truck was a pain in the butt," Gary said. "It didn't want to start and everything took way longer than expected. We didn't have any trouble at the office, but we ran into a roadblock where you turn off Route 19 onto Kent's Ridge Road."

"Cops?" Dave asked.

"No," Gary said. "Dumbasses."

"How did you get by them?" Will asked. "Did you run the roadblock?"

Gary shook his head. "There was no running it," he said. "That truck doesn't have a lot of clearance and I was afraid I'd get stuck. Besides, what if I got through but Alice didn't? As much as I didn't want to, we had to stop and deal with them."

"How'd that work for you?" Will asked.

"One of them tried to get romantic with Alice and she shot him through the car door," Gary said.

"Ouch!" Dave said.

"Yeah, I think she's been through some... *stuff* while she was on the road," Gary said. "She's clearly a different person than the woman I knew from work. So, of course, after she shoots one of them, the guy I was dealing with went to draw his gun and I had to kill him. Then all hell broke loose."

"You guys get hurt at all?" Will asked.

"No," Gary said. "The rest of them scattered like flies when I turned my surprise on them."

"What kind of surprise?" Dave asked.

"A Slide Fire stock," Gary said.

"What's that?" Dave asked.

"Think full auto without the hassle. It uses recoil to bounce the rifle back into your finger, making it fire at a really high rate," Will said. "I didn't know you had one of those."

"I didn't *want* anyone to know I had it," Gary said. "I like to keep a few tricks up my sleeve."

"Can I see it?"

"Later, Will," Gary said. "I want to get something to eat right now and take a break. Tonight we need to have another family meeting. It's not one I'm excited about."

"Are there any more surprises like that we need to know about?" Dave asked. "Like that special stock?"

"I think when we pack up tomorrow you'll be seeing several things you didn't know I had," Gary said.

THAT NIGHT, after the sun set and the light began to fade, Lana insisted on a fire in the backyard fire pit so she could roast marshmallows. Will and Gary were both apprehensive about spending so much time in the open. It bothered them deeply that the home where they'd experienced so many happy times had become a place where they couldn't even relax and feel comfortable anymore. If anything, that in itself was a sign that they should move if there was a better option available.

After a lot of pleading from the little girl, they conceded to her. After all, the next two nights could be their last ones in their home for who knew how long. Gary needed to talk to everyone about it, and he hoped that having the conversation around the fire pit might improve everyone's mood. They had to know it was coming.

"These are the last of the marshmallows," Debra said as she set them and the sticks on the table. "If you want one, get one now or forever hold your peace."

"How do you even make a marshmallow?" Charlotte asked, examining one. "Is there, like, some backwoods recipe for making them?"

"Not that I've ever heard of," Gary said. "The marshmallow is purely a product of high technology."

He smiled at Charlotte. He was being sincere. Gary had no idea how to make a marshmallow and it wasn't like you could just Google it now.

Seeing no time like the present to ruin everyone's mood, he decided to dig right into the topic of the meeting. "You've all seen the truck," Gary said. "I don't know if you all put two and two together yet, but it means that we're going to have to leave our houses. At least temporarily."

Gary paused for the collective groan and he was not disappointed. There was a groan, a lot of mumbling, and a chorus of rapid-fire questions, all of them from his daughters. He let them vent, then raised his hands like a politician to bring the cacophony to a halt.

"Surely you all know that this isn't something I *want* to do, don't you? This is my home. I raised you girls here. I've put a lot of sweat and labor into this place to make a home for all of us and the thought of a vandal breaking into it makes me sick. You know what makes me sicker?"

No one said anything.

"The thought of one of you getting hurt because I made the wrong decision about staying."

Debra leaned over and took his hand. He smiled at her and continued.

"If we stay here because I can't stand the thought of people breaking into the house, then I'm making the house more important than your lives and that's not how I feel at all. You all are the most important thing in the world to me. I truly believe, with all my heart, that our best chance of survival is to get out of this town until things settle down and order is restored. Until then, I feel that the safest place for us is to get way out in the country with a group of people we can trust. That's the only way we can maintain any level of security."

"Do we have a group like that?" Sara asked. "I mean, I know you've talked about Jim and his family, but that's not really a group. Is that going to be enough to really improve our chances? I don't want to move and then have to move again if things get worse."

"We've got to take one step at a time. Moving to Jim's valley is a start. I never thought having a group was important before," Gary said. "I concentrated on storing food and ammunition, buying weapons and solar gear, but I never thought about the importance of building a survival community. On the long walk home, Jim, Randi, and I had a lot of time to think about that. We started out as three people, but we made it home as a team. While I know it sounds corny, it was clear by the time we made it home that none of us could have made it without each other."

"So that's who we'll be living with?" Charlotte asked. "Jim and Randi?"

"No. Jim has a neighboring farm that's empty now. He's going to talk to the owner's relatives about us staying there and taking care of the place until they decide what to do with it. As far as I know, Randi is staying with her parents. She's a nurse, though, and would be a darn good asset to any survival community. I'm sure that Jim would welcome Alice and her family too if we could find a place for them to stay."

Alice raised an eyebrow at that, but had no comment. She was acutely aware that the spot her family was currently living in was completely unsuitable. She hoped that her husband and son were somehow faring well. She really hoped that they had chosen to go to her mother's farm at the other end of the county. If they weren't home when she got there, that was the first place she'd look. She knew there were resources there, though she was unsure about security. She couldn't imagine her mother having to fight off people wanting to steal a cow.

"Is it really that unsafe here?" Alice asked. "Unsafe enough that you all are ready to leave your homes?" It worried her, because if it was unsafe here then her family was probably facing a similar situation if they remained in her neighborhood. Even with what she'd been through, it was just hard to imagine that suburbia was falling apart. After all, wasn't a home in the suburbs supposed to be the American dream?

"It's been scary at times," Debra said. "We've had some... encounters. It's hard to even relax because you never know who's going to show up next and try to take your stuff. I don't like it but you have to be suspicious of everyone you see. No matter how innocent they look, you can't know their true intentions."

"But what about the *good* people?" Alice asked.

"What about them?" Gary asked.

"Where the hell are they?" Alice asked, raising her voice. She noticed the startled look on the children's faces. "Sorry. I just want to know where all the *good* people are. Why is it that the bad people are driving everyone's decisions? Why are we all at the mercy of bad people? I've about had enough of it."

"I imagine the good people are hiding in their homes, trying to keep their families safe," Gary said. "They might be doing what we're doing, trying to hold on as best they can and avoid contact with people. Either way, you can be surrounded by good people and all it takes is one bad person to screw up everyone's day."

"Then why isn't someone doing something about the bad people? Why are good people allowing bad people to call the shots? Why are we even allowing bad people to live if they're causing so much trouble?" Alice would have never said such a thing a year ago, thinking all people were basically good and salvageable. Now she was not so sure about that.

Gary was surprised to hear Alice speak this way. "I guess that's an age old question, Alice," Gary said. "In the modern world, we try to understand bad people, make excuses for them, and try to fix them if we can. That can't work the way things are now. We need to get rid of them. You get one chance, and if you screw up a second time, we're done with you. I don't know. Maybe that's the only way we save the good people."

Alice shook her head, plainly frustrated at the state of things.

"It reminds me of this story," Gary continued. "There was this bus full of ugly people and it crashed, killing everyone on board."

"Seriously, Gary?" Debra said. "A bus full of ugly people?"

"Bear with me," he said. "A bus full of ugly people, a wreck, and they all die. So they get to Heaven and Saint Peter meets them at the gate. He says he'll give each of them one wish before they enter the gates of Heaven. The first is a woman and she tells Saint Peter that she wants to be beautiful. He grants her wish and she immediately becomes the most beautiful woman you've ever seen."

"Everyone else in the group sees how beautiful she becomes so all of the rest of them wish for the same thing, until Saint Peter gets to the last person in line. He's laughing as he approaches Saint Peter and Saint Peter asks him what he wants for his wish. 'Make them all ugly again,' he says."

Gary looked around the fire while everyone pondered the story.

"That's an awful story," Sara said, her eyebrows crinkling. "I don't like it."

"The point is that it only takes one jerk to screw things up for everyone," Gary said. "It's a parable. A lesson. There's a moral."

Debra rolled her eyes and placed a fresh marshmallow on Lana's stick. "So what do we need to do to make this move happen?"

"It's a major undertaking," Gary conceded. "With the extra fuel I got, I think each family can take a car and try to pack as much of your personal stuff in there as you can. Take durable clothes and remember that the weather will get colder eventually. Take raincoats, gloves, hats, socks – everything you can. We can't count on our stuff being here when we come back. Try to take warm clothes for everyone. It's about durability, not looks. You won't need high heels, black dresses, or a selection of purses. Leave all that. I'm going to try to pack all of the food and preparations into the big truck. If there's any room left, we can fill it with more of your stuff, but don't count on doing that. Between guns, tools, food, and gear, there may not be much room left."

Alice stood abruptly. "I'm sorry to interrupt, but I've been having some stomach issues. Where are you all... doing your...business?"

No one responded quickly enough.

"I really need to know," Alice said. "*Soon.*"

"Behind that storage building is a shower tent with a camping toilet in it," Gary said, pointing. "Do you have a light?"

"I'll be okay," she said, trotting off quickly.

"That's what can happen when you don't filter your water," Gary said. "She had to drink out of a ditch because she couldn't find fresh water. Remember that. Explosive, projectile diarrhea – for weeks."

AFTER EVERYONE HEADED off to bed that night, Gary retreated to his old office/junk room/gun room in a spare bedroom. He turned his Baofeng HAM radio on, put on some headphones, and began scanning channels. He picked up some folks in Asheville, North Carolina, having a conversation about the state of things there. That city was an odd mixture. There was a large hippie population and they were using the disaster as an excuse to get back to Mother Earth. Those hippies that had farms out of town were opening their doors to anyone willing to contribute free labor. They were accepting everyone who requested to join them. It was the communal living movement of the late 1960s and early 1970s all over again.

There was also a thriving survival and prepping culture in the area. Those folks were quietly retreating to their homesteads and bug out locations, shutting their gates to the world. They were certain that the hippies would not find surviving the winter to be very easy. While the hippies didn't mind gardening, a lot of them were vegetarians and it was hard for a vegetarian or vegan to take in enough calories in a subsistence lifestyle. You couldn't just pop into town for a falafel, feta, and arugula pita.

The survival groups were most concerned that the hippies and others with even fewer resources would come knocking on their doors any day. The hippies, on the other hand, worried that the survivalists were armed and would come take their food. Had the hippies understood the survivalists better, they would have realized that the survivalists offered nothing but encouragement to those willing to try and make their own way. It was those who tried to live off of the back of others that they had no love for. The survivalists were of the "teach a man to fish" school rather than the "let me give this man a fish" school.

While listening to this conversation was entertaining to Gary, it reached the point of containing more ranting than news and he switched to another frequency. Eventually, he came to rest on another conversation, catching a retired machinist from Richmond speaking with a retired Navy Radioman in the Virginia Beach area. By all accounts, neither city was doing well at all. Richmond, with a scarcity of resources within the boundaries of the city, had descended into chaos. It was controlled by street gangs on the north side and by bikers on the south side. Each sought to keep the other group on the opposing side of the James River. The machinist lived on the west end of the city and wanted to flee, but had no means to do so.

The criminal elements of Richmond spread northward from the city and tried to subsist by robbing and stealing along the I-95 corridor. Farther to the north, Washington, D.C. was under martial law. Under military rule, many of the residents of the city had been pushed out, toward Richmond to the south. The folks living in the rural areas between Washington and Richmond were pinched in the middle, dealing with constant raids, thefts, and murders.

The entire Hampton Roads-Newport News-Virginia Beach area

was also under martial law. With such an enormous military population and a concentration of vital military assets, the government felt they had no choice but to lock down those cities. Criminal elements quickly felt the heat and migrated westward, also toward Richmond. While Richmond had once come back from being in the top five murder capitals in the nation, per capita, it was uncertain if they could come back from this. Anarchy ruled the former capital of the Confederacy.

The state government had fled from the capital city of Richmond and was now operating from somewhere in the Alexandria area. There had been talk of locating westward to Roanoke, but it was felt that their efforts might be more sustainable if they moved to a region of the country that was under martial law. The side effect of that was that Virginia quickly fell in bed with efforts to contain the disaster by restricting freedoms. These actions only resulted in hobbling those who were law-abiding enough to try and adhere to the state government's new emergency regulations. Those unwilling to comply were branded outlaws. As the capability to disseminate the new emergency regulations by TV, radio, and the internet was limited due to widespread power outages, most of the outlaws did not yet know that they were outlaws.

Gary listened for as long as he could before he had to retreat to his bed for the night. He felt so depleted from his journey home that he was not sure how long it would take for him to feel energetic and well-rested again. As tired as he was, the news he heard on the radio was disturbing to the point that he almost wished he hadn't even listened. He missed the ignorant bubble he'd been in a few days ago, but he couldn't un-hear what had been heard any more than he could un-see the many horrific sights he had seen on the way home.

14

The Valley
Jim's House

AT LLOYD'S INSISTENCE, Jim let Lloyd pick him up in the Scamp and drive him to town the next morning. Jim tried to explain the whole fuel conservation concept to Lloyd but it was against his nature and he only had one response.

"Fuck it," he said.

So Jim let him drive. It was his gas after all, and who was Jim to tell him that he couldn't burn it up? Jim had not been on this particular road into town since he'd made it home. The section where he lived was not crowded with abandoned vehicles. It didn't receive much traffic except for the folks who lived back there. If one of their cars broke down, they'd move it out of the road for safekeeping since they were close to home. That did not appear to have been the case on this road.

The connecting road between Jim's valley and town ran along a small river. The road was on a high bank beside the river but it was close enough that care was required. There was no guard rail. In the winter, when the roads were icy, everyone drove slowly as to not end up in the river. It was clear that some cars had run out of fuel along this road, but they were no longer blocking the road. Someone, probably for purely entertainment purposes, had pushed all of those abandoned vehicles off into the river. While Jim likely would have done the same thing when he was younger, he was certain the fluids in the vehicles would not help the fishing situation, and that was unfortunate. The river had also once been the source from which the town drew its drinking water, although Jim assumed the plant was no longer running.

The first sign that they were nearing town came in the form of a shopping center housing the local superstore. There were also several other stores offering cash advances, manicures, discount clothes, and an excellent Mexican restaurant. They were on an access street that provided a shortcut between a back road and the shopping center.

"God, I miss that place," Jim said. "We went there every Friday for food and cold bottles of Dos Equis."

Lloyd cast a glance in that direction. "There's something going on up there now, it looks like." He slowed the vehicle.

Jim leaned over and took a look. The shopping center was shaped like the letter L and someone had taken vehicles and created a line that bridged across the parking lot, joining each end of the L. They had turned it into a triangle comprised of all the stores and a wedge-shaped section of the parking lot. It looked like someone had turned the store into a fortified encampment.

An opening had been left in the wall and a cop stood blocking it, an M4 held across his chest. He wore riot gear, like he was ready to engage an angry mob. Jim saw a flash of light that drew his eye to the roof of the store. He saw something breaking up the shape of the roofline. From the glimmer of light, he assumed it was a sniper's scope and that they were in his cross-hairs. They shouldn't linger too long.

There was a generator running somewhere behind the barricade. The smell of grilling meat carried across the parking lot. Jim could swear that he even heard the sound of children playing, but that sound did not go along with the serious bearing of the guard and the menacing wall of cars.

"They're going to need more than one guard if the smell of that meat carries too far," Lloyd said. "People will come in droves."

Jim said, "I think the cops have created some kind of base up there. It looks like a command center for the emergency operations folks."

A drone about two-feet square rose from behind the barricade and flew off to the east.

"What the hell was that?" Lloyd asked. "An alien?"

"A drone," Jim replied. "I definitely think it's the cops. They must be using that drone to do recon."

"For what?"

"To look for resources and see what people are up to. It's a hell of a lot safer for them to send that drone out than to let officers go knocking on people's doors under the current circumstances. Someone would probably get shot. It also uses less fuel."

"That Big Brother stuff makes me paranoid. I was happier thinking it was an alien," Lloyd said. "Let's get out of here."

"This is a situation where paranoia is exactly the correct response," Jim said. "Let's move it."

BANNER STREET FELT DISTINCTLY different than most of the places Jim had seen over the course of this disaster. With so many houses in close proximity to each other he had no idea what to expect, but there were actually people moving and walking around in the neighborhood. It almost looked like any other summer afternoon. There were kids out playing and folks talking on porch steps. All of this changed when the loud Plymouth pulled onto the street.

Folks flew into high alert. Mothers called to their children and steered them into houses, locking the doors. The people talking on porches pulled their neighbors into their living rooms and closed the doors behind them. Blinds were shut. Jim even saw a group of teenagers who hid in the bushes because they couldn't get to a house fast enough. These people appeared to be fairly relaxed but were exercising an entirely appropriate degree of caution. They'd either had some bad experiences or were just smarter than most. Perhaps that would keep them alive a little longer than some of the other people he'd met.

Thirty seconds ago, Jim's plan had been to ask the nearest person in the street which house David's family lived in. Now, with the streets abandoned, he had no idea what to do and he said as much to Lloyd.

Lloyd responded by slamming on the brakes, stopping the car in the middle of the street. "I got this."

They were at a more populated section of the street and the houses were packed tightly around them. From where they sat, they were in sight of almost all of the houses in the neighborhood. Lloyd climbed out of the car and onto the hood of the vehicle.

"What the hell are you doing?" Jim hissed, staring through the windshield at his friend.

Lloyd ignored him and stood on the hood. Jim was reminded that it was a good thing this was a vintage car with a hood strong enough to support someone standing on it. On a newer car, Lloyd would have sunk to his knees. Lloyd raised his hands to his mouth.

"Attention people of Banner Street!" he yelled, doing an imitation of a town crier. "We're looking for David Sullivan's house. We have important information for his wife. We are not here to cause any trouble."

Lloyd hopped down from the hood and walked around to Jim's window. "What did you think about that?" he remarked. "Simple and direct."

"I thought I was watching a Broadway play," Jim said. "Such delivery. We'll see if it works."

People must have been discussing Lloyd's statement behind closed doors and trying to determine if he was telling the truth. Apparently, they found him credible. In less than a minute after he climbed off the hood, the door of an immaculate brick cottage opened and a man in khakis and a polo shirt stepped out. His clothes looked expensive but were wrinkled and a little dirty. He had his hands in his pockets and it was obvious there was a gun in there. Jim didn't blame him for that. It was a logical response.

"What are you looking for?" the man asked.

"David Sullivan's house," Jim replied, getting out of the car. "I need to speak to his wife."

"Why?" the man asked. With his bluntness, it was clear he had no intention of sharing any information unless he was satisfied with the answers to his question.

"Because I need to tell her that her husband is dead," Jim said. If bluntness was the shared language of the new era, then he had no trouble using it. In fact, it came pretty natural to him.

The man appeared startled by this, then looked down at the ground. "Sweet girl," he said. "She knew something had happened. Said she could feel it."

"It happened a few days ago," Jim said. "I just wanted to talk to her about it."

The man raised his eyes to Jim. "She's with her parents," he said. "They managed to come up with some fuel somehow and they came and got her and her kids. I think she knew by that point that David wasn't coming back home."

"Where do her parents live?" Jim asked. "I really need to talk to her."

"Abingdon," the man replied. "Not sure where though."

"Shit," Lloyd said. "That's another thirty miles each way. I'm not sure I have the gas for that."

Jim shook his head at Lloyd. "That's okay," he said. "We're not going to Abingdon. We definitely can't spare gas just for that."

Jim stepped up on the sidewalk and moved closer to the man. This obviously made the guy a little nervous because the hand in his pocket closed around the grip of the gun he was carrying. Jim had no bad intentions, he just didn't want the whole street to hear his business. He spoke quieter. "Can I leave her a note? If I write her one, can you give it to her if she comes back?"

The man looked relieved that this was all Jim wanted. "Sure," he said. "I got no guarantee that I'll see her again, but if I do I'll give it to her. Let me get you something to write on." The man withdrew back into the house and returned with a ledger pad and a pen.

While Jim wrote, the man said, "I hate that about David," he said. "He was a good boy. They had small children."

Jim nodded. "I agree. They were good people. His dad, Henry, was a good friend of mine."

"*Was*? Is he dead too? How...?" the man asked, not quite sure how to put the question.

"One of the criminals they released from the jail came through and killed several folks out in the valley, including David's parents," Jim explained. "I buried them all together behind the house, in case she asks. There's a marker on their graves."

The man considered this for a moment. "What about that man? The one who killed them? Is he still out there wandering around somewhere?"

Jim looked up from his note and caught the man's eye. "No. He's dead too. I killed him myself and left his body for the coyotes. He didn't deserve a proper burial."

The man's eyes widened and he swallowed hard, but Jim sensed that he was pleased by the answer. He certainly didn't want someone like Charlie Rakes showing up at his house. Things were obviously insulated there in his neighborhood. They'd not seen that kind of ugliness. They'd not had to kill to save themselves or their friends.

Yet.

Jim finished writing and folded the note. He handed it to the man, along with the writing supplies. "So how are you folks getting by?" he asked.

The man sighed. "Things are tight," he said. "We're working together, though. We've kind of pooled our resources. We're cooking as a group to make the best use of what we have. Everyone on this street gets along pretty well and we're trying to take care of each other."

"That's good," Jim said. "I'm glad you folks are getting by okay. Not many folks are out there trying to take care of each other. It's kind of an ugly world right now."

The man nodded. "We're worried about winter," the man admitted. "Some of us have fireplaces and we're starting to lay in wood, but I dread it. Except for the older folks, most of us have never had to heat with wood before. I worry about someone catching their house on fire. Some of these old chimneys might not be safe. In this tight neighborhood, it could jump from house to house."

Jim knew that it would be very difficult for folks not used to heating their homes with wood. It was important what type of wood you used. The wood also needed to be dried and cured. It was important that your chimney was in good condition and that you kept the fire a reasonable size for the type of fireplace you were using. Wood stoves and fireplace inserts were more efficient and offered more control over the fire. If it got too hot, you could shut off a damper on the stove or in the chimney and choke the fire back. With a fireplace, there were fewer options.

Jim started to tell the man that he was getting ahead of himself if he was already concerned about winter. Chances were that most of them in that neighborhood wouldn't make it that far if the electricity stayed off. If government projections were accurate, there would probably be fewer of them to feed by winter also, but he held back. He wanted to keep this positive and he had other things to do.

"I would encourage you to add a gate or something at both ends of your street," Jim said. "It would be good if you could limit traffic into the neighborhood to just those folks that belong here. I'm not sure if you'll get any response if you call the cops right now."

The man snorted sarcastically. "The cops," he spat.

"What about them?"

"They've set up a base of operations over at the shopping center," the man said. "They've basically taken over the store." He was obviously bitter over that.

"Really? They've taken over?" Jim asked. "I saw the barricade but I wasn't sure what was going on."

"Oh yeah, they definitely took over," the man said, his resentment building. "There was still food left. The fresh stuff was gone but there was still canned food and other things that could be used. Things that people might need like blankets and first aid supplies."

"What exactly did they do?" Jim asked. "They just moved in one day?"

"Basically," the man said. "They were out there to provide security while folks were shopping but things were getting hairy. There were no lights and they were having to ring up purchases by hand. People were having to pay with cash. There were fights breaking out and not enough cops to keep a lid on it. The cops on duty finally just decided that the doors had to be shut and locked. They said it was for everyone's safety, then word got out that they all started moving their families in. Now there's like this whole fortified compound of cops in the middle of town and they're not sharing the food. Folks have asked to get in and been turned away."

"I doubt that there's all that much food left," Jim said. "I don't know that it would be very helpful if they did decide to open things back up."

"It's the point of it," the man said. "They're cops. They shouldn't be doing things like that."

"I'm not taking up for them, but they're also people," Jim said. "People with families. They're looking out for their families the same way that you're looking out for yours. I have a hard time blaming them for that."

"So you're okay with it?" the man asked, his voice rising.

Jim shook his head. "No, I'm not okay with it. I'm just not surprised by it, is all. Like I said, they're people and people do desperate things. It's in our nature. As long as they stay on their side of the fence, we'll get along. If they try to cross my fence and steal from me, then I'll have a problem with them too."

"That's kind of a selfish attitude," the man said. "What do you recommend for the rest of us?"

"It's a selfish world now," Jim said with a shrug. "My best suggestion would be for you all to find a similar place if you could. Find a building that you can secure and that is strong enough to fend off attack. Something you can heat this winter."

"Well, a lot of us here in town have talked about storming the shopping center," the man said. "We could just take it back for the people of the town."

"That would be a wasted effort and a lot of you would die," Jim said. "And even if you succeeded, I think you'd have little to show for it. Like I said, there's probably not that much left in there at all. You'd probably be better off moving everyone into one of the abandoned factories."

The man considered this. "What if the cops do run out of food?" the man said. "If that happens, won't they come looking to take our food?"

"There are already people out here looking to take your food," Jim warned. "If it's not the cops, it will be someone else. I assure you of that. Remember, that's why David and his parents are dead. They had something that someone else wanted. That's why I am suggesting you get a gate up, or even better, find a more secure location."

The man nodded. "That's a good idea. I'll talk to the others."

"I need to be going. Good luck to you," Jim said, turning back to the vehicle.

He slid into the passenger seat and turned to Lloyd. "Those people don't have a fucking clue what's going on out there in the world."

"What are you going to do now?" Lloyd asked. "What are we going to do about finding a place for Gary?"

Jim sighed. "I'm going to talk to any other neighbors I can find and see how they feel about it."

Lloyd started the car and accelerated out of the neighborhood. "What do you think they'll say about some stranger moving in like that?"

"I think if I tell them that I have a heavily armed friend with his own supplies who wants to move in and help us defend the valley, they'll see that as an asset for the community. Especially if things get uglier."

"Uglier?" Lloyd asked. "You don't think they're ugly enough already?"

"Oh, I think they're plenty ugly already," Jim said. "But I still think there are levels of ugliness that we've not seen yet."

"You are just a ray of fucking sunshine," Lloyd mumbled under his breath. "You should be writing greeting cards or something."

FOR THE NEXT TWO HOURS, Jim and Lloyd visited the families that remained in Jim's end of the valley. This was done with extreme caution. Lloyd pulled up to each gate and honked the horn, while Jim stood in front of the vehicle with his arms raised and a white pillow-case in his hands as a flag of surrender. Jim was well aware that many of his neighbors were older and couldn't see well. He hoped that he didn't get shot by an overzealous, nearsighted farmer.

They visited the Wimmers first. The Wimmer clan was one of the largest families in the valley. The old man had been a local politician back in the day. He had a half-dozen kids who all had more kids and now those kids had kids too. Altogether, it seemed like there were hundreds of them, but it was probably closer to fifty scattered out over several houses, all located within sight of each other on the same farm. After he waved his white flag, someone very cautiously came and met Jim at the gate. He and Lloyd were invited back up to the house. You couldn't visit the Wimmers without being invited to the parlor.

They exchanged stories with the family and Jim was not surprised to learn of their run-in with Charlie Rakes. The Wimmer family was pleased to learn that Mr. Rakes had been sent to meet his maker, although some expressed a little disappointment that they had no role in his demise.

The Wimmers were an old-time farming family who had lived in the valley for nearly a century and a half. As was their heritage, they all had tremendous gardens and canned much of what they ate. Their big farmhouse, which the patriarch and matriarch called home, still had a wood-fired cook stove in the kitchen. They had an electric stove as well, but had installed it without removing the old one. They just couldn't put all their trust in some newfangled electrical gadget.

When the electricity had failed a few weeks ago, Mrs. Wimmer had simply said, "See, I told you that would happen," and set about building a fire in the old cook stove.

Mr. Wimmer had rolled his eyes skyward, recalling that Mrs. Wimmer had indeed told him that such a thing might happen, but also knowing that it had roughly been around the time of World War II. However, as a kind and loving husband, he did not point out to her that her prediction on the relative undependability of electric ranges had taken around seventy years to manifest itself.

They also had hundreds of head of cattle, that being how most generations of the family had made their living. They had also supplemented their income with tobacco when it had been profitable to do so. The Wimmers assumed that if they could keep their cattle safe, they might be able to trade butchered beef for some of the other things they were unable to produce on their property. They specifically mentioned diesel fuel and ammunition. Jim had plenty of the latter. He let them know that he might be interested in trading for some beef down the road and told them he'd get back with them shortly.

When Jim broached the topic of his friend Gary moving into Henry's empty house, the Wimmers offered no opposition. Jim explained that he thought it was in the best interest of all living in the valley for them to collectively agree to gate off their road. Although it was a through road and connected to other roads on each end of the valley, there were other ways around. It was not a road that people *had* to travel unless they lived back in there. Jim's plan was to install two locked gates, one just past the house that Gary would be moving into and the other at the intersection near the Akart Farm. Jim hoped it didn't prove necessary to man those gates with armed guards. He hoped that a gate with an appropriately menacing sign may serve to deter any potential bad actors from coming into their neighborhood.

"I think some new folks in the neighborhood would be real nice," Mrs. Wimmer said. "All of these empty houses just depress me." She was around 87 years old and was practically the matriarch of the valley. At least half of the folks that lived back there were related to her or her husband. She'd spent her entire life there, even attending school in the valley and going to church there. Of those two structures, only the church still stood.

"My friend Gary is a good man," Jim assured her. "He'll take good care of his end of things and he'll help keep us all safer."

"That's just fine," Mrs. Wimmer said. "And don't leave without taking some mulberry jelly with you. We've been making it all week."

"We tried to talk Mom out of making her jelly this year, what with all that was going on in the world," her son said. "She told us that was nonsense. She'd learned to make it on a wood cook stove when she was a little girl and she wasn't going to let a power outage stop her."

"Modern conveniences have made all my children weak in the body and mind," Mrs. Wimmer complained. "We never should have taken the electricity when they brought it through the valley. It was Mr. Wimmer's idea. He was determined to have a radio in the house."

Her son rolled his eyes and Jim smiled at them both. "Thanks for the jelly, Mrs. Wimmer. You just let us know if you need anything."

She waved her hand at Jim. "We'll be fine," she assured him. "Wimmers are like poison ivy. Can't hardly kill us if you try."

Next, they went to the Bird Farm, home to a family of gun-loving goat farmers. They weren't particularly violent people, but from the largest Bird to the smallest Bird they loved to shoot and gunshots rang from their farm daily. As a shooting enthusiast himself, Jim had spent many afternoons up there shooting on the Birds' homemade range.

While Jim knew that the Birds wouldn't shoot at him if they recognized him, they might just see two strangers in a loud old car and decide that they should drive them off with a little gunfire. Rather than take a chance on that, Jim left them a short note explaining the situation with Henry's farm. He asked them to stop by one day and see him just so they could exchange information. He also left them a radio channel that they could use to reach him if they wanted to. He honked the horn, then left the note in their mailbox.

Next was the Weatherman Farm, although it was more commonly known as the Weatherman Zoo. While many farmers in the region had cattle, goats, or sheep, along with a few dogs and cats, that was not sufficient for the Weathermans. They had a little over thirty acres and raised llamas, emus, ostriches, alpacas, and over a dozen varieties of goats, from the dwarf to the fainting. They had miniature horses and miniature cows and pot-bellied pigs. They had a donkey named Petunia that wore a hat with holes cut out for her ears. They also had chickens, ducks, quail, and geese. There were hutches with rabbits. Peacocks roamed the property making strange noises that scared anyone who heard them, except for Mrs. Weatherman, who was the ringmaster of the whole circus.

The farm was overseen by Mrs. Weatherman, her three daughters, and a very tired Thomas Weatherman. Thomas was Jim's age but had been able to retire early, something Jim had only been able to dream of. Thomas had told Jim his story one day when Jim helped him wrangle a loose emu from the road. According to Thomas, after watching his wife buy tons of Beanie Babies off eBay, he said these simple words: "I think that's going to be big. A feller ought to get in on that."

When Thomas sold his few cattle off that year, he used the money to buy eBay stock at around thirty-five dollars a share. After the dot-com explosion and numerous stock splits, Thomas had nearly a million dollars. It was the only financial investment he'd ever made in his life, other than in his home and farm. When the market got squirrely in the late nineties, Thomas cashed out with no regrets and never bought another stock. He renovated his house, built some new buildings on the farm, and took early retirement from his job as a federal mine inspector. Now, he pretty much spent his days helping his wife with her menagerie.

The Weathermans were pleased to see Jim. Like Jim, they were not born into the valley but had moved there at some point. With no relatives there and no close friends among their neighbors, they were fairly isolated socially. This was not a big deal in regular times, when they had the phone, the internet, and the ability to drive and see friends. Without that ability, though, a rural family's social circle could instantly drop from being global to simply extending from one end of the house to the other. When the power went off, the Weathermans initially treated the event like the occasional snow and ice events experienced in this part of the country. Then when gunshots and the lingering smell of home fires began reaching their homestead, life changed for the family.

"Don't take this the wrong way," Jim said, "but I was almost surprised to find you guys still alive."

Thomas Weatherman had met the two at the gate and they stood there talking. Thomas wore a Glock on his hip and Jim was pleased to know that there were more people in the valley comfortable with carrying, and hopefully using, firearms.

"We weren't too worried at first," Thomas said. "Then when I caught sight of that strange family going in and out of Henry's place, I got worried."

Thomas and his family lived a little distance off the road, but were Henry's closest neighbors. There were fewer families at this end of the valley.

"What did you do?" Jim asked. "How did you stay off that scumbag's radar?"

"We circled the wagons, as the saying goes," Thomas said. "We moved all the livestock to the barn or to back pastures that can't be seen from the road. No one goes out by themselves and everyone carries a gun."

"That's sound practice," Jim said. "I still wonder why Charlie Rakes didn't wander up here, since you guys were the closest to Henry."

Thomas laughed. "Years ago, when I was single, I lived in a rough hollow over in Buchanan County. There was a lot of stealing went on over there. I asked my neighbor what I should do to keep from having someone break in on me. He told me to shoot up a box of shells the day I moved in and to keep shooting often so that everyone knew I was armed. "

"Did that work?" Lloyd asked.

"Damn right it did," Thomas said. "We took that same approach here."

"How?"

"The fires didn't worry me at first," Thomas said. "I thought it was campfires since the power was out. Then, about the same time as the shooting started happening, I started seeing faces I didn't recognize wandering up and down the road. We moved the animals, like I said, and then I told my family that I expected each of them to fire off a few rounds every day as a deterrent. They came and got me when they did it so I could make sure they were practicing good gun safety. Now I know they're safe with their guns so they don't have to come get me anymore, but I still want each of them firing rounds every day. I think guns send a message that people like that Rakes character understand loud and clear."

"Must have worked," Jim said.

"What happened to him?" Thomas asked. "Did he move off or did someone move him?"

"He killed Henry, his wife, and their son. He also kidnapped my mother and was going to kill her and my son. When I got home, I killed the bastard and fed him to the coyotes. Then I ran his whole family off."

"I appreciate that," Thomas said. "He deserved no better."

Jim went on to explain why he was there and Thomas was excited to hear that he was getting a new neighbor, especially when he found out that they had a large family. His children were tired of just seeing each other.

"My daughter is getting the same way," Jim said. "Maybe she can get together with your girls one day and visit."

"That would be great," Thomas said. "When should I expect the new neighbors?"

"Any day now," Jim said. "Then we're going to gate off this valley and hope we can keep things calm until the lights come back on and the fuel starts flowing."

Thomas had one last question. "How many of us are left back here, Jim?"

"About a fourth of what lived here before," Jim replied. "Maybe less."

"How many people is that?" Thomas asked.

"About seventy."

Thomas grinned. "How many of those are Wimmers?"

"At least fifty," Jim said.

Jim shared the information about the radio frequency that they could all use to keep in touch on the family band radios, asked if Thomas had any of the radios, and was pleased to learn that he did.

"If you can, leave one on," Jim said. "It's the closest thing we've got to 9-1-1 for now."

15

G ary's House
    Richlands, VA

THE MOOD WAS somber as Gary and his family packed up. No one
thought they were going to be able to fit everything into the cars.
Although Gary tried to assure his family that they could come back
for more stuff if fuel was available, even he didn't believe it. They all
felt like the moment they left their house there would be wolves
descending from the hills and the house would either be looted or
someone would move in. Gary had seen it on his way home. Abandoned property became community property. Regardless of the care
or attention paid to a home over the years by its rightful owners, in
their absence it simply became a roof under which a traveler could
take shelter. Any room could serve as a bathroom. Any corner a
receptacle for garbage. It was heartbreaking.

Gary had every intention of coming back as soon as he could to
check on things but he wondered if it was even worth it. He couldn't
defend his home from fifteen or twenty miles away. Even if he could

come up here and try to drive folks out, was it worth the expenditure of fuel or ammunition and the risk of death? As soon as he drove out squatters, more would probably come. It would be an endless cycle.

Debra had all the children gathered in the living room. Gary had hooked up a portable DVD player to an inverter and a deep-cycle marine battery. The kids were all watching a movie while the adults tried their best to reduce their lives to a carload. They were using every trick in the book to maximize what they could carry. They gassed up their largest vehicles with the most interior space. They chose vehicles with luggage racks on top so they could tie as many things as possible to the top. Debra even managed to find two of those zippered car-top carriers made of weatherproof canvas that they could stuff full and strap to the tops of vehicles. Gary also had one of those luggage carriers that slipped into a receiver hitch. He used it for carrying coolers to the beach so they didn't leak all over the car. He put it on Charlotte and Dave's minivan and it gave them just a little more space.

Based on criteria known only to him, Gary assigned vehicles. He would drive the box truck with Alice riding with him. Gary wanted someone in there with him to literally ride shotgun. Will was going to drive Debra's SUV and pull Gary's utility trailer behind it. Gary had made that decision because Will had hauled trailers before and wasn't likely to forget it was back there or run a tire off into the ditch. Charlotte was going to drive her minivan while Dave drove his Subaru Forester. Gary had intended to limit each family to a single vehicle but the Subaru had the gas for the trip so why not use it? Sara also had a minivan and was going to be driving it. That left Debra driving Gary's beat-up old Nissan Pathfinder with Karen riding with her.

Once they had figured out who was driving what, Gary was surprised to see just how many vehicles they had in their fleet. He drained the gas from the vehicles they weren't taking and from all the gas-operated equipment he owned. He really didn't want to dig into the gas cans he'd taken from the maintenance shop at work yet because he hoped he could use those for the generator when they got settled. Not for entertainment, air conditioning, and microwave popcorn, but for operating tools and lights when needed. Through careful fueling, he managed to get a quarter tank in each vehicle and he thought that would be enough to get them to their destination as long as nothing crazy happened. If something crazy did happen, he had the backup cans.

The loading itself was dizzying. Everyone felt the sense of urgency and worked quickly. Gary convinced them that the use of soft-sided luggage and stuffable bags would allow them to get more in the cars. Outside his house, Dave stood by their vehicles, a rifle close at hand, and Charlotte threw stuff out the windows and door to him. He mercilessly crammed the items into every nook and cranny of both vehicles. As the cars filled up, he began strapping luggage, duffel bags, and garbage bags onto the roof rack and into the zippered carrier. When he was done, he laced two hundred-foot ropes over the entire mass of luggage and strapped it all down. It looked like the Beverly Hillbillies moving cross-country. Gary hoped that it all stayed on when they started driving because he had no intention of stopping on the side of the road.

The rest used similar methods, filling large spaces with bigger items and cramming clothes into every miniscule space within the vehicle. This was not packing for vacation, so little care was given how things would look when unpacked. The primary concern was just trying to find room for the things they really wanted to take.

Alice helped Gary since Debra was watching the kids. They loaded the emergency preparations first – dozens of totes, ammo cans, five-gallon buckets, and cardboard boxes. They loaded solar gear, tools, vacuum-sealed containers of heirloom seeds, cases of canning jars, and a pressure cooker. They loaded tents, sleeping bags, lanterns, camping stoves, cans of Coleman fuel, and a half-dozen unopened tarps. There were the diapers that Gary had mentioned, as well as unopened cases of toilet paper, tampons, paper plates, and garbage bags. They loaded hanks of rope, spools of wire, a tote of fishing and trapping supplies, and several types of water filtration. The food alone took up about thirty percent of the truck.

Gary intentionally delayed loading the weapons and ammunition. He'd been working on a plan for distributing them throughout vehicles. He wanted the majority of them to be in the truck with him, but he also wanted a few in each vehicle just in case they lost the truck. He couldn't stand the thought of it, but he knew it could happen and that it would be a good idea to make contingencies just in case. Every vehicle would have a shotgun, a pistol, and a rifle, with ammunition appropriate to them.

The day was exhausting for everyone, a combination of nerves and frustration. When everything but the guns was loaded, Gary began to work on those. Alice helped him. Her husband hunted but he did not buy the kind of guns that Gary bought. As a matter of fact, she had not even seen guns like the ones Gary had except in the movies. Her husband's guns had wooden stocks and blued barrels and these guns were nothing like that. They were black, with different attachments and handles on them. She did not have any idea how you fired something that looked like that.

As a non-hunter, Gary preferred tactical and defensive weapons. Over the years, he'd bought a lot of them. So many, in fact, that he had hidden dozens of them from his wife. She wasn't bothered by his interest in weapons and she would never have said anything to him about them, it was his own guilt about spending money on what seemed like an extravagance. His most recent acquisition, motivated by an interest in precision shooting, had been a Savage 110 in .338 Lapua Magnum. He'd fitted the rifle with an MDT Tac21 chassis. With the correct loads, he could hit at two thousand yards, using a Schmidt Bender scope he'd purchased for nearly twice the price of the rifle. Altogether, with the rifle, stock, scope, Atlas bipod, and a supply of ammunition, he had nearly ten thousand dollars in the rifle. His most expensive weapon.

Gary sat on an upturned bucket beside the massive pile of weapons, drinking a warm Gatorade, when his family filed into the garage. They stood around him, their clothes sweat-soaked and a general cloud of weariness hovering over them.

"You all done?" he asked, trying to force his voice to sound cheerful.

"Not yet," Debra said. "I have to add a few things to the truck."

Gary groaned. "It's nearly full," he said, losing some of his cheer. "Most of what space is left is for the guns. I'm not sure you can get anything else in there."

When Debra didn't respond, he turned to look at her and saw that she was carrying stacks of photo albums. Every memory, from dating to their wedding to the birth of their children and grandchildren, was in those books. She looked heartbroken and fragile. He knew what had happened. She had gone to move the albums and had opened them. Once you did that, your entire life flashed before your eyes.

"We've got room," he said.

He stood and helped Debra find a safe spot for the albums, then leaned back against the truck, taking another swallow of his drink. His damp shirt was sticking to the aluminum truck body behind him.

Alice popped up from her own bucket. "Darn, I've got to go again," she said, walking off briskly. "How long before this medicine fixes this?"

"Soon," Gary called after her.

"What did you give her?" Debra asked.

"Metronidazole," Gary said. "At least the fish version. And some Imodium."

"It doesn't seem to be helping," Karen said. "Are you sure those fish antibiotics are safe?"

"They're safe, it just takes time," Gary said. "You have to stick with the medicines and stay hydrated. Take it seriously, though. Diarrhea kills over a million people worldwide every year. A hundred years ago it was one of the leading causes of death and could easily become so again."

"Can we talk about something else?" Charlotte moaned.

Karen took a seat on Alice's bucket. "What time is it?" she asked. "I'm hungry."

Debra looked at her watch. "A little after six p.m."

"How about we eat dinner and call it an early night," Gary said. "Let everyone get some rest."

"Now that I'm packed, I'd just about prefer to go tonight," Sara said.

Charlotte nodded in agreement. "Me too. Let's get this over with. It's just too sad looking at our empty houses."

"I would agree under other circumstances," Gary said. "However, I don't want to have an emergency and get stuck on the road in the dark. I also don't want to have to find our way to a strange house in the dark. The whole thing is just too risky. It's best to try and get an early start tomorrow. I'm going to try and radio Jim tonight and let him know we're coming and then I want to get out of here first thing in the morning. Like sunup. We get up, gather our stuff, and go."

"Do you have to go back up on the ridge or are you going to try and radio him from here?" Debra asked. "I worry about you being away from us again."

"I'm going to try the radio from here and see what happens," Gary said. "And I guess I should get on it. Sitting here isn't getting anything done."

As Gary stood, Alice quickly walked around the corner of the house. "I think I saw something," she said.

Everyone immediately went on high alert.

"What?" Gary asked. "What did you see?"

"A flash back at the edge of the woods," she said. "I thought it was nothing at first, but it moved. Then it went away."

"Someone is watching us," Will said. "She probably saw binoculars or a spotting scope."

"Dave, you stay here with everyone. You girls keep a weapon close. Close this door and lock yourselves in the house," Gary said.

"Where are you all going?" Debra asked, apprehension in her voice.

"We need to see what's out there," Gary said, grabbing his Bushmaster and a sling pouch with spare mags. He kissed Debra. "It will be okay."

"Be careful," Alice warned.

Gary nodded, then he and Will stepped out of the garage.

IT TOOK them at least five minutes to approach the location where Alice said she'd seen the flash. Despite having worked in the open all day, they now felt exposed and did their best to stick to the cover available. Whoever had been there was long gone, although there was a clear indication that someone *had* been there. The weeds were flattened in a manner suggesting someone had been there for a long time, someone watching what they had been doing.

Had this someone seen them loading the trucks? The idea that someone may know their plans filled Gary with anxiety.

When they returned to the house and relayed their findings to the family, the anxious feeling spread through the group. As if the exhaustion and stress of the day weren't enough, they now had this to deal with.

"This is simply confirmation of why we're leaving," Gary reminded everyone. "We knew that we were not safe here. I've been telling you that. We knew we could not secure this location."

Gary could tell that they were hearing his words but not experiencing the reassurance that he hoped his words would give them. They all needed to stay on high alert until they got off this hill and out of this town. He hoped that the confrontation with that Molloy kid the other day would scare them off, but it obviously hadn't. This was becoming personal.

Gary would have to reconsider his thoughts on when it was justifiable to kill someone. Jim had told him that you didn't leave people alive to deal with later, when you might be less prepared for the encounter. Better to finish them off when you had the upper hand. While Gary was not completely convinced, he was beginning to see the logic of it. If he killed someone in cold blood like that, then it became his *individual* problem. All he had to deal with was his conscience and any guilt he felt. If he failed to kill someone and they came back and hurt his family, then it became a group problem and *everyone* had to deal with it. It was a lot to wrestle with.

"I want you all to go ahead and fix dinner. If you need to cook, do it in the garage with a window open. Go ahead and set up a portable toilet in one of the bathrooms. Consider yourselves on lockdown. I don't want anyone going out again this evening," Gary said.

"Will," Gary said, turning toward his son-in-law. "I want you and Dave to pull every vehicle over here as close to the house as you can get them. One of you drives, the other maintains watch. After they're all here, I want you to keep watch until dinner is ready," Gary said. "We'll eat in shifts. We do not leave these vehicles unguarded. That's our life and our future out there."

"Got it," Will said.

"I'm going to go make that radio call right now, before it gets any later," Gary said. "Then I'll be back and we'll come up with a watch plan for tonight."

Gary grabbed the radio from his pack. It was part of the set that he, Jim, and Randi had taken from the ranger station on Mount Rogers. He went upstairs and stood in the window of the bedroom, hoping that it would give him just enough reach. The hilltop upon which his home sat was in a bowl-shaped dip atop the hill. Not only did the signal have to climb out of that bowl, it had to clear a significant ridge, then go fifteen miles beyond that to reach Jim.

Gary brought the radio up to his mouth, embarrassed that he, Jim, and Randi had not taken the time to establish some type of radio protocol. They'd been on the move then, and even establishing *this* means of contact was kind of an afterthought. They'd not had time to establish any codes or anything like that. As a result, they were on an open channel discussing their activities. He could only hope that that they were vague enough that nothing too critical hit the wrong ears.

"Jim?" he said. "You read me, Jim?"

Gary waited a moment and stared out the window, his eyes scanning the tree line.

"Jim?" he repeated. "You read me, Jim? It's Gary."

There was a crackle of static and then a voice. "Gary, it's Jim. Good to hear your voice, old buddy."

Gary breathed a sigh of relief. "Transmitting from home this time, Jim. I wasn't sure if I'd get you or not."

"Not as loud as the last time," Jim said. "But I can hear you. What's going on up there?"

"We're bugging out." Gary paused a moment, almost unable to believe that the words were coming from his mouth. "We just can't hold this position. Too risky, and it keeps getting worse. I want to do what we talked about last time."

"Everything on my end is done," Jim said. "I won't go into the details on here, but when you get to my house it's taken care of."

While this had been the plan, he'd had no assurance until this moment that everything he and Jim had talked about had been arranged. There was a home on a farm and they could work with Jim and his family to make the best of things. Gary felt a wave of emotion despite the distance they still had to go. It was the most hope he'd felt in days.

"When should we expect you?"

"I hope to be out of here first thing in the morning if there's no trouble. Give us an hour to get there. So, hopefully by 8 or 9 a.m."

"We'll be watching for you, Gary," Jim said. "I'll have the radio with me just in case you get in a jam. If that happens, don't hesitate to call."

"Anything going on over that way that we need to be worried about?" Gary asked. "Any hazards or highwaymen?"

"I don't know about any hazards on your end of the road," Jim said. "There's a roadblock at the Route 19 and Route 80 intersection near here. A couple of days ago, it was manned by a trooper named Travis I went to high school with. I don't know if he's still there or not. The road between my house and there was clear when I took Randi home but I can't make any promises. Use caution and we'll be ready to come help you on the road if you need us."

"Appreciate it, Jim," Gary said. "You've got no idea how much."

"You don't have to thank me," Jim replied. After a pause, he added, "Okay, maybe you do have to thank me. I prefer it to be in the form of a pie or cobbler. We can work out the details once you get settled."

Gary grinned. "If you wanted one of my wife's pies all you had to do was ask, Jim."

"Okay, I'm saying," Jim replied. "I'll see you when you get here. Out."

Gary signed off, turning off the radio to conserve batteries. He would turn it back on in the morning and keep it on until they got to Jim's house. He stared out the window, watching the tree line, trying to catch a glimpse of anything out of place. At this time of day, with the angular light casting long shadows, it would be hard to detect someone hiding, especially someone in dark clothing hidden back in those shadows. Especially someone with a mask.

"Dinner's ready, Dad!" Karen called from the bottom of the steps. It would be their last meal in this house for who knew how long. He turned away from the window.

Had he lingered there a moment longer, he might have caught the movement, the shadow that was *not* a shadow moving among the trees.

A WATCH SCHEDULE was agreed on by the end of dinner. With their long, hectic day, time had crept up on them and the sun was already setting. Everyone was exhausted and lethargic. Muscles were sore and stiffening. Even the children were fussing and over-tired. Gary bagged the dinner trash and set it outside the back door. He normally wouldn't do that because of animals getting into it and scattering it around the yard. Now, he thought it might not matter. Let the animals tear into it, let the wind blow it – he didn't care. All the cooking gear and uneaten food was packed into the vehicles. In the morning, they would not eat until they arrived at their destination. The goal was to leave as quickly as possible, before most of the world awoke.

Will and Sara would take the first watch of the night and be on duty until midnight. Dave and Charlotte would take the second watch, from midnight until 3 a.m. Gary and Alice would come on at 3 a.m. and stay on until the whole group bugged-out. Debra and Karen would not pull a shift as they were staying in a room with the children, both of them armed and the door to the room locked.

Gary had spent some time discussing his watch plan with Will. Their goal was to make sure no one approached the house and no one stole the vehicles. Their lives were in those vehicles now. Gary had even thought about sleeping in the truck but knew that he needed to get at least a few hours of comfortable sleep if he could. The next best thing was to place the female guard of the team on top of the box truck armed with a shotgun. It would give them a high point where they could see all the vehicles and a good part of the yard. Hopefully it would also keep them out of the way if things went bad. The male guard's duty would be to walk a circuit around the house and vehicles.

Gary still had the body armor he'd worn on his trip home. While it was not as substantial as a military-grade plate carrier, it was all he had. It was better than nothing, and he planned that each man on foot patrol should wear it. When he explained this to Dave and Will, they disagreed.

"I won't wear a protective vest when my wife doesn't have one," Will said.

"Same here," Dave agreed.

"The women will be in a concealed position," Gary said. "They'll be out of sight on top of the truck. The man on patrol will be the one exposed to fire."

"Not going to happen," Will said.

"Nope," Dave said. "Not going to happen."

After Gary relented and agreed that the women could wear the vest, they developed four patrol patterns that the man on foot duty was to utilize. Each was assigned a letter from A to D. Each shift, the first pattern walked would be the A, then the B, then the C, then the D. Then B-B-C-D, followed by C-B-C-D and D-B-C-D. Although Gary and Will had no training in tactics, they knew it was important that the patrol be randomized and less predictable while still systematic enough to cover all the ground that needed covering.

Gary hated to expose anyone to the danger of patrolling the property but he didn't know what else to do. His biggest fear was of someone setting the house on fire with all of them inside it. Someone *had* to keep watch and he didn't know of any safe way to do it. He didn't want the foot patrol to go too near the bushes or anywhere else that someone might be lying in wait. At the same time, having them keep away from cover forced them to walk in the open. Even though he'd instructed them not to use a flashlight unless they absolutely had to, there was still enough of a moon that anyone out walking in the open would be silhouetted by it. Despite his unease, he didn't know what else to do. He was nearly dead on his feet with exhaustion. They only had to make it another ten hours or so and they could hopefully start over in a more secure location.

THE FIRST SHIFT went off without a hitch. At midnight, Sara climbed off the roof of the truck box using the blue fiberglass ladder that Gary had left for that purpose. She went inside and woke her sister and Dave. In less than five minutes, they were out in the cool night air, switching places. Sara handed the body armor over to her sister and helped her get it adjusted properly.

They also received the pair of walkie-talkies Will and Sara had used to maintain contact with each other during their shift. Charlotte climbed the ladder, the shotgun slung over her shoulder, and Dave started his foot patrol. Every few minutes, they made radio contact, and touching base with each other made them feel a little better about being out there alone in the dark.

At around 2 a.m., Charlotte heard the door to the house unlock and swing open. She immediately went on alert.

"Charlotte?"

Charlotte twisted around on the roof. She was laying on a blanket to keep her from getting chilled by the dew-soaked metal of the roof. "Yes, who is it?"

"It's Alice."

Charlotte relaxed a little. "What are you doing up?" she asked. "Your shift doesn't start for another hour." She crawled to the edge of the tall truck box and looked down at Alice, who was standing there in sweatpants and an oversized t-shirt, but no shoes. She was clutching both arms around her stomach.

"These stupid cramps woke me," Alice said. "I need to go to the bathroom again."

"There's a camping toilet in the bathroom in the house," Charlotte said. "It's there so you don't have to go outside at night. Dad doesn't want anyone out here."

"I know," Alice said. "But it's *really* bad and I'd like a little more privacy, if you know what I mean."

Charlotte took one look at Alice's face and knew instantly what she meant. It was that explosive diarrhea her dad had been talking about.

"You want to use the outside toilet?" Charlotte asked.

Alice nodded. "Yes. Preferably without getting shot."

"Let me get on my radio and tell Dave," Charlotte said. "If you get shot, diarrhea will be the least of your problems."

"Please hurry," Alice pleaded.

Charlotte crawled across the roof of the truck and picked up her radio. "Dave?"

His response was immediate. "Everything okay?" he asked, concern evident in his voice.

"Yeah, it's fine," she said. "Alice is out here and she wants to use the outside toilet."

"Why? There's one inside."

"You know, the explosive diarrhea thing."

"Oh yeah," he replied. "I got it. Does she need me to come get her and make sure she gets there safe?"

"No," Alice said from the ground since she could hear Dave. "I just don't want to get shot."

"She's good," Charlotte said into the radio.

Knowing she was safe now from being shot, Alice tore across the yard barefoot, running for the toilet tent that still sat behind the storage building. It was little more than a folding camp toilet over a hole in the ground but it didn't have to be emptied, which made it preferable to using the toilet inside. Out of necessity, it would be one of the last items packed. Alice gratefully unzipped the door and stepped inside. She started zipping the door back closed behind her, but the urgency of her situation was upon her and she did not have the time to finish it. She abandoned the task and focused her attention on getting her pants unbuttoned.

Through the unzipped door, she saw a shadow, a flash of movement.

"I'm in here," she said, taking a seat. "It's occupied. I'll be out in a minute."

There was no response.

"Dave?" she asked. "Is that you? I'll be out in a few minutes. Give me some privacy."

Still no response.

In the tight quarters of the tent, the door was within arm's reach. She leaned forward, grabbed the tent flap, and pushed it to the side. Immediately outside the tent stood a figure in black, its face a grinning skull.

She screamed as loud as she'd ever screamed. While the scream was a fear reaction, it was also an attempt to summon help.

On the far side of the house, Dave had altered his foot patrol to allow Alice her privacy. At the sound of her scream cutting through the quiet night, he felt a surge of terror. He could not tell who the scream came from but his first concern was for his wife. Not being of the mindset that usually ran toward danger, Dave did not react as a person with tactical training might. He did not ready his weapon and go into fight mode. Instead he reacted out of instinct and fear for Charlotte's safety. Wanting to get to her as quickly as he could, he slung the rifle over his shoulder and took off running blindly toward the garage end of the house.

As he ran past the broad flowering cherry tree Gary had planted upon moving into the house, a black figure peeled away from the trunk and stepped to intersect his path. By the time Dave discerned the figure and began to understand that he should react, it was too late to do so. The moonlight gleamed from the edge of the machete as it arced toward Dave's neck. He did not even have time to raise a hand in his defense before the machete buried itself in his neck, jarring against his spine, and nearly severing his head. He sprawled into a lifeless heap, dark blood spurting into the wet grass.

In the driveway, Charlotte spun toward Alice's scream, knowing exactly who it was but having no idea what she should do about it. She could not see her. She stepped as close to the edge of the roof as she could, trying to see around the corner of the house.

"Alice?" she called. "ALICE?"

There was a gunshot from that direction, which only scared Charlotte worse. She had no idea what was going on. Who was shooting? Why was Alice screaming?

She fumbled to pick up her radio. "Dave!" she yelled into it. "Dave!"

There was no answer. She dropped the radio back onto the blanket and clicked off the safety on the shotgun. "DAVE!" she yelled as loudly as she could.

She heard the creak of the ladder behind her and spun around, hoping it was him. A hulking black-clad figure the size of a pro football player rose over the edge and sprang onto the roof, his leering skull mask pulled up to murky, emotionless eyes. The figure immediately rushed across the short distance toward her. She fired the already raised shotgun, striking the figure center mass with buckshot. He was still coming, and she didn't know if it was from inertia or some overpowering desire to kill her. She tried to fire again, forgetting in her panic that the action of the weapon had to be pumped to chamber a new round. When she pulled the trigger again, nothing happened.

It was too late anyway. The figure was too close now and moving too fast. She dropped the shotgun and raised both hands. He ran full into her and she had the fleeting thought of feeling like a quarterback being sacked before she realized that she was now flying through the air, the man falling with her. They fell ten feet before they landed, Charlotte on her back, crushed beneath the weight of her massive attacker.

The shot Charlotte heard had come from Alice killing the man outside the toilet tent. She had learned that hesitation got you killed and she showed none at all. After her experience with Boyd, she would never again be caught without a weapon. Considering the state he found her in, the masked man who'd surprised Alice had probably expected that the hand she raised toward him would contain a roll of toilet paper and not a .38 revolver. He bled to death in the yard with a look of confusion on his face, apparently wondering how such a thing had happened to a nice guy like him.

The shots and screaming had now awakened the whole house. There was yelling and confusion inside. The children were crying, while the adults stumbled around blindly, trying to find their weapons in the dark. Will and Gary, with their weapons a little closer at hand than the others, were the first into the garage. They paused there together, looking out the window.

"I can't see anything," Will said.

Gary cracked open the door, surprised to find it unlocked. "Charlotte!" he yelled.

There was no response. He threw the door open and yelled again. "CHARLOTTE!"

A voice came from his left. "Gary, it's Alice."

"Alice? What—"

Before he could get the words out, he heard the cab door to the box truck slam shut.

"Charlotte?" There was the sound of footsteps running down the driveway, running hard and running *away*. Gary pushed by Will and ran between the vehicles. He threw up his rifle and touched a button on the quad rail of his rifle. His weapon-mounted light came to life. It was a short-range light, designed for use inside his home, but it was still bright enough to catch the back of a black-clad figured sprinting toward the end of his driveway. When the light hit the man, he turned and looked over his shoulder, the reflective ink of the skull mask glowing brightly and making the moment even more surreal.

Gary was beyond the edge now. He'd had enough of being under siege and feeling like a prisoner in his own home. He flipped the safety lever off, pushed forward on the handguard, and the Slide Fire stock engaged the trigger. Flames shot from the muzzle brake as a six-shot burst erupted from the rifle. The figure at the end of the driveway screamed and staggered. Gary gritted his teeth and pushed forward on the handguard again. The weapon fired, rounds spraying from the barrel, and Gary fought to keep it on target. He had no idea how many rounds hit the man but he fired until the mag ran dry and his target was still.

When he turned to tell Will to check the man for signs of life and to finish him off if he wasn't dead, Will wasn't there.

"Will?" Gary hissed.

"Over here," came a voice from the other side of the truck. "Get over here now."

Gary ejected his spent magazine and slammed a new one home and chambered a round. He killed his light, not wanting to present a target, then realized his night vision was blown now by use of the white light. He couldn't see anything and would have to use the light. He flipped it back on and moved carefully around the front of the truck. On the other side, he found Will and Alice crouching over a blood-soaked Charlotte.

"No!" Gary cried, stepping to his daughter and dropping to his knees.

"She's alive," Alice said. "I don't know what happened to her yet. That guy was on top of her."

Only then did Gary notice the bulky black form of the man that Charlotte had shot and killed on the truck roof. "Is he dead?" Gary asked, his anger flaring again.

Will nodded.

"Did you check him?" Gary asked. "Are you sure he's dead?"

"I didn't check for a pulse," Will said. "His eyes are open, and blood is pouring from his mouth."

Satisfied, Gary put a hand under Charlotte's head and started to pick her up.

"No," Alice said, putting a hand on Gary's arm.

Gary swung his rage in Alice's direction, his eyes filled with fury. He was in...*a place* ...and Alice could see it.

"I think she fell off the truck," Alice explained quickly. "That hedge broke her fall, but we need to make sure she's not hurt badly before we move her. I don't want to make her injuries any worse."

"Will," Gary snapped, "check the one at the end of the driveway. If he's still alive, slit his fucking throat."

Alice stared at Gary, unused to seeing him so filled with hate.

"We can't find Dave," Will said. "I need to look for him."

"Check on the man I shot first. We don't leave anyone alive," Gary ordered. "Then we'll look for Dave."

"You put thirty rounds in his back," Will said. "He's not coming back from that."

Gary ignored Will and looked at Alice. "Get my wife. Now!"

Alice rose without a word and ran into the house, yelling for Debra. She'd never seen Gary this way before, and it scared her.

Gary checked Charlotte's breathing and found no difficulties. He raised her shirt and was relieved that she had on the body armor. He saw no wounds that matched the volume of blood covering her clothes; it was definitely someone else's. He gently rolled her onto her side, then raised her shirt and body armor to examine her back. There were scratches and gouges outside of the area covered by the vest but it had offered her some protection against the bushes. While the bush had taken its toll in scratches, it may also have saved her life by breaking her fall.

Will came jogging up, startling Gary enough that he reacted by reaching for his sidearm.

"It's me," Will said quickly. "That one's dead. I'm looking for Dave now."

"Be careful," Gary said. "When Debra gets out here, I'll come help you."

Seconds later, Debra came running out of the house, a headlamp on her head. "I need a first aid kit, but I can't find one!"

"They're all packed," Alice said.

"Where, Gary?" Debra said in a panic. "Where do I look?"

"Calm down and look under the seat of my Pathfinder!" Gary yelled. "I keep one in there."

"What do you need me to do?" Alice asked Gary.

"Help my wife," he said, getting to his feet with his rifle. "We can't find Dave. I'm going to help Will find him."

Debra returned with the first aid kit from Gary's vehicle, which reminded Gary that he had a powerful battery-operated spotlight in there as well. He ran and got it, then took off after Will, playing the light around the tree line and in every shadowy recess on their property. He saw no one and nothing out of the ordinary, until he turned the corner.

The first thing he saw was Will on his hands and knees in the grass. When the light hit him, Will threw up an arm in Gary's direction and expelled a sobbing, screaming torrent of vomit into the grass. His body heaved and he screamed again, his body knotting and spewing the contents of his stomach yet again. It was like watching the dying contortions of a poisoned animal. Will pounded the earth with his fist, screaming again. *"NOOOOOOO!!!!!!"* It echoed away into the night.

Only then, at the perimeter of the circle cast by his light, did Gary notice the still body in the grass. A cry escaped him as he ran across the yard, sliding to his knees in the dewy grass and dropping his light and weapon. It was instantly apparent that nothing could be done to repair the body in front of him. No amount of preparation, planning, or foresight had prepared him for this. What the hell had he been thinking? They were not soldiers, and in sending his son-in-law out to play one, he'd gotten him killed. The realization hit him like a shovel to the head. He found himself screaming too, pounding the grass in the same futility that Will was experiencing.

"There could be more of them," Will croaked. "We've got to check. I hope we find some too."

Gary realized he was right and staggered to his feet, picking up his weapon and his spotlight. "You check around back," Gary said. "I'm going to get a blanket and cover Dave's body."

Gary started to walk off as Will headed in the other direction. Gary paused, then turned. "Will!"

Will stopped. "What?"

Gary jogged back over to him. "I'm going with you," he said. "We stay in sight of each other. I'm not letting anyone else die tonight."

"That's not your fault, Gary," Will said. "He wasn't doing anything the rest of us weren't doing. You can't blame yourself."

"Even if I'm not responsible, I'm still the one who has to tell my daughter that her husband is dead," Gary said. "I'll have to look at my grandbabies every day knowing it was my plan that got their father killed."

Will started to remind him that it was his plan too, but he knew that there was no arguing with Gary at this point. Gary had to work it out for himself. He had to come to terms with it and find a way to live with it.

Around back, they found the dead man by the toilet tent and figured out what must have happened there. When they returned to the driveway, they found Alice standing there armed and waiting on them.

"They went inside," Alice said before anyone could ask. "Your wife used smelling salts and woke her up. We helped her inside and they're checking her for injuries. I'm guessing that Dave is dead?"

Gary nodded, choking down a sob at the memory of the gruesome sight.

"I heard you all yelling," Alice said. "I figured that's what happened."

"Did *they* hear?" Will asked. "Has Charlotte figured it out?"

Alice shrugged. "We were going inside when I heard you screaming. I assume Debra heard you, but she didn't say anything. Charlotte was still pretty out of it so I don't think she noticed."

Alice pointed to the box truck. "It looks like the one that ran off down the driveway was trying to hotwire that truck. There's some wires pulled loose under the dash. He must have jumped in there after Charlotte fell, before you guys came out. It's a good thing he didn't get it started."

"It wouldn't have started," Gary said. "I disconnected the battery cable earlier in case someone tried something like this."

"That was a good move," Alice said. "You think of everything."

"Not everything," Gary said sadly. "Not nearly enough."

16

The Valley
Jim's House

THE MOOD at Jim's house was almost festive considering the state of the world. Jim let everyone know that his friend Gary and his family would be moving into Henry's place tomorrow. Everyone was excited at the prospect of new people to talk to. Without work for Jim and Ellen, and with no school for the kids, everyone was getting a little tired of seeing the same people all day long. They did love each other, but seeing new faces was nice too and would keep them from getting so crabby and put out with each other.

Jim had also recruited his children to help the new residents unload and get settled. He planned to help, and even Lloyd and Buddy had volunteered. The pair had been invited to stick around for dinner that night. Even though they'd tried to leave, Ellen and Jim had assured them that they had plenty of food. After some arm-twisting, they relented and agreed to stay.

Over dinner, Jim talked about his own excitement at Gary's family joining them.

"In hindsight, I can now clearly see two areas where I should have spent more time preparing," Jim said. "I'm hoping Gary's arrival will take care of one of them."

"I think you did well," Nana said. "While you might not have known the particulars, you knew what was coming long before it happened. That's more than most people can say."

"I didn't know exactly what would happen, now," Jim replied. "I only knew that there was a lot that could happen and I wanted to be prepared for as much of it as I could. I don't see how anyone could watch the news and not see how fragile our society is."

"What did you miss?" Pete asked. "What are the two things?"

"There are probably more than two. The things that became obvious pretty quickly are, first, I would feel more comfortable with the self-defense end of things if I'd taken more training," Jim said. "I wish I'd learned a martial art, spent more time on firearms training, and some basic tactics like how to work as a team in a gunfight. That kind of thing. Some days I feel like it was simply dumb luck we ever made it home from Richmond."

"You expect to do much of that?" Pops asked. "I was hoping the worst was over. I don't want to think we're going to have to be fighting people off all the time."

"I don't know how much more unrest there will be. I've already had to do more fighting than I ever thought I would, and I'm just winging it. I would feel a lot more comfortable if I really knew what I was doing. There's only so much you can learn from watching videos on the internet."

"And we don't even have that now," Pete said ruefully.

Jim laughed. "Ain't that the truth? There are tactical schools all over this country, run by veterans and law enforcement trainers, and they teach all that kind of stuff. I should have spent some money on that, but I never did."

"What's the other thing?" Buddy asked.

"The other is that I wish I'd had a plan for other folks to join us,"

Jim said. "If I had it to do over again, I would have built a couple of cabins around the property with the plan of offering them to prepared friends if a situation like this occurred."

"That makes sense," Buddy said. "They could store some of their survival gear and stuff there in the cabins and have it already waiting on them when they got here."

Jim nodded. "Exactly. It would be mutually beneficial. I provide a place for them to bug-out to and in return they would help out with the gardening, food storage, and security."

"Which is kind of what you're doing now, right?" Pete asked. "With your friend Gary coming?"

"Yeah," Jim said. "The bad part is that it's a lot harder to do now than it would have been a couple of months ago. It would be better if we had cabins here on this property already instead of having to put Gary and his family in a house up the road. We'll have a bigger area to try to secure, although we will be close enough to come to each other's aid if we need to."

"It's better than nothing," Pops said. "I guess you'll know next time the world collapses and try to do a little better."

Nana rolled her eyes at his attempt at humor.

"What are your plans for when they get here?" Ellen asked. "If this is supposed to help us secure the area and improve our situation, will that work? Like you said, they'll be in a house up the road."

"While you all are talking about this, I'm getting dessert out of the oven," Nana said, getting to her feet and heading for the kitchen.

"The first goal is improving the security for this whole end of the valley," Jim said. "I've already talked to the other families that live back here and we're going to gate off the road to keep out people who don't belong. We're going to do it unmanned first, with a warning sign on it, something menacing. If that doesn't work, we'll put a man on it. If we put a gate by the Wimmers' house and one by the house where Gary is going to be staying, that should cut out some of the traffic."

"There aren't many people driving," Pete pointed out.

"That's right," Jim said. "Most people are still using the road, though, since it's the easiest walking. The gate sends more of a message than anything else. While we can't really secure thousands of acres with a few families, we need to do the best we can. Next, I think we still have time to get out some end-of-season crops. We can still plant kale, spinach, carrots, broccoli, cauliflower, and some greens, and have time for them to come up. If we take care to protect the plants, and cover them when the frost is coming, they'll last for a good while. We might even be able to throw a greenhouse together with a little work. All that will give us some fresh food to supplement the stored stuff. That's something that every family in the valley should try to do."

"We also need to be looking at some livestock," Jim continued. "There are probably folks with more stock than they can take care of since they can't go out and buy supplemental feed now. We could probably trade for some chickens, rabbits, goats, and a couple of cows. That would greatly help out our situation if this goes long-term."

"Is it too late to build cabins like you were talking about?" Buddy asked.

"No," Jim said. "I'm still thinking about doing that. They'll just have to be more primitive with the limited availability of commercial building materials."

"You could probably just build some real log cabins," Lloyd suggested.

"We might have to do that," Jim acknowledged.

"Who wants cobbler?" Nana called from the kitchen.

There was a chorus of positive responses. Nana and Ariel had picked fresh berries earlier so that they could make the cobbler. Despite the fact they didn't have ice cream, it was still delicious.

"Thanks for picking these berries," Buddy told Ariel as she brought him a bowl of cobbler. "I think this is probably my favorite dessert in the whole world."

Ariel smiled. While she was the smallest of the group and had the least to say when they were all gathered, Buddy always went out of his way to find some reason to call attention to her. He complimented her on her hair or her efforts at helping Nana in the kitchen. It was not lost on the group that he'd once had a little girl of his own and had recently lost her. It broke their hearts to hear how he spoke to her, and knew he must have been a good father. They did not know the lengths he'd gone to make things right. If Jim had known, as a father, he would completely understand.

After dinner, they retreated to the backyard. The sun had set over the hillside and left the sky in layers of orange and red for which no one had any words. They stared, small in the large world, and forgot for a short time the state of things.

There were chairs, benches, stools, and rocks for seating. A fire was built in the circle of stones that served as a fire pit. Lloyd brought out his guitar, playing and singing mountain ballads that sounded utterly suitable in the world as it now was. Those were songs written in the days before rural electrification and widespread ownership of automobiles. They were the songs of barn dances from a day when more folks would have come on foot or horseback than in a Model T.

"I have to go to the bathroom," Ariel told her mother.

An outhouse stood at the end of the yard. Upon Jim's return home, it had been one of the immediate needs that had to be dealt with. Using scrap lumber, Jim threw together a traditional outhouse pretty quickly. He dug a hole in a far corner of the yard using his excavator and then used the same machine to place the outhouse on top of the hole. It was far enough to keep the smell distant, and close enough that it was still convenient.

"Can you go by yourself?" Ellen asked.

Ariel looked at the sky, already turning dark. She wasn't so sure.

"I can see you from here," Ellen assured her. "If you need me, just yell."

"Can I have a flashlight?"

"You have one on your head," Ellen pointed out.

Ariel reached up and felt the headlamp on her head. "Oh yeah. I forgot." Ariel bounded off across the yard and locked herself in the outhouse.

They sat outside until the stars emerged and the night turned cool. It reminded Jim that cutting firewood would get a little harder once he ran out of chainsaw gas. He always cut a year ahead to allow the wood time to cure. While he had plenty of wood for the upcoming winter, it was time to start cutting for the one after. Without the ability to turn on the heat pump on the extra cold mornings, it would be more critical than ever that he kept them well-stocked with wood. In his twenties, he'd lived in a house with two woodstoves and no other form of heat. They'd had a record cold spell that year and he'd learned a lot about never letting the fire burn out. A cold house took a long time to warm back up when all you had was a wood stove.

The fire dwindling, they closed up shop and headed for bed. They would not be having a watch tonight. Things had been quiet and Jim felt comfortable with the perimeter alarms he'd set up upon his return. There were battery-operated motion sensors all around the property and they set off loud alarms in the house if triggered. There were also solar motion lights. Some of those had the bulbs replaced with what was referred to as a "buzz bulb." Instead of lighting up, it produced an ear-splitting buzz that served as an alarm if the motion sensor was activated.

Another step Jim had taken was to place his solar-powered motion lights at established distances from the house. His long-range rifles were zeroed at two hundred yards. At several locations, such as the driveway, he had lights set up at exactly two hundred yards from the house. If a solar motion light was triggered by someone, Jim knew the exact distance to target. He had others set up at five hundred yards. If they were triggered, he would know the exact holdover on his scope for the target illuminated under that light.

He'd also learned in his visit to the Weathermans' farm that they had pups ready to be weaned. Jim had asked for two of them. They were Great Pyrenees and would be excellent for maintaining a watch on the property. Jim would feel a lot better when they were in place. They were big dogs and would require a lot of food. He hoped he could develop a prolific hutch of rabbits that would help provide food for the dogs.

Lloyd and Buddy had walked down from Buddy's house that

afternoon instead of driving. Lloyd wasn't known for his love of physical activity, but as his fuel gauge got closer to E, even he realized that perhaps he should attempt to preserve some of it. They had flashlights, and both carried guns. Lloyd also had a jar of his grandfather's moonshine he'd discreetly been nipping from over the course of the evening. He and Buddy both bespoke its character and excellence.

After they wandered off into the darkness, Jim locked his house up tight. He made sure all of the windows were secure. He climbed into his bed and laid out his bedside kit for rapid deployment: headlamp, M4, Beretta, LCP backup, an ESEE tactical knife, a SOG folder, and his tactical vest with spare mags and rounds for everything.

BUDDY AND LLOYD started walking the paved road to Buddy's house. It was a beautiful night, the moon brilliant and the sky brimming with stars in the way that can only be seen away from the lights of cities. Both men were pleasantly drunk. Two owls hooted back and forth as the quart jar passed between them. Lloyd found himself humming as he walked, then singing aloud.

"Would that be *Down In the Willow Garden* that you're singing?" Buddy asked.

"It would be," Lloyd replied.

"Brings to mind my mother. She sang that one while she worked sometimes."

Buddy slipped back into the warm pool of his thoughts. It was a sad song, and there was a lot of sadness in his life. His mother had been a good woman and he missed her. She'd died before his daughter was old enough to remember her. He couldn't help but wonder if his mother's influence may have helped keep Rachel on the right path. So many bad things in this world and he couldn't do a damn thing about it except for the one thing he'd done already. He'd avenged his daughter's death and that was something.

He started humming along with Lloyd and the words came back to him. Before long, they were proceeding up the road, singing at full volume. Neither had the polished voice of a recording artist but there was a purity and trueness that made the song beautiful. It carried through the night like the sound of a creek, almost belonging.

Buddy wasn't sure how many verses they sang, but when the last notes died both men were smiling. "I reckon if there was anyone out tonight with ill intent, we have clearly broadcast our position," he said.

"It would require a callous and Godless man to kill someone singing the ballad of Rose Connelly," Lloyd pointed out.

Buddy stopped in his tracks. Lloyd, his reflexes slowed by persistent jar-nipping, took another step or two before he could get word to his feet to stop.

"Do you recall me leaving a light burning in my house?" Buddy asked.

Lloyd looked up the hill, squinted, and could make out a dim glow in the windows of Buddy's living room. "No. We turned the lamp out last night and didn't turn one back on this morning," Lloyd said. "We've had company."

"We may still have company. Are you armed?"

"Hell yeah." Lloyd withdrew his infamous nickel-plated .32 caliber from his waistband.

"Is that the .32?" Buddy asked.

"It is."

"Are you planning on killing them or just piercing their nipples with that thing?"

"Everyone is a damn comedian around this place," Lloyd said.

Buddy started up his driveway, moving off the gravel and into the quieter grass. He had his .45 automatic in his hand. "I'd feel better if I was a sight less drunk," Buddy admitted.

Lloyd followed behind. "My family has historically done some of their best killing while drunk."

"It wasn't their best killing if *you* know about it," Buddy replied. "The best killing remains a secret between you and your maker."

Despite their drunkenness, they were soon at Buddy's porch and found no one outside waiting on them. Buddy walked entirely around the house while Lloyd watched the front porch.

"I didn't see anything," Buddy said. "I'm going to go up on the porch and look through a window."

"Be careful," Lloyd warned. "One creaking board and we're busted."

Buddy took the steps slowly, avoiding those spots he knew were creaky. Moving from the steps to the porch, he froze when a board emitted a loud pop as he put his weight upon it. Lloyd cringed and readied his pistol but no sounds came from the house. Buddy started breathing again and resumed his creep toward the living room window.

With no electricity, natural light was of more importance than it had been a month ago. For that reason, Buddy had left the curtains completely open. As he neared the window, he could see fully into his living room. He waved at Lloyd to come up.

Lloyd started up the steps, then tripped, his pistol skittering noisily across the porch. Fortunately, Lloyd had put the moonshine jar in his pocket when he drew his pistol or it would have shattered. Buddy cringed and anxiously watched the men in his living room, both hands closed around the grip of his pistol. They didn't stir.

"I guess we know they're deaf now," Buddy whispered. "That's useful intel. Now get up and get over here."

Lloyd slowly rose to his feet and finally made it to the window. He took in the scene. "Ain't that a sight. It's like they're watching television or something."

Buddy nodded. "More like some damn Goldilocks story from the end of days." He turned away from the window. "The back door is quieter. I'm going around. You stay here and try to hold the noise down. Did you find your gun?"

Lloyd held it up.

"Try not to hurt yourself," Buddy said, then disappeared around the house.

Lloyd stood watching through the window, his eyes moving from man to man and seeing no movement. In less than a minute, he could see a shadow and knew that Buddy had made it in the house. Buddy crept into the living room and stood crouched behind one of the men. Still, the men did not move. Buddy used his pistol to poke one of the men in the head, receiving no reaction. He moved to another, then the last, and came and opened the front door.

Lloyd stepped in cautiously, his pistol raised and aimed in the direction of the men. "Are they drunk too?"

Buddy shook his head. "Dead."

"Dead?" Lloyd was confused. "How?"

"I have an idea," Buddy said, then went to the kitchen.

Lloyd stepped to each man and verified for himself that they were not breathing. When Buddy came back, he had an open pill bottle in his hand.

"They each took a few of these pills," Buddy said.

"And they all overdosed?" Lloyd asked incredulously.

"No," Buddy said. "They were poison. I needed them for a little project. You remember the one I told you I'd been working on when you found me walking up the road?"

"I remember that, but I don't remember anything about any poison pills," Lloyd said.

"I might not have mentioned them," Buddy said. "The pills were what you might call *tangential* to the story."

"So you've had those in the kitchen the whole time I've been here?"

Buddy nodded.

"What if I had taken one of them?" Lloyd asked. "For a headache or something?"

"These ain't headache pills," Buddy said. "They're serious pain meds."

"Well put them in a safe place," Lloyd said. "I don't want to wake up with a hangover and die trying to find a Tylenol."

AFTER A PEACEFUL NIGHT and a sound sleep, Jim felt like a new man.

Every morning, he awoke with a new appreciation for his bed and blankets. Despite his wife's insistence that they needed some fancy bedspread called a *duvet*, each night Jim folded the duvet off to the side and climbed under a stack of quilts his grandmother had made for him when he was young. Except for a few scattered nights here and there, most of them in hotels, he'd spent nearly every night of his life under his grandmother's quilts. He wondered if she'd considered that as she made them, that they would follow him for his entire life and never leave his side. While they may not have had any magical powers to dispel bad dreams or bring happiness, Jim attributed them with helping him maintain a connection to his past and his family. If he had anything to say about it, he would take his last breath one day while under one of those quilts.

Jim went to the kitchen. As usual, his parents were up already. Nana was reading and Pops was out enjoying the cool of the morning.

"Have you had coffee yet?" Jim asked.

His mother shook her head.

Jim went out back onto the screen porch and shook the red tank that attached to the Coleman stove. It still held enough fuel for making coffee. He pumped the tank to pressurize it, then started the stove. He wasn't a fan of percolated coffee, so he put a teapot on instead. He preferred to make his coffee with a GSI Outdoors H2JO. It was a coffee filter that screwed onto the top of a Nalgene water bottle. You put coffee in it, then poured hot water over it until the filter was sitting in the water. The filter was made in such a way that the water bottle's lid would then screw onto the top of the filter, making a leak-proof assembly. As the coffee steeped in the filter, a good shake every few minutes assured a nice strong brew. Jim thought it made the best cup of coffee he'd ever had in his life.

When he'd made coffee for his mother and himself, Jim took a cup out to his dad. He was sitting in the backyard watching the fields from a camping chair.

"What are we getting into today, Jim?"

"Gary is supposed to be here early. He's probably already on the road. I'll radio him in a few minutes and see how it's going. Then I guess we'll spend the rest of the day helping them get settled."

"I'm going to drink this coffee and sit right here for now. Let me know when breakfast is ready," Pops said. "I'm hungry."

Jim went inside and found his radio. He'd also turned his off last night to preserve the battery. He checked the time: 7:05 A.M. He turned the radio on and held it to his mouth. "Gary, you on?" No response, so he tried again. "Gary, this is Jim. You read me?"

Jim went back outside with his dad and set the radio in the cup holder of his camping chair. "Breakfast will be in about twenty minutes," he told his dad.

"I guess I can make it until then."

The radio crackled. "Jim, this is Gary."

"There he is," Jim said. He picked up the radio and held the transmit button. "Jim here."

"We got held up," Gary said. "We'll be there but it may be a couple of hours."

Jim's brow furrowed. There was *something* in Gary's voice. "Every-thing okay, buddy? You guys okay?"

"Not really," Gary replied.

Jim could hear him struggling to speak. He was getting worried.

"What's going on, Gary?" he asked. "Is everything okay?"

There was a long pause.

"Gary?"

"We've got to dig a grave, Jim," Gary said, struggling to keep his voice steady. "We had trouble last night."

Jim had to ask *who* but he hated to say the words. He'd known Gary for a long time. If he'd lost a daughter...

"It wasn't one of the girls, was it?" Jim said, struggling now with his own words. "Tell me it wasn't one of the girls."

"No," Gary said. "It wasn't. We lost Dave, though."

"Ah shit," Jim muttered to his dad. "I can't believe that. They were so close to getting out of there."

Jim thumbed the transmit button. "I'm sorry, Gary. Is there anything we can do for you?"

"No," Gary said. "Just give us time to dig a grave and have a little service. Needless to say, Charlotte is a wreck. She also got a little banged up last night."

"What happened?"

"I'd rather not get into it on the radio," Gary said. "Give us a few hours and we'll see you."

"Okay," Jim replied. "Be careful."

Jim dropped the radio back in the cup holder.

"Did he say what happened?" Pops asked.

"No," Jim said. "I do know they've been having trouble with thieves and trespassers."

Pops shook his head. "I was hoping things were getting better. I don't like hearing things like this."

"Keep hoping, Dad," Jim said. "Keep hoping."

Jim had a selection of rusty farm gates in his scrap pile. Every time he saw a neighbor replacing one, Jim would see if he could get the old one. With a little welding, he made them into a variety of different things for his farm. His woodshed, for example, was entirely made of welded together gates with a roof on top of them. He used gates the way thrifty crafters used pallets.

He selected two of the least decrepit to install on the road in and out of their valley. Since Gary wasn't coming for a few hours, Jim could use that time to put the gates in place. He attached bolt-on pallet forks to his tractor bucket and used those to carry the sixteen-foot steel gates. He stopped at one of the sheds and picked up a tamping bar, a pick, and some old, rusty gate hardware. From his shop building, he grabbed a brace-and-bit, a pipe wrench, a tape measure, and a four-pound hammer. At the barn, he attached a PTO-driven posthole auger to the back of the tractor. Outside the barn, he had a stack of old locust posts and he selected four of the larger ones.

He went back in the house and told everyone his plan.

"Do you need me to go with you?" Pops asked.

"No," Jim said. "I'm going to take Pete and we're going to swing by and get Lloyd. That should be enough."

"Good," Pops said. "I hate anything to do with digging holes."

Jim smiled. He understood.

"Pete, you ready to go?" Jim asked.

"What do I need to take?"

"I'm taking my weapons, a bottle of water, and a snack. You should do the same."

"You all be careful," Ellen said.

"We will. It's a simple job and we won't be long."

Jim drove the tractor up toward Buddy's house with Pete riding on the fender. When they reached Buddy's gate, Pete hopped off to unlock it so that Jim could drive through.

"It's locked," he said, holding up the chained padlock for Jim to see.

Jim nodded. "I guess I can't blame him for that," he said. "I'll just walk up to the house."

"All the way up there?"

"It's not that far," Jim said.

"How about you go and I guard the tractor?" Pete offered.

"Okay," he said. "If you see anyone coming, I want you to get off the tractor and come straight to the house. Understood?"

Pete saluted. "Aye aye, Captain."

Jim shook his head, and set off at a jog up the hill. Buddy's house was about two hundred yards off the road, sitting on top of a low, treeless hill. Jim paused at the edge of the yard to catch his breath. That was when he noticed the dead men stacked like firewood on the porch.

Jim immediately threw his rifle up and went on alert. He ran to Lloyd's Scamp and ducked behind it. He continued to watch the house for a minute but saw nothing out of the ordinary.

"Lloyd!" he yelled. "Buddy!"

There was no response and he yelled again. This time the front door creaked open. "What in the hell are you yelling about?" Lloyd asked.

Jim stood up and gestured toward the bodies on the porch. "I saw that and got a little worried. Sorry that you find my concern for your safety to be disturbing."

"Disturbing because it's too damn loud," Lloyd said, shielding his eyes.

"You're hungover, aren't you?"

"As a towel on a rack," Lloyd confirmed.

"Glad you find your current circumstances comfortable enough that you can let down your hair and relax. I'd hate for the collapse of modern civilization to interfere with you getting drunk," Jim said. He slung his rifle over his shoulder and approached the house.

"We didn't set out with the intention of getting drunk."

Buddy came out of the house with a cup of coffee in his hand and nodded to Jim. "It's a fact," he confirmed. "We had every intention of going straight to bed when we got home, but we came home to the damndest sight you ever did see."

Jim nodded toward the stack of bodies. "I'm assuming it had something to do with them?"

"That it did," Buddy said.

"Hold that story for a second," Jim said. "I'm going to get Pete up here. I told him I'd only be a second. I don't want to leave him down there by himself for too long."

"I'm going to get some coffee," Lloyd said.

Jim walked back to the driveway and could see Pete atop the tractor. "Pete, come on up here!" he called.

Pete waved in acknowledgment, climbed off the tractor, and started up the hill.

Jim took a seat on the edge of the porch. He caught a whiff of the bodies and relocated himself further away. He appraised Buddy as he sat on his porch. "Am I to assume that you killed all these men?"

"That would be both a *yes* and a *no*," Buddy replied cryptically.

"How can it be both? Either you did or you didn't."

"I indeed killed them, but I wasn't here to enjoy it," Buddy replied.

Jim looked for the gleam of humor in the man's eyes and found none. This didn't make any sense.

Lloyd returned to the porch and took a seat, quickly discovering that sitting in close proximity to the bodies did not agree with his booze-weakened stomach and he moved. He was looking a little green around the gills.

Jim could hear Pete coming up the road about that time and didn't want him to have to look too closely at the bodies on the porch. "Keep watch over there, Pete," Jim told him. "Make sure no one gets the tractor."

"Are those dead people?" Pete asked, gesturing toward the bodies.

"They are," Jim said.

Pete considered that information, then took a seat in the gravel and did as he was told.

"Do you think they just randomly found your place?" Jim asked. Word of new criminals active in the valley was not welcome news. The experience with Charlie Rakes was still too fresh.

"I expect that they were acquaintances of my daughters," Buddy said. "Drug addicts and criminal-types. That's all I care to say about it."

Jim understood. It wasn't that Buddy cared to tell him the story in general, it was that it had arrived at a painful juncture where further discussion cut too close to the quick. The wound of his lost daughter was still too fresh for Buddy to discuss her with men that were still little more than strangers to him. Jim respected that. He stood. "I came to ask you all if you wanted to help me hang a couple of gates this morning but it's clear that you all have more pressing matters before you."

"Gates?" Lloyd asked. "I thought we were helping your friend unload today? I thought that was the plan."

"Shit," Jim said. "These bodies sidetracked me and I forgot to tell you my news. Gary had trouble last night. They got hit by someone, and he lost a son-in-law."

"What happened?" Buddy asked.

Jim shook his head. "He didn't want to go into detail on the radio so I don't really know. He sounded pretty shook up."

"That's a crock of shit," Lloyd said. "He's that close to getting out of town and they get hit with something like that?"

"I know. It does suck," Jim agreed. He turned his attention toward the bodies. "You all want some help burying those?"

"I'd appreciate it," Buddy said. "I'm too old to dig graves and this here banjo player's hands are too soft. He probably gets a callous when he uses a Kleenex."

That broke a smile on Jim's face. "You got a sinkhole we can toss them into?" Jim asked. "I don't have the excavator with me for digging holes but I can use the loader bucket to spread dirt over them if you have a hole to throw them in."

"I got just the place," Buddy said. "There's an old sinkhole on the back of the property where people used to throw their trash. There's a pop machine in there, box springs, rusty fence wire, and a bunch of other crap. We'll just bury all of it."

17

G ary's House
    Richlands, VA

GARY FELT he and Will should deal with Dave's body before sunup.
He didn't want the morning to shine light on the scene and allow
the rest of the family to see what he and Will had already
glimpsed. If was not a sight for children, nor anyone that loved
the man.

Debra had suggested they wrap the body in a sheet, but Gary had
deferred.

"Thanks, but I think I'll stick with a tarp," Gary said. He didn't
want to go into the details of how Dave had died. No one needed to
know what shape his body was in. Gary simply told them that Dave
had received a knife wound that hit a major artery and he bled to
death quickly. Charlotte was still too disoriented from her fall to ask
to see him, which was a blessing. Gary hoped to get his body in the
ground before she thought to ask about seeing him. She knew he was
dead, but for now she was lying on the sofa with Debra and Sara

taking care of her while Alice watched the kids. It looked like she had a concussion.

"A tarp is disrespectful, Gary," Debra said. "This isn't a deer we're talking about, it's our son-in-law. It should be a sheet or a blanket. It's much more suitable. We have them to spare, it's not a big deal."

"I know what I'm doing and we can't use a sheet," Gary replied. He turned to walk off.

"Of course we can," Debra insisted. She couldn't give it up. It was a sign she wasn't coping well that this had become such a big issue for her. She was melting down. "People wrapped the dead in sheets for centuries. It will be fine." She thrust the sheet at him again.

He turned back to her, lowered his eyes to the sheet, but still would not take it.

"Gary," she said, her voice louder this time.

When he didn't take the sheet from her, she threw it at him. "Take it," she said, her voice shrill and bordering on hysteria. "Take the stupid sheet."

Gary stepped closer to her and lowered his voice. "Dammit, Debra, a sheet won't work," he hissed. "They nearly cut his head off his body. There's blood everywhere. We have to use something that won't soak through."

He turned and walked off, leaving the sheet in the floor. Debra was still standing there, her mouth open in shock. Tears spilled to the floor but Gary did not see them. Debra covered her mouth and sagged against the wall.

As they stood over his body, Gary pulled his headlight from his head and tossed it into the grass. He did not want to see too clearly what had to be done. It was bad enough to only infer in the darkness the damage that had been done to Dave. To shine light fully upon it and be confronted by the obscenity, the desecration of his flesh, was too much for them.

Gary spread the blue tarp beside the body, trying not to look at it. He pulled Nitrile gloves from his pocket, handing a pair to Will and stretching a pair onto his own hands. He took a deep breath, pushed it out through clenched teeth, and bent over the body. He placed a hand on Dave's shoulder, finding it cold to the touch, and attempted to roll him over. Dave was on his side, facing away from the tarp. Gary had thought he would roll easily in this position but that was not the case. Rigor mortis had already set in.

Gary got on his knees in front of the body and pushed on Dave's shoulder with both hands. The body finally moved and rolled to its back, breaking loose with it a clotted mass of blood that had glued the body to the grass. Gary's stomach rolled. The body had been in a fetal position on its side, the head curled down toward the chest as Gary rolled it onto its back. Now on its back, gravity broke loose whatever forces were holding the nearly severed head in position. With a wet croaking sound, the head yawed slowly backward until it rested on the ground, the gaping wound opening like the enormous mouth of some legendary beast. The movement of the head cleared the airway and a burbling of air escaped the corpse. Gary turned away and began dry heaving, his body wracking both from his convulsing sobs and the spasms of his stomach.

Will took Gary's place then, steeled himself, and rolled the body the rest of the way. He gritted his teeth, pushing with his legs until he got his brother-in-law onto the tarp. He quickly threw the loose end of the tarp over the body, concealing it from his sight. When he started to get to his feet, he realized that his knees were damp, Dave's blood having soaked into his pants.

The contents of his stomach were rising into his mouth. Will tried to choke it down, to stay strong, but he could not contain it. He erupted, spewing vomit in the other direction. He staggered to his feet and walked off into the darkness, bent at the waist, throwing up the whole way. He cried at this point. Not for Dave or Charlotte or even their children, but for the thought that this could have been him. His wife could be in there mourning him. His daughter could get up tomorrow and have to face life without him. He could not leave her to this world alone. Who would protect her?

He would have to become the kind of man that Gary accused Jim of being, the kind of man who sometimes used killing as a preventative measure, the kind of man who killed offensively rather than defensively. Gary was always saying that he only wanted to kill if he had no other choice. Every time they faced such a situation, Gary would point out that his friend Jim would have handled it differently. Will did not fault Gary for being the way he was, but he was beginning to see an efficiency in the way Jim handled things. He put out fires *before* they spread. He killed when he had the advantage. He killed so that he didn't have to worry about the bad guy killing him or someone he loved later.

Certainly, Gary had to deal with this new world in a way that he could live with. For his part, Will was not sure he could live in this new world *without* becoming the kind of man that Jim was. He could not sleep at night with loose ends haunting his sleep. He would rather deal with the consequences of his overreaction than have to bury his child.

Gary was so enraged by Dave's death that he took a step he would not have taken even a few days ago. He gathered the bodies of the three men they'd killed, tied them by the ankles to the back of his lawnmower, and dragged their bodies all the way down to the bottom of his driveway. He stopped at the nearest road sign, one posting the speed limit. He stood the first body up against the sign and removed a two-foot long zip tie from his belt, looped it around the man's neck and the sign post, then yanked it tight. When he stood back, the man hung there, kept on his feet only by his bound neck.

Gary did the same with the next man, standing him by the first. The third man got the same treatment. When he was done, the three dead men encircled the signpost. Gary had carried a plywood sign down in his lap and he hung it from one of the men's necks, facing the road:

THESE MEN WERE THIEVES

ON HIS WAY back up the hill, one thought nagged at Gary. Wesley

Molloy was not among the dead men. That meant he was still out there. Shortly though, his continued existence would no longer be Gary's problem. Molloy could have this town and everything in it.

They all agreed it was better to bury Dave there today than to take him to the new place. They didn't know how long they would be there and they didn't want to have to abandon him to strangers if the new arrangement didn't work out. If they buried him in the yard of his own home, he'd be there among the fruits of his labor and hopefully they would all rejoin him one day when things got back to normal.

There was a short debate about whether the children should attend the graveside service or not, and it was Karen who settled it. She had seen how Charlotte was sinking into a dark hole and needed something to pull her back. She convinced her parents that it might be beneficial for Charlotte to see that she still had responsibilities in this world. Debra was not so sure they could pull Charlotte out of her grief. Charlotte had moved past the violent sobbing and gone to a constant wail that was unsettling to everyone. It was similar to the howl of a dog and had the same spine-chilling effect.

Will and Gary dug the hole, only making it down to around four feet before they hit a rock that they could not pry loose or move around. It would have to be deep enough. They went ahead and placed the body there so that it was already in the ground when everyone came out for the service. Karen had snipped some flowers from the perennial bed in front of the house. She gave everybody, even the children, some to toss into the grave.

There was no one but Gary to say words over the body. In a family, all of the worst duties always fell to the patriarch or matriarch. Debra had to tell Charlotte that her husband was dead, Gary had to wrap the body, and now Gary had to speak over him. There was plenty of unpleasant work to go around.

Standing there over the grave, Gary realized that the last time he'd celebrated Dave's life was when he offered a toast at his wedding to Charlotte. He was neither a minister nor an orator by nature. He spoke plainly and honestly of his son-in-law in his role as such, as a father, and as a husband. The adults fought to maintain composure. Of the children, only Sara's daughter, Lana, seemed to have any comprehension of what was happening, but she may have just been feeding off the uncontainable sadness of the adults. Charlotte crouched at the foot of the grave, still wailing, as Gary and Will filled it. Only when it was full did she allow Karen to lead her away, the wail tapering to a moan due to sheer exhaustion.

She still had not acknowledged her children.

WHAT FEW THINGS they'd needed overnight were hastily shoved into the packed vehicles as they prepared to leave. Gary started to lock the house, but ended up leaving it unlocked. Perhaps it would discourage any vandals from breaking the windows out and leaving the house exposed to the elements.

It's only a house, Gary reminded himself. Still, it felt like more than that. It felt like a part of his life he was leaving behind.

The truck required a boost and a blast of starter fluid to get the engine cranking. As they started the other vehicles and prepared to leave, it became clear that Gary's vehicle assignments were going to have to be modified. With Dave dead, his already packed vehicle needed a driver. It was also clear that Charlotte was probably not in any shape to be driving a vehicle. In her state of mind, she could intentionally drive herself off an embankment just to put an end to her suffering.

Alice agreed to drive Dave's vehicle. There was probably gear in there that they didn't need now that Dave wasn't going with them but it was too late to sort it out and repack. They could do that later.

Karen would switch with Charlotte, who would now ride with Debra while her kids remained in her minivan with Karen. Gary knew that his family was capable, but they were a man down and vulnerable. They were traumatized and sleep deprived. He hoped they didn't run into anything too challenging. He just didn't have a lot of faith in their abilities right now. Timing, judgment, stamina – it was probably all impacted by the night they'd had. Everyone had earned an easy day and he hoped they'd get it.

Gary assigned an order to the vehicles and instructed them not to pass each other, even on the four-lane highway. They were to remain in the assigned order. Each vehicle received a handheld radio set to a common frequency. Each driver was reminded to have a weapon available and ready.

"When I say I want your weapons ready, I mean one in the chamber ready to go," Gary said. "You may have to drive with one hand and shoot with the other. You can't count on having time to chamber a round first. I want you to be able to pick up your weapon and start firing."

Everyone got in their vehicles and belted up. Gary got on his radio. "Whenever you're ready, Will."

Will eased out, the trailer tracking behind him, rattling and creaking under the load.

"We took out one threat last night," Gary said into his radio. "We killed off the punks on the dirt bikes, but we don't know what else is out there. Keep your eyes open for anything suspicious. If something doesn't look right, stop in the road and we'll check it out. I do not want to lead this whole group into a trap."

"Got it," Will replied.

"Everyone else with us? Sound off in order," Gary said.

"I'm here," Debra said.

"Me too," Karen replied.

"Here," Sara piped in.

"I'm here," Alice said.

"Good," Gary said. "Let's keep it tight and call out if you have trouble."

While he wasn't sure what everyone else was experiencing, Gary felt a nearly overwhelming anxiety. Years ago, he'd rented an RV for a family trip. The vehicle was enormous and he'd never driven anything like it before. He was constantly worried he was straying out of his lane or going to hit a curb when he took a turn. There was the fear he was going to hit an awning when he refueled or that he was going to get into some jam he couldn't back up out of. It was exhausting and that was how this felt at the moment, like he was maneuvering some awkward and barely controllable behemoth down a narrow, unfamiliar road. He would be glad when this day was over.

They approached the intersection with the four-lane Route 19.

"This is where Alice and I got hijacked, Will," Gary said into the radio. "Keep your eyes open."

Gary did the same, scanning every clump of bushes, trying to see beyond the guardrail and over every embankment. He saw nothing out of the ordinary.

"Looks clear," Will said. "I don't see anything."

"Then hit it," Gary said. "Keep moving."

Will pulled onto the highway without incident. Gary came next. He drove slowly and saw the blood-smeared asphalt where he and Alice had encountered the men asking that a toll be paid. He scanned his mirrors and saw each trailing vehicle enter the highway without incident.

"We're all good," Gary said into the radio. "Let's crank it up to about forty-five miles per hour. Will, if you see anything in the roadway, go ahead and stop so we can check it out. We've got to watch for traps."

"Roger that," Will said.

In a few minutes, they passed the office complex where Gary, Jim, and Alice worked and where Gary had gotten the truck. Immediately beyond it, they passed the armory where people on the grounds stopped what they were doing to watch the convoy move past. Gary watched in his mirrors to see if anyone came out and attempted to pursue them. He had no reason in particular to think that they might, but he wasn't taking any chances. Any moving vehicle with fuel, any truck that might be carrying food or supplies, could be targeted.

"Alice?" Gary said into his radio. "Anyone pull onto the road behind you?"

"Nope," she replied. "Highway is clear behind me."

"Perfect," Gary said. "Everyone keep your eyes open. Let me know if you see anything concerning."

They crossed the county line, leaving Tazewell County behind and entering Russell County. They passed through a community known as Belfast, seeing houses at a distance but no one out moving around. The kept their vehicles at the appointed speed, continuing to the open pastures of the Rosedale area. Gary picked up his radio.

"Jim said we might hit a police roadblock at the intersection up here where the traffic light is," Gary said. "I don't expect any trouble, but we need to be ready for anything. Even if it's manned by cops, that doesn't mean there won't be trouble. Once we get past this intersection, it's another fifteen minutes or so to Jim's place."

As they approached the non-functioning traffic light, Will slowed. "I can see some kind of obstruction up there," Will said into his radio.

"I see it," Gary said. "Looks like a MRAP or something. Slow it down a little." An MRAP was a military surplus Mine-Resistant Ambush Protected vehicle. A lot of law enforcement agencies had been obtaining them since the wars in Iraq and Afghanistan had been slowing down.

"Whatever is going on here, we've got no choice but to go through this intersection," Gary said. "Drive slowly, all of you keep your hands on your steering wheels and in sight. If there's a cop there, don't give him any reason to shoot you. We'll just have to play this one by ear. If we're cool, he should be cool."

Gary didn't know if the pep talk was for his family or himself. He didn't feel like he had anything to hide, but he still felt uneasy. Just being on the road again, being away from home, brought back all of the anxiety of his journey home with Jim.

Approaching closer, he could definitely see that there was an MRAP sitting beside the intersection. There were concrete Jersey barriers placed through the intersection to slow and funnel traffic through a narrow choke point. They didn't block the intersection completely, only forced drivers to slow down and go through single-file. From the impact craters on the concrete barriers, it was evident that not everyone had seen fit to comply with the request to stop.

There were several four-foot long sections of concrete culvert placed on end behind the Jersey barriers.

Gary tried to understand what the upended culverts were for. He figured it out pretty quickly when a helmeted figure popped up out of the culvert and leveled an Israeli Tavor rifle at his group.

"Easy everyone," Gary said into his radio. "I'm going to handle this. Everybody stay cool."

Gary got out of his truck, raised his hands over his head, and stepped to the front of the vehicle. The figure in helmet and goggles followed him with the rifle. Gary couldn't help but admire the culvert idea. All the man had to do was duck back down and he was surrounded by a barrier that would stop most small arms fire. It was like a rodeo clown ducking into a barrel to hide from the bull. He would have to get a couple of those.

"Are you Travis?" Gary asked.

"Who's asking?" the man replied.

"My name is Gary Sullivan. My family is in these vehicles."

"Sullivan," Travis said, thinking. "There was a Sullivan working at the county offices. Any relation?"

"No, I don't have any family over this way," Gary said. "So you *are* Travis?"

"Why would you think my name is Travis?" the man asked. "I don't know you."

"My friend Jim Powell lives about fifteen minutes from here," Gary explained. "He and I just walked back from Richmond together a few days ago. My family and I have had some trouble at home and Jim offered us a place to stay until things get back to normal."

The man hopped out of the culvert and approached the convoy of vehicles. Gary could see now that the man had a Virginia State Police patch on the sleeve of his shirt.

"Tell everyone to keep their hands visible," he instructed.

"Already did," Gary said.

"We're off to a good start then. Are you armed?"

"Of course. Everyone, including me, is carrying a concealed

weapon and they have permits to do so," Gary said. "Is that a problem?"

"Not as long as they keep their hands clear of those weapons," the Trooper replied.

"So you are Travis, right?" Gary asked yet again.

The man finally nodded. "I am. Jim and I grew up together. I've known him a long damn time."

"He and I have been friends for about twenty-five years," Gary said, smiling.

"I never said we were friends, or that I liked him," Travis said, moving up the line of vehicles and looking inside each of them. "The sneaky bastard always seemed like he was up to something. What kind of trouble did you run into back at your home? Must be bad if you're bugging out."

"Looters and thieves, I guess you'd call them," Gary said. "They kept trying to break into our house. It got to where we couldn't even go outside without some kind of run-in. Last night they killed my son-in-law in the front yard. We just buried him before we left this morning."

The trooper nodded, continuing to move along the line of vehicles, scanning both the contents of the vehicle and the person driving it. When he got to Debra's vehicle, he stopped by the passenger window and stared at Charlotte. Her eyes were swollen from crying and she still moaned with the pain of loss, though exhaustion had sapped some of the fury from it.

"There's a lot of shitheads out in the world right now," the trooper said.

"That's a fact," Gary said.

"Where did you get the fuel for your trip? It hasn't been available to civilians for several weeks."

"It's what we had at home," Gary said. "I was out of town when the crap hit the fan and I walked home with Jim. My family didn't drive anywhere while I was gone. They were afraid to even leave the house. We're using every last bit of fuel we have for this trip."

Travis nodded, seemingly satisfied with that response. "One last question," he said. "Why are you driving a vehicle with Local Government Use Only tags on it?"

That question took Gary completely by surprise. He'd not considered that there may be some fallout from using a public vehicle for his private move. In the scheme of things, it seemed a minor detail. Leave it to a cop to notice something like that.

He decided that honesty was easiest. "Jim and I work at the mental health agency together. He lent me the vehicle. It's from his division."

The trooper considered this. "I'm not sure that the law allows him to lend a public vehicle for private use. As a matter of fact, I'm pretty sure that the law strictly forbids it."

"Look," Gary said, "we're just trying to get moved. The truck is full of my personal belongings. I'm going to take it back once this mess is all over. It's probably even safer with me than it would be back at the office. You could probably even say that I'm assisting the Commonwealth of Virginia in preserving one of its assets."

The trooper looked Gary in the eye. He knew BS when he heard it, but he appreciated it when it was used skillfully. "How do I know it's full of your personal belongings? How do I know that you didn't steal a bunch of food and fuel from your work? Supplies paid for with public money? You prove to me that it's your personal belongings in there and I'll let you through."

"Look if you want to," Gary said, frustrated now. "We've got nothing to hide. We're just trying to get moved. We've had a really bad night and today hasn't been so hot either. We just want to get to our destination."

The trooper slung his rifle over his shoulder. "I'll take you at your word about borrowing the truck," he said. "I still need to look in the back. If it's full of personal stuff and not stolen goods, you'll be free to go on your way. If I see any property tags indicating that the contents are state property, I'm confiscating the truck and everything in it."

"Fair enough," Gary said. "Knock yourself out."

Gary led the trooper to the back of the vehicle and reached for the handle on the sliding door. The trooper put out a hand to stop him.

"I think I can take care of that," he said.

Gary raised both hands and stepped back. "Sorry, just trying to help." He had no idea what he was going to do if this went south. Was he willing to kill this trooper? He wasn't sure he could do that.

"You can help me by going back there and standing by that next vehicle," Travis instructed. "I don't turn my back on people I don't know."

Gary did as he was told, walking back and standing by Debra's window.

"Everything going okay?" she asked.

"I have no idea. This guy is a jerk," Gary replied. "I think he's just hassling us because he's bored. I don't know what he's getting out of it."

"Did you tell him that you were friends with Jim?"

Gary nodded. "Yeah, and I'm not sure that it helped. As a matter of fact, I think it may have had the opposite effect."

Debra grimaced. "Sorry. Jim can have that effect on people."

Gary shrugged. There was nothing that could be done about it now.

The trooper's rifle slid awkwardly from his shoulder as he leaned over to open the back door the truck. He unslung his rifle and propped it against the bumper, threw the heavy steel latch on the door, and tugged on the canvas strap that lifted the door. As the door rose, no one noticed the black clad figure standing in the darkened interior until it was too late.

Travis shaded his eyes to better see inside the truck. When his eyes adjusted and he saw the grinning skull face of the tactical mask, his hand dropped to his pistol and he opened his mouth to say something. It was then that everyone noticed that the masked man was holding a shotgun. The trooper yelled and began to draw his sidearm but it was too late. The skull-faced man pulled the trigger once, then twice, each shot pushing Travis further back.

Despite the mask, Gary recognized the hair. He recognized the eyes. It was Molloy. Somehow he'd slipped into the back of the truck during the confusion of the night. He was planning to go with them to their new home.

Stunned, Gary reacted, crouching beside the vehicle and drawing his Glock. The gunman noticed Gary's movement and pointed the shotgun in his direction, firing off another round. Gary ducked and the windshield shattered. He popped back up, leveled his Glock across Debra's hood and fired four times, each shot striking the black figure center mass. He twisted and jerked, dropping the shotgun. As he fell, he sagged to the truck bed, then slithered out the door onto the pavement. Gary stepped out of cover, keeping his gun leveled at the black figure. He saw no movement.

There was a scream behind him. Karen had heard the shot and run to her mother's aid, finding the shattered windshield and two bodies covered in glass fragments.

"Mom?" Karen cried.

Gary ran back to the car and flung open the driver's door. "Debra, are you okay?"

Debra rose slowly, glass fragments raining down from her. "I'm okay. Check Charlotte."

Gary ran to the other side of the car. "Charlotte! Baby, are you okay? Charlotte?"

She didn't move.

Gary pulled her door open and touched her shoulder.

"Charlotte!"

Karen was helping Debra brush the glass from her hair and out of her clothes.

"Tell me my baby is okay, Gary," Debra pleaded. "Tell me she's okay."

Gary grabbed Charlotte by the shoulders and pulled her from the vehicle. Glass scratched and sliced at his fingers and the palms of his hands. He lay Charlotte on her back and brushed glass from her face and hair. He didn't see any blood but her eyes were closed and she was unresponsive. Alice was suddenly at his side with Sara. They were watching him in silence. He noticed Will in his peripheral vision, checking the dead man, then joining them also.

"Charlotte, are you okay?" Gary asked, his voice breaking. "Please, baby, are you okay?"

Her face screwed into a mask of pain and a furious scream erupted from her. Gary recoiled from the intensity of it, realizing it meant she was alive. It was like the first cry of a baby, the indication that the child survived birth. He began sobbing. Debra, finally free of glass, came running around the vehicle. She dropped to her knees and hugged her daughter.

"Charlotte, it's okay. You don't need to cry. You're alive," Debra whispered. "You're alive, sweetie."

Charlotte opened her eyes and looked at her mother. "That's *why* I'm crying," she said. "I'm crying because I'm still alive and I don't want to be."

There was a moan from behind them. Gary had forgotten about the trooper in the midst of his fear for his family. He found Travis lying on his back, attempting to staunch the spurt of arterial blood from his neck with his fingers. Gary knelt beside him. The man had been wearing a heavy military plate carrier but several buckshot rounds had gone above the armor and caught him in the throat. The blood ran like a faucet. Gary tried applying pressure by placing a bandana over the wound but it was hopeless. In the days of 9-1-1, he might have had a fighting chance. In this world, he had none.

Gary noticed Travis looking him in the eye.

"Why did you do it?" he whispered. "I was going to let you go."

"Do what?" Gary asked, confused.

"Let your people shoot me."

"I-I... didn't d-do anything," Gary stammered.

"I would have let you go," Travis said. He was weaker now, his voice slowing, his eyes shocky.

"He wasn't one of my people," Gary rushed to explain. "He's one of the people that killed my son-in-law."

The explanation fell on deaf ears. The trooper was gone.

"Shit!" Gary yelled. He beat on his thighs with his fists. He stood and yelled it again. "Shit!"

Will came running up with his rifle in his hand. "We need to get out of here," he said. "There are a lot of houses up in that neighborhood and people are starting to come out and look. We need to be gone before someone comes down here."

That thought cleared Gary's head quickly. He grabbed the trooper's Tavor rifle and handed it to Will. "Put this in the truck and shut the back door." He grabbed six spare mags from Travis' vest and the Sig that he'd dropped beside him. He found two spare Sig mags on his belt and he took those as well. It wasn't so much a calculated move as a reaction to gather what resources he could immediately lay his hands on.

"I'm sorry," Gary said to Travis' body.

"I'm not," Will said.

"How can you not be sorry?" Gary said. "He was just doing his job. He didn't deserve this. He died thinking we did this to him on purpose."

"If that cop hadn't opened that door, who would have been the next person opening it?" Will asked. "Who?"

The realization dawned on Gary. It would likely have been him. Or it would have been Will. Either way, his family would have lost another man. As badly as he felt about it, he would rather it be the trooper than he or Will. His family couldn't sustain another loss.

"We need to get going," Will urged.

Gary ran to the cab of the truck, which he'd fortunately left running, because they didn't have time now for boosting cars. People were getting closer to the road. He snatched up his radio. "Let's get out of here."

Everyone piled into their cars and pulled out, the vehicles in the back swerving to avoid the two dead bodies. As they slipped through the concrete barriers and past the intersection, Gary could see people coming down the street from a nearby neighborhood. Some of them appeared to be carrying weapons. The obvious conclusion that those strangers would arrive at when they came upon the scene would be that Gary and his people had killed the trooper. It's what he would think under the same circumstances. They would have to hide the truck when they got to Jim's and then get rid of it at the first opportunity. It was the most obvious of the vehicles and if there was any sort of law enforcement in place at all, they might be looking for it.

Gary took the radio off the dash. "Jim, you read me?"

The response was immediate this time. "Jim here."

"We're coming in hot," Gary said. "We hit stormy seas."

"Understood," Jim said. "You know the road by the old school near my house?"

"I do."

"Turn there and go four miles," Jim said. "Then turn right and take the first left. Go about one half mile and I'll be waiting for you by the side of the road. There will be folks with me to help."

Gary felt better already. "Appreciate it," Gary said. "We'll see you in a few."

18

The Valley

AFTER RECEIVING Gary's radio transmission from the road, Jim drove to the end of his driveway to wait on him. He'd sent Buddy, Lloyd, and Pete up to Henry's farm earlier to get the house presentable. It wasn't like they were staging it for HGTV or anything, but there were a few things that needed immediate attention.

They opened the windows to let in some fresh air. They pulled up the hallway carpet, removing the bloodstain from where Henry's wife bled to death at the hands of Charlie Rakes. They also gathered and removed the accumulation of trash from when Charlie and his family had lived in the house. What could be burned was dealt with in the backyard. Non-burnable trash went to a sinkhole back away from the house. It was the same way they did it in the country a century ago, before landfills, transfer stations, and community dumpsters. Garbage pickup had never been available out this far and, at this rate, wouldn't be for a long time coming.

Ellen and Nana had fixed a box of ready-to-eat food for the family. It wasn't like in the old days, when Gary could just send out for pizza since it was moving day. Jim didn't know what they'd fixed, but it smelled good in the cab of the truck.

When Jim heard a truck approaching, he recognized it. The exhaust on that truck had been rusted out for years and had a particular sound to it. He'd told his crew to get it fixed but they kept putting it off. There was no sense in Gary stopping his whole entourage in the road just for a greeting when they were this close to their new home. Jim pulled out in the road, waved to Gary to follow him, and led the convoy directly to Henry's farm.

Jim found the gate open and eased through, the truck bouncing a little on the cattle guard. Pete, Buddy, and Lloyd were sitting in the shade of the porch. He saw Buddy spin the lid back onto a mason jar and pass it to Lloyd, who tucked it into a bucket of tools. Pete was sipping on a Dr. Pepper he'd come up with somehow. Jim drove toward them, then pulled out of the way to make room for the mass of vehicles following him.

Gary pulled in behind him and killed the engine on the box truck. He slid out the door and slammed it shut behind him. Jim got out and walked toward the man. He extended a hand, then withdrew it and instead hugged his friend. Over the course of walking hundreds of miles, he figured the grade of their friendship had gone up a notch.

"It's good to see you, Gary."

"You too, Jim," Gary replied.

"I'm sorry things have been so rough up your way. I didn't come back to a picnic either. I had to kill a man within fifteen minutes of getting home."

"Yeah, it definitely wasn't the homecoming I imagined," Gary said. "I thought after what we'd been through, I kind of deserved more. I thought the world owed me at least a couple of good weeks of wearing flip-flops in a lawn chair."

"So much for that," Jim said.

"No kidding."

Gary's family had been hanging back and allowing the two men a moment to reconnect, then began filtering over. Everyone was introduced.

"Jim, you remember Will, don't you?"

Jim nodded and extended a hand to Will.

The rest of the introductions were rushed since Charlotte needed to get off her feet. Jim quickly showed Debra and Sara to the master bedroom and they escorted Charlotte, making sure she laid down on the bed. Jim had warned Lloyd, Buddy, and Pete not to mention anything about the death in the house or the bloody carpet. He hoped they remembered.

Outside, Jim found Gary speaking with Alice in the front yard. Jim hadn't seen Alice. She'd not gotten out of the car when he was out before and he had no idea she was even with them. Gary hadn't mentioned it.

He approached the two. "Alice, I want to apologize for being such a—"

His apology was cut off when Alice grabbed him in a tight embrace. "You have nothing to apologize for, Jim. I had a lot of time to think on my way home. I should have realized that you had a better idea of what was going on. I just couldn't admit it, either to myself or to you all. I guess I'm hardheaded."

"I was still a dick," Jim mumbled.

"Just because you were a dick didn't mean you were wrong," Alice said. "I've known you long enough that I should have been able to separate the messenger from the message."

"I've been trying to work on that same thing for years," Jim chuckled wryly. "If you won't allow me to apologize, I at least want to express that I'm sorry for whatever hardship led to you being here."

Alice smiled. "I'll accept that. Thank you."

"Where's Rebecca?" Jim asked. "She still convinced that FEMA is going to get her home? I wonder if she made it yet."

Alice's smile dropped like a rock. "She didn't make it. She was murdered."

Jim was genuinely shocked. He and Rebecca had butted heads

over the years but he did have kind of an admiration for the woman. "How?"

"We met up with a man in the camp. He wanted to leave with us, but they made it hard to leave. When we finally got out of there, he came with us. He turned out to be mentally ill. I was pretty much done with the two of them but he killed Rebecca before I could part ways with them. I got up one morning and found her dead. He'd stabbed her repeatedly. I still have nightmares about the sight of it."

Jim didn't know what to say. He touched Alice's shoulder. "I'm sorry."

"Why didn't you tell me this, Alice?" Gary asked. "I had no idea what you'd been through."

"You had your own problems, Gary," Alice said. "You didn't need to hear about mine."

Gary shook his head.

"Then I had the misfortune of crossing paths with the same man again in Bluefield. How's that for luck? I went to sleep in an abandoned car on the highway and woke up zip-tied to a pole in his basement. His mental illness was getting worse and, besides Rebecca, it turned out that he had already killed his mother. He was going to kill me too."

"Oh my God," Gary whispered.

"You obviously got away," Jim said. "How?"

It was part of the difference between Jim and Gary that Jim did not dwell on the fact that Alice had experienced such an awful event, and instead chose to focus on the fact she'd escaped it.

Alice looked Jim in the eye and he found a cold practicality that had not existed there before. "I severed his femoral artery with a broken piece of wire. Then I stabbed him with his own knife and shot him in the face."

There was something in the way she said it. It was almost a challenge. She was throwing out her deed and seeing if they could accept who she was now. Seeing if they would believe her. Gary looked taken aback; Jim was impressed.

"I knew there was a fighter in there," Jim said. "I knew it because of the way we used to fight."

Alice found her smile again. "Speaking of that, I stayed in the office the other night and I found the message you left on the wall. I knew you left it for me. I can't tell you how much it lifted me up to find that."

"Did you find the note I left on the candle? About how you must have missed it in your *safety inspections*?"

"I did," she said. "I'm pretty sure I laughed about it, but I may have cussed you too."

"Have you been home?"

"No, she hasn't," Gary answered for her. "When I found her, she was weak from a stomach bug and I offered to let her take one of our cars if she'd wait a day and come with us."

"That was a good plan," Jim said. "Safer than traveling alone."

"Trust me, I know," Alice said. "And now that you all have safely arrived, I'm going to empty this vehicle and go check on my own family."

Lloyd and Buddy conveniently strolled up at this point to introduce themselves.

"I'll be glad to help ya'll unload," Lloyd said. "Unfortunately, if we wait too much longer I'm going to be too drunk to be any help."

"I second that amendment," Buddy said, extending a hand to Gary.

After introductions, they quickly emptied the vehicle that Gary was lending Alice. The contents were piled in the yard to haul inside later. As they prepared to say their goodbyes, Gary moved forward and hugged Alice.

"Thanks for being there for us," he said. "You were a big help."

"You're welcome," she said. She turned to Jim and extended her arms.

Jim smiled, then hugged her. "I think there's going to be safety in greater numbers," Jim said. "If you and your family need a group, you're welcome to come join us."

They broke the hug and Alice smiled at Jim. "I sincerely appreciate that," she said. "I may be back." She turned to walk off.

"Alice," Jim called. "We've been keeping in touch with radios. We're monitoring channel ten. If you need to get up with us, that's how."

"Got it," she said. "Channel ten. Thanks." She got into the vehicle, pulled out, and was gone.

"She's different," Jim said, watching her drive off. "You can tell her experiences have changed her."

Gary nodded. "No kidding. The woman nearly blew my damn head off," he said.

It was so unexpected that Jim started laughing. "What?"

"In the hallway at work," Gary said. "When I went to get the truck, I stopped by my office and startled her. If I hadn't ducked, she'd have killed me. She actually fired at my head and the door deflected it."

Jim shook his head. "Well, do you want to unload the big truck or leave it until tomorrow? I know you guys have had a long day already."

"We need to unload it now. It will have to be hidden as soon as possible," Gary said. "We had trouble at the roadblock and people may be looking for this truck."

"You kill Travis?"

"*We* didn't kill him, but he's dead and people probably *think* we killed him," Gary said.

"I never did like him."

"Apparently it was mutual," Gary said. "Which you might have mentioned before I went ahead and told him that you and I were friends. It didn't help things."

"Sorry."

"We'll talk about it later," Gary said.

"There's food," Jim said. "I forgot to mention that. My wife and mom sent it."

"I'm starving," Will said.

"We can eat while we unload," Gary said. "I won't be able to rest until this truck is out of sight."

"When it's unloaded, there's an equipment shed we can put it in for now," Jim said. "It's tall enough that we can drive it in and shut the doors."

They worked for two hours to unload the contents of the truck. The men did most of the unloading while the women kept the children out of trouble, looked after Charlotte, and set out the food that Ellen and Nana had sent for them. Jim had originally planned on having a little get-together at his place to welcome Gary's family to the neighborhood, but the mood was too somber after Dave's death. It was not the time for a party.

When the unloading was done, Gary and Jim made plans to catch up the next day and start on their security plan.

"I appreciate this, Jim," Gary said. "I don't know how things would have turned out if we'd stayed in our home."

"You're welcome," Jim said. "I'm pretty sure you would have done the same for me."

Jim gathered his weary crew and loaded them into his truck for the short drive back to his place. Lloyd climbed in the front to ride with Jim. Pete and Buddy rode in the back. It was just past sunset and the sky was beautiful in a way that made conversation unnecessary.

When Jim reached the turnoff for his driveway, he asked Lloyd if he wanted him to take them the rest of the way up to Buddy's house, but Lloyd declined.

"We had a good time walking the other evening," Lloyd said. "I think I'd like to do it again. An evening stroll is good for the soul."

"The next time you walk up the road singing in the dark, you might not be so lucky. Someone might hear you and shoot your dumb ass," Jim warned.

"Then I would die a happy man," Lloyd said, meaning every word of it.

"Have it your way then," Jim said. He turned off the road and crept up his driveway. He approached the house and Pops, Nana, and Ellen came out, waiting on the porch. They were obviously anxious to hear about Gary's experience. Jim was glad Ariel was not there on the porch to hear it. It was not a story fit for young ears.

Jim stopped the truck and everyone piled out.

"How'd it go?" Pops asked.

"I don't even know where to start," Jim said. He took a seat on the steps and Pete lumbered up and sat beside him. Jim put an arm around his son and patted him on the shoulder. The evening was pleasant and the lightning bugs were flickering through the pasture. The moon and a few planets were beginning to emerge in the darkening sky. The night would be every bit as beautiful as the evening had been.

"Excuse me, but I ain't got the stomach to hear this story again," Buddy said. "Once was bad enough. Are you staying, Lloyd, or are you ready to head back to the house?"

Lloyd had just plopped himself down on the steps, too. "I just got comfortable but I suppose and I can get uncomfortable just as easy." He started to get up.

"Don't rush," Buddy said. "I ain't leaving without saying goodbye to that little peach. Where's she at?"

Ellen smiled. "Ariel is in the backyard," she said. "The last time I looked, she was lying in the hammock reading a book."

Buddy smiled too. "That little girl..." he said, trailing off. "Enjoy every second of it. Every second." His sentiment pulled at each heart. They all knew where he was in his head right now. He was remembering his own daughter, remembering when he and his wife were all that mattered to her, remembering when each thing she did was precious to them.

"Do you mind if I go tell her goodbye?" he asked.

"No," Jim said. "That's fine. She likes the attention."

Buddy started off around the side of the house while Jim began his telling of Gary's recent experiences. Pops, Ellen, and Nana had settled into chairs on the porch and were listening eagerly when a scream tore through the evening.

Jim sprung up from the steps and looked for his weapons. He recalled leaving his M4 in the truck. His Beretta was in there too, slid up on the dash when the paddle holster became drenched in sweat.

He started toward the truck to get them but another scream from the backyard pulled him away and he ran as fast as he could.

ARIEL WAS CURLED up in the two-person hammock that hung between a poplar and a maple in the backyard. It was a colorful Guatemalan hammock woven of coarse fabric. Ariel loved it because it was so big that it wrapped around her completely when she lay in it, the sides coming together over her head so that it seemed like she was in a cocoon. She was reading the latest *Kingdom Keepers* book. It was one of her favorite series.

She thought she heard a sniffing sound outside of the hammock, like when you met a dog for the first time and it smelled you. She went back to her book, then she felt something poke her in the back. She giggled.

"Pete," she said. "I know that's you."

She waited for his response, knowing he would usually start giggling, too. Instead of a giggle, she heard a growl. Ariel started to raise up and poke her head out of the hammock where it was closed over her head. She wanted to see what was out there, but she was too scared. She wanted to yell but was frozen with fear. Then she worried that her scream might provoke whatever was out there growling at her. She had no idea what to do. Tears forced their way out and rolled down her cheeks.

There was a scratch against the hammock where her arm lay. She yanked it away. There was a snarl and something nipped her back through the fabric of the hammock. It hurt. That was when her paralysis broke and she let go with the most powerful scream to ever escape her lips. As her scream faded, a chorus of yipping began around her.

She screamed again.

BUDDY HAD JUST COME around the back corner of the house and was looking for the hammock when he heard what sounded like growling. In the low light it took him a moment to find the hammock, everything blending together into the generalized grayness of twilight. It looked like the hammock was swinging, but his old eyes had a hard time assembling all the information.

Then he heard the scream and the yipping sound that he recognized instantly as the sound of coyotes. They heard it every night in this farming country. It was the sound of hunting. Of predation.

Buddy could just barely make out the coyotes from the distance. It looked like a tangle of fur encircling the hammock. One latched onto the hammock and violently shook its head back and forth. Ariel screamed again and Buddy loped toward her.

"I'm coming, baby girl!" he yelled. His heart rate soared and he reached for his pistol, but the shoulder holster was not there. They'd all gotten so sweaty helping Gary unload the truck that they'd removed their guns and left them on the truck dash. His was still there, where it helped him not one damn bit. There was no time to run back for a weapon. As he passed the fire pit, he saw an axe sunk into a pine log and wrenched it free. It would have to do.

In seconds he was at the hammock and stomped at the spine of the nearest coyote nipping at the hammock. It was larger than he expected, and faster. It turned its head and snapped at his pants leg. He yanked his leg back, then another coyote sank its teeth into his calf. He cursed and kicked, the animal letting go just in time for Buddy to break its back with the axe. It dropped with a whimper. He looked toward the house but saw no one there yet. Surely they were coming.

Ariel screamed again and he looked down to see a coyote biting into the hammock, tearing away a small section of coarse fabric. The coyote tugged harder, opening the hole further. Buddy struck at it with the axe, but missed as the coyote sprang beyond his reach.

Buddy yelled when another set of teeth latched onto his calf again, not letting go this time. The teeth pulled at him and he felt a tearing deep inside his leg. Then he heard those teeth grinding against his bone. He swung down with the axe, having trouble getting any force up because of the coyote's position behind him, but he connected with the animal's head. It turned him loose and stood there, stunned. Another blow dropped it and it lay there kicking, its eyes rolling crazily in its head.

The pain in Buddy's leg made it hard to stand but he knew if he dropped, he would die. There were too damn many of them. He could not run with Ariel – he was too old and the coyotes were too fast –but he had to get her out of that hammock. One of the mangy animals squeezed its head into the opening in the torn fabric. When Ariel screamed again, Buddy parted the top of the hammock and grabbed the child into his arms just as the coyote snapped at her face.

One of the coyotes leapt at her dangling foot and Buddy twisted his body, yanking her just out of reach of the powerful jaws. With all his remaining strength, he pushed Ariel skyward.

"Grab onto a branch, Ariel!" he yelled. "Pull yourself up!"

Ariel latched onto the branches of the tree. She climbed quickly. Buddy embraced the tree, trying to keep himself upright. He had dropped the axe when picking up Ariel and he didn't see where it went. The coyotes were trying to pull his legs out from under him. He struck at one with his fist, only to have the beast latch onto his hand, crushing the fragile bones of his fingers. He cried out in pain. Ariel recoiled in horror and let loose with another long scream.

There was a powerful blow to his back as one of the coyotes sprang onto him, trying to bite him on the back of the neck and take him down. He elbowed it and it dropped off him. Buddy looked up into the tree and saw the pained face of Ariel looking down at him. She was reaching a hand toward him as if she could pull him into the tree with her.

The coyotes continued to bite and tug at him. Buddy felt himself getting weaker. He was going kind of numb, which made him think he might be going into shock. He'd seen it happen to people before, usually just before they died. He looked up again and this time saw his daughter Rachel when she was Ariel's age. They were playing in the yard and he'd set her in a tree. Now she wanted down and she was reaching for him with her little arms, those little grasping hands. Buddy let go of the tree and reached for his daughter.

"Shoot them!" a woman's voice screamed. "SHOOT THEM!"

It was the last thing Buddy heard.

ELLEN AND NANA ran ahead and cleared the kitchen table while Jim and Lloyd carried the bleeding man into the dark house. Jim barked orders.

"Pete, get my headlamp now!" he yelled. "Ellen, I need the big first aid kit. Pops, I need lanterns and flashlights."

They slid the bleeding man onto the kitchen table as Pete ran up with Jim's brightest headlamp. He slammed it onto his head just as Ellen returned with the large nylon bag that had the advanced first aid kit they took on their camping trips. Jim unzipped a pocket and removed a pair of EMT shears, cutting Buddy's pants legs off at thigh level.

"Get me a couple of big towels," he told Pete.

While Pete was gone, Jim removed a liter bottle of saline from the kit. When he returned with the towels, Jim unfolded them and placed them under Buddy's legs while Lloyd held them in the air. Jim poured saline over Buddy's legs, rinsing away the blood and making it easier to see the numerous wounds. The sight of that did nothing to instill Jim with confidence.

"Shit," he said. "I'll never get all these closed up."

"You have to," Ellen said. "What else are we going to do?"

"Give me some gloves," Jim said.

He examined Buddy's legs. There were so many teeth marks that it was impossible to tell how many times they'd gotten him. One bite on his calf seemed to be the worst, with a chunk of flesh missing and blood continuing to seep from it. Jim let out a deep breath.

"There's a pouch of celox powder in a side pocket," Jim said. "It's orange and says Quick Clot on it. Hand it to me."

Ellen thumbed through the contents of the pocket and located it. Jim tore it open and sprinkled the granular powder over the wound.

"I'll need a trauma pad next," Jim said. "It's a thick, absorbent bandage. Then I'll need a rolled bandage to hold it in place."

Ellen located the items and passed them to Jim. He placed the thick bandage over the celox powder to press it into the wound, then wrapped it tightly. He'd need to check it again in five minutes and make sure it had stopped bleeding. With that wound dealt with, there were at least two dozen others seeping blood and that was just on his lower legs.

"One at a time," Jim mumbled, trying to keep himself from getting overwhelmed. "One at a time."

He pinched a wound shut. It looked like the deep puncture from a canine tooth.

"Ellen, give me an irrigation syringe," he finally said. "Then I'll need a suture pack. Pops, hold a light for me. Keep it where I'm working."

Jim took the irrigation syringe and filled it with sterile saline. He did his best to thoroughly flush out each of the puncture wounds from the bites. Then he opened the suture pack, retrieved some forceps, and stared at the instruments. Despite all of the violent things he'd done lately, he'd never threaded a needle through living flesh.

"How do you know how to do this?" Lloyd asked.

"I took a class," Jim replied. "Good old Dr. Bones."

"Have you ever done it before?"

"Only to an amputated pig's foot," Jim said. "That's what they gave us to use in the class."

Lloyd raised an eyebrow and Jim noticed it.

"You got something to say?" Jim asked.

"Nope," Lloyd said. "Not a thing."

"That's what I thought," Jim said. He saw Ariel standing in the corner, silent tears running down her cheeks. "Ariel, can you get a blanket for Buddy?"

She nodded and ran off, returning with her favorite fleece blanket. Ellen helped her arrange it over Buddy's upper body.

Wanting to get the sutures in place before Buddy woke up – if he woke up at all – Jim started working. He stitched each cleaned wound. They found an additional large wound on his back, which they also irrigated and stitched. For the shallower cuts from smaller teeth, Jim irrigated the wounds and then closed them with butterfly closures.

Some of Buddy's fingers were clearly broken. Jim did his best to straighten them and applied several foam-lined aluminum splints. For the rest of the swollen hand, he wrapped it in a protective bandage until he could figure out more about what damage had been done to it. He applied antibiotic ointment to all of the superficial scratches, then pulled off his gloves and sat down. He checked his watch. It was nearly midnight.

"I'm exhausted," Jim said.

Nana looked at Buddy's still form in the harsh lantern light. "Do you think he'll make it? He looks awful pale."

"He'll need antibiotics, but I only have them in pills so he'll have to be awake to take them," he said. "And he lost a lot of blood, but he's a tough old bird."

Ariel approached the table and gently took Buddy's hand in hers. "Thank you," she whispered. "I hope you get better." She turned to her father. "He can have my bed. Okay?"

Jim smiled. It was a way she could help. "Okay, sweetie. You clear off those stuffed animals and I'll get Lloyd to help me move him in there."

LLOYD SAT in the corner watching his friend, the lantern turned down to its lowest setting and casting a yellow light. He plucked at his banjo, muting it with his hand so that only the hint of a note emerged. He sang quietly, pausing when Buddy stirred. He'd been singing "Down in the Willow Garden" again, the song that Buddy seemed to like so well.

"What did you do with the money?" Buddy asked.

Lloyd sprang from the chair and set his banjo down. It was the first sign of consciousness they'd seen since Buddy had gone into shock and passed out.

"What money?" Lloyd asked. "What are you talking about?"

"The money I gave you for singing lessons," Buddy said, a tired smile reshaping his lips.

"That ain't no way to act, you cranky old bastard," Lloyd said. "I was just practicing your funeral song in case we had to plant you."

Buddy moved his head as if trying to shake the cobwebs from it. "Well, I hate to say this, but without the counterbalance of my voice, your singing would be an atrocity. Were your voice to ring out over my proceedings, I dare say I might be forced to get up out of my own coffin and seek a more peaceful final resting place." Buddy cracked his eyes open and looked at his new friend. "No offense intended, of course."

"None taken," Lloyd said, patting his friend on the shoulder. Outside, the sky was lightening. This long night would soon be over. "If you can tolerate my absence, I'll let the others know that the reaper found you distasteful and sent you back."

Buddy smiled again and closed his eyes. Lloyd slipped from the room and was back in a moment with Ariel, Ellen, and Jim. Ariel approached Buddy slowly. She'd always been timid around illness and injury. She reached out a hand and patted Buddy on the forearm.

"Thank you, Buddy," she said. "You saved me."

Buddy opened his eyes and looked toward the little girl. It required a surprising amount of effort to maintain focus on her. He gave her a smile. "If I had let those coyotes eat you, who would make me pies and cobblers?"

Ariel grinned. "Would you like me to make you one today?"

"More than anything in the world," Buddy replied.

Ariel grabbed her mother's hand. "Let's go, Mommy. We have to make a pie."

"Ariel, it's 5 a.m.," Ellen said. "You're going to have to wait just a little bit. Mommy needs to wake up and have some coffee first."

"You can drink coffee while I peel apples," Ariel said, pulling her mother from the room.

Jim approached the bed and laid his hand on Buddy's shoulder. "You'll need to take it easy," he said. "You lost a lot of blood and you'll be weak until it's replenished. There might be some damage to the muscle, too, and that will have to repair itself."

Buddy nodded and closed his eyes. He was getting tired already. "Make sure that banjo player doesn't rob me blind while I'm laid up," Buddy said. "Musicians are a shady lot."

"You better be nice to him," Jim said. "You'll need his help while you're recuperating."

"Maybe you can make a rickshaw out of a wheelbarrow and let him pull me around," Buddy whispered. "I'd like that."

Lloyd shook his head. "Even near death the old coot can't be nice," he said.

A silence fell over the room.

Jim cleared his throat. "I know you need to rest, Buddy, but I want you to know that I can't even begin to thank you enough for what you did."

A tear leaked from Buddy's closed eyes. "I didn't do it for you," Buddy said. "I did it because I was a dad once and it's what dads do."

"You're still a dad," Jim said, his voice cracking and his own eyes filling with tears. "I see it in you every day. Nothing changes that."

"Maybe, but I managed to save your girl when I couldn't save my own," Buddy said.

"I owe you," Jim said. "I owe you a lot."

Buddy waved him off with a hand he could barely control. "I need to rest," he said. "We'll talk later. Right now, I'm tired as a groundhog in hard dirt."

JIM SAT on the back porch, drinking a cup of coffee and watching the sunrise. While he was pleased that Buddy was alive, the whole experience with the coyotes had shaken him. His biggest fear on the long walk home from Richmond was that something might happen to his family before he could get home to protect them. When he got home, he knew things wouldn't be easy but at least his family would be protected. He would be there to defend them against all attackers. They would be safe.

That was not to be the case.

He was there when the coyotes attacked and his presence hadn't changed a damn thing. Had it not been for Buddy's intervention, Ariel might have died. Buddy had prevented that through guts and sheer luck. It left Jim with the painful awareness that if his family wasn't safe with him here, then there was no chance of them ever really being safe at all. That thought both hurt and terrified him.

At the beginning of this national crisis, he'd convinced himself that the only way he'd make it home from Richmond alive was to become as hardened as the worst of men. He felt like his grandfather was whispering a reminder in his ear the whole way home, reminding him that the world he found himself in now was not a place for the soft and considerate, for the delicate of heart. It was a world where you had to kill those who would try to kill you, where you had to make hard decisions about who lived and who died, and where you had to be selfish to keep those you loved alive. If he had to kill a hungry thief, he'd do it. If he had to drive off hungry beggars at gunpoint, he'd do it. If he had to dig discreet graves every week to keep his family alive, he'd do it. All without a second thought.

Weeks ago Jim would have handled last night differently. He would probably have flipped out to a degree. He'd never handled stress well, but he was adapting because this world required it. Surviving was about more than food and firepower. Jim was learning every day that it was about mindset too. It was about putting your feelings aside and doing those things that had to be done.

Later, he would get Gary and they would finish putting up those gates on the road. Jim knew they would not be enough. The world would press at them, wanting their livestock, their fields, their supplies, or whatever it was that they had and the world wanted. The gates were just a symbolic gesture, really. Several times recently, Jim had heard sounds that he thought might be drones, like the one he and Lloyd had seen in the superstore parking lot in town. What good was a gate against a drone?

More than anything, the gates were a symbol of people pushed to the edge. Gary had been displaced from his home and found a new one. He would not want to leave again, unless his family was able to return to their real homes.

Jim sat, watching the day emerge. He was making his stand too. He'd fought to get back to his home and family. He'd killed for it, and he would not be leaving, no matter what came at them.

Made in the USA
Columbia, SC
17 October 2024

44589010R00152